# THROUGH
# FIRE AND WATER

# THROUGH
# FIRE AND WATER

*A NOVEL SET IN THE RÍO SAN JUAN*
*REGION OF NICARAGUA*

## Tom Frist

iUniverse, Inc.
Bloomington

**Through Fire and Water**
**A Novel Set in the Río San Juan Region of Nicaragua**

iUniverse books may be ordered through booksellers or by contacting:

iUniverse
1663 Liberty Drive
Bloomington, IN 47403
www.iuniverse.com
1-800-Authors (1-800-288-4677)

Photographs are by Tom Frist.

ISBN: 978-1-4759-5226-1 (sc)
ISBN: 978-1-4759-5228-5 (hc)
ISBN: 978-1-4759-5227-8 (ebk)

Library of Congress Control Number: 2012918308

Printed in the United States of America

iUniverse rev. date: 10/11/2012

"We went through fire and water, but you brought us to a place of abundance." Psalm 66:12

"If I give all I possess to the poor and surrender my body to the flames, but have not love, I gain nothing." I Corinthians 13:3

"I tell you the truth, unless a kernel of wheat falls to the ground and dies, it remains only a single seed. But if it dies, it produces many seeds." John 12:24

# DEDICATION

I dedicate this book to my wife, Clare Strachan Frist, the love of my life and my best friend. Born in Costa Rica of Christian missionary parents and grandparents who devoted their lives to helping others in Latin America, Clare has inspired me with her goodness and shared with me a love for the people and the region, where we lived and worked together for some eighteen years—three of which were in Nicaragua.

# ACKNOWLEDGMENTS

Nicaragua has long suffered from wars, military intervention, natural disasters, poverty, and corruption. Today, however, its future looks bright because many patriots have learned from the past and are determined to do better in the future.

I would like here to acknowledge and thank some of these catalysts for change who have inspired me in the writing of this novel:

First, my brother-in-law Harry Strachan. He and some of his prominent philanthropist friends from Central America have created family foundations to give back to their countries. They also gave me the opportunity to live in Nicaragua from 2002 to 2005 and try to promote in small and informal ways development programs in the Río San Juan Region.

Second, my nephew Robbie Lindenberg. On a pro bono basis, he has played a key role in keeping those programs going from 2005 to the present.

Third, the Gustavo Parajon family. Their health work in rural Nicaragua through Providenic and AMOS has helped thousands and partially inspired the fictional Acción organization in this novel. They have been peacemakers and bridge builders in Nicaragua for many decades and are dear personal friends.

Finally, I want to acknowledge all of my friends on the Río San Juan—from Solentiname and San Carlos to San Juan de Nicaragua. I hope that this novel will be of help to them as a means of interesting others in the Río San Juan—a true national and world treasure!

Although these catalysts for change are of different political persuasions, they are all united in their determination to bring peace and prosperity to this little country of important economic potential, breathtaking natural beauty, and outstanding music and poetry.

# PROLOGUE

In 1848, soon after gold was discovered in California, a great migration began of Easterners to the west coast of the United States. Since no continental railroad yet bridged the country, many fortune hunters and settlers were forced to sail around the tip of South America to get there.

Cornelius Vanderbilt thought that he had a better solution. In 1851, he established a quicker, safer, and cheaper route to San Francisco through Nicaragua. Passengers embarking from New York or New Orleans on Vanderbilt ships disembarked at the mouth of the San Juan River in Nicaragua at the small town of San Juan del Norte ("Greytown" to the British). There they began their voyage across Nicaragua on river and lake boats and on mules and in stagecoaches operated by Vanderbilt's Accessory Transit Company. The trip took them up the San Juan River, across Lake Nicaragua, and by land to the Pacific Ocean—a total of 189 miles. At San Juan del Sur, they embarked again on other Vanderbilt ships for the final leg of the journey to San Francisco.

Tens of thousands used this Nicaragua route to and from San Francisco, and disputes over the route's ownership and over profit sharing often broke out between Nicaragua and the United States, between Vanderbilt and his partners, and between the town of San Juan del Norte and the Accessory Transit Company. As for the latter disputes, the townspeople of San Juan del Norte resented the refusal of Vanderbilt's company to pay any fees to the town, to allow its passengers to shop in the town, or to obey arrest warrants for company employees who committed crimes.

When the Accessory Transit Company failed to remedy these matters, the town council of San Juan del Norte decreed the destruction of the company's headquarters at Punta de Castillo, a headland across the bay from the town. Some armed citizens took it upon themselves to fulfill the order, and they succeeded in burning a few company buildings and stealing some goods before company employees chased them off. The directors of the Accessory Transit Company immediately sought the support of the

U.S. ambassador to Nicaragua, Solon Borland, to seek recompense and to prevent future attacks.

Borland, who was a vocal proponent of the incorporation of Nicaragua and other Central American countries into the United States of America, took a personal interest in the matter as he, too, was attacked by some of the same angry citizens when he passed through San Juan del Norte on his return to the United States. Once home, he convinced the U.S. Government to send the U.S. warship *Cyane* to San Juan del Norte to defend American honor and property.

The *Cyane*, under the command of Captain George Hollins, arrived off the coast near San Juan del Norte on July 11, 1854. Captain Hollins immediately posted an ultimatum in the town demanding that the town apologize to the U.S. Government for its treatment of its ambassador. It also insisted that the town pay reparations to the Accessory Transit Company for the damages done to its property. Hollins made it clear that if these demands were not met by 9:00 a.m. on July 13, he would destroy the town with his ship's canons. Since no response was received by that time, the guns of the *Cyane* opened fire at precisely 9:00 a.m. The actual barrage lasted for an hour and thirty-five minutes, and the town was totally destroyed, although with no loss of human life.

# PART I
# 1984

# CHAPTER 1

Like a child's stick thrown into a muddy stream, a long, narrow passenger boat slowly made its way down Nicaragua's Río San Juan, oblivious to the upcoming rapids. A sudden burst of rain had broken the heavy heat and humidity of this April midafternoon, but now the sun reappeared from behind the clouds above the giant Guanacaste trees that bordered the river.

The boat carried six passengers—two Americans and four Nicaraguans—all heading to the Roberto Romero State Farm to spend the night before devoting two days to treating patients at the small medical clinic in the nearby river town of La Esperanza. In the middle of the boat, beneath the craft's wooden canopy, dozens of cardboard boxes of medical supplies were stacked. Clear plastic sheeting protected them from the downpour and from the spray of water from the river.

From the back of the boat, Nicaraguan music blared from a shortwave radio hanging by a frayed chord from a support beam. The radio belonged to the boat's owner and pilot—a burly, unshaven man in his late thirties nicknamed Chino. Gripping the control handle of the two-stroke outboard motor, Chino guided the boat around fallen branches and other hazards floating downstream to the Atlantic. Sitting right in front of him, a young *Sandinista* soldier in uniform named Benito cradled an AK-47 assault rifle on his lap and stared at the far riverbank looking for signs of *Contra* rebels.

When the music stopped and a familiar drumroll announced the Sandinista anthem and afternoon newscast, the older of the two Americans perked up and emerged from his long silence. With an ironic grin and a flourish of his hand, Stan Hollins took off his red and black baseball cap, put it over his heart, and sang in an off-key voice his favorite verse of the anthem, "*Luchamos contra el Yankee, enemigo de la humanidad*—We are fighting against the Yankee, the enemy of humanity."

1

"Good thing they're no Yankees on this boat," Stan said, "just us good old Southern boys!" Stan, a six feet tall, athletic, handsome man in his mid-forties with thick brown hair, directed his joke to his new son-in-law, Clay Danforth, who sat on the bench beside him and was also from Nashville. Clay, who was a little shorter than Stan and wore a floppy L.L. Bean hat to cover his small bald spot and to shade his pale, scholarly face, smiled back politely, although he didn't seem to understand the joke.

On the bench behind them, Stan's friend Luis Romero, now a high-ranking official in the Foreign Ministry of Nicaragua's new revolutionary government, however, laughed out loud. His own great-grandfather had Southern roots, and Luis could easily be confused for a white Southerner because of his light skin, sandy hair, and European facial features. Only his slightly accented English and his *guayabera* shirts gave him away as a Nicaraguan.

Stan and Luis had been friends now for eleven years, since January of 1973 when Stan drove to Nicaragua a twenty-six foot truck packed with relief supplies that he had personally collected from Nashville for the victims of the disastrous Christmas Eve earthquake in Managua. For the three weeks that he was in Nicaragua to distribute the supplies, Stan had stayed with Luis's family in their Granada home, and Luis had served as Stan's translator. In the following years, their friendship had deepened as Stan returned often to Nicaragua to help in some of Luis's community development projects. Usually when Stan came, he brought with him small groups of volunteers from his church and from the elite boy's preparatory school in Nashville where he taught history.

In 1980, after the overthrow of Somoza and his government, Luis invited Stan to move to Nicaragua permanently to help him and his political party, the Sandinistas, create in the country what he called "a model society of equality and justice." Fascinated with this new challenge and bored with his life in Nashville, Stan quickly accepted the invitation despite the strong protests of his daughter Laura who didn't want to miss her senior year of high school with her friends. Within six months, Stan quit his job, sold their house, raised some support from his church and friends, and moved with his wife Elizabeth and Laura to Managua. That same year, with Luis's help, Stan founded *Acción para la Paz,* the small international relief and development organization based in Managua that sponsored the health clinic on the Río San Juan to which they were now heading.

"How much farther is it?" Clay asked. Stan noticed that his usually cheerful son-in-law had a new weary tone in his voice. This was Clay's first time outside of the U.S. and Canada, and his initial enthusiasm for the adventure had been deflated by the long trip and the heat and humidity of the day.

"Not more than ten minutes," Luis answered. "We pass by an island on the left, and then you'll see the farm on the right bank. Actually, you can see its radio antenna now." Luis leaned out from under the boat's blue wooden canopy and pointed to what looked like a silver pin sticking up from a hill in the far distance.

Clay let out a sigh of relief, took a sip from his canteen, and put it back into his leather knapsack. He then zipped open another pocket and pulled out an expensive Nikon camera. With one hand grasping its strap, he clumsily moved forward to the bow. There he positioned himself so that he could get a full picture of the boat, its passengers and supplies, as well as the wake in the river behind them.

Stan figured that, during the last hour of their boat ride from San Carlos, Clay had already used his zoom lens to shoot some three rolls of pictures of river shacks on stilts, women washing clothes in the river, dugout canoes, majestic jungle trees, white egrets, a snoozing alligator, and several turtles sunbathing on limbs sticking out of the water. Everything on the river was new and exotic to him, and he wanted to share his adventure with his parents, his medical intern friends at Vanderbilt University Hospital in Nashville where he worked, and most of all with his new wife, Laura.

Laura, who was now a junior at Vanderbilt, had stayed in Managua with her mother, Elizabeth. Her original plan had been to come with Clay and her father to help out in the *Acción* clinic, but when she found out she was pregnant, she changed that plan on her doctor's advice.

As Clay returned to his seat, Stan noticed a barge in the distance filled with people leaving the right bank of the river and heading downstream. He pointed it out to Luis and asked who they were.

"Day laborers at the state farm heading home to La Esperanza about five kilometers downstream," Luis explained. "They come each morning and leave each evening." Luis then turned to the young Nicaraguan woman sitting beside him. "If you look up at the top of the hill behind the barge, you can see the house where we will stay tonight."

Sandra Espinoza, the sixth person and the only woman in the boat, shaded her eyes with her hand and looked. Her face and eyes reflected the intensity of her strong personality. Thirty-two years old and a reporter and photographer for *La Barricada*, the official newspaper of the Sandinistas, she was known in Nicaragua for her dark beauty, her combative feminism, her bravery, and her guile. Now dressed in loose-fitting khaki pants and shirt that hid her shapely body, she had once used her feminine charms to entice a high-ranking Somoza official into a trap where he was kidnapped for ransom.

Luis had invited her to come along on the trip so that she could write an article for the newspaper on "Good Yankees"—international volunteers like Stan Hollins who came to Nicaragua to help the Revolution instead of to oppose it. At first, Sandra was reluctant to do such a story because she had no love for the U.S. Government and didn't want to portray any Americans in a positive light. She finally relented on the condition that Luis would come along with them on the trip so she could use their time together to gather material not only for the "Good Yankee" story but for two other articles—one on Luis and his family and the other on the Roberto Romero State Farm. Stan was happy that Luis had finally agreed to Sandra's conditions despite his natural modesty. Stan had no such modesty himself, and he knew that a favorable article in *La Barricada* would be a considerable help for raising support for himself and his work.

Stan looked at his watch. It was 4:00 p.m., and they had been traveling since 4:30 a.m. It had been a tiring trip, starting with a nine-hour ride in Stan's battered, blue Toyota Land Cruiser on the torturous dirt highway from Managua to San Carlos. An army pickup truck, which Luis had arranged, followed behind carrying donated medical supplies from the U.S. that Stan had gathered. Much of the distance, they swerved like drunks, trying to avoid the thousands of gaping ruts and potholes in the road. When they were unsuccessful, their bodies jolted and crashed into each other and into the roof of the car.

After finally arriving in the sleepy river capital of San Carlos, they had spent an hour in courtesy visits with the mayor and with the regional military commander, while the supplies they had brought were reloaded from the army truck onto the boat. Even though the military commander reported that there had not been any recent Contra activity in the upper region of the river, he still insisted on sending with them one of his soldiers—at least until they got to La Esperanza, where a small army contingent was stationed. He then radioed the state farm administrator,

Cesar Rodrigues, advising him that Luis and the American medical team would be arriving within two hours.

Those two hours had just passed when Chino cut off the motor and glided their boat the last ten meters towards the farm visitor's dock, bouncing softly off the white tires that protected the heavy wooden planks of the wharf. Benito, in the stern of the boat, stood up, grabbed one of the pier posts, and pulled himself out of the craft onto the dock. At the same time, Stan reached for the rope hooked to the bow and slung it up to him. The soldier grabbed it and tied it to one of the pilings. When the boat was secure, he held out his free hand to help Clay, Sandra, Stan, and finally Luis climb onto the pier.

Stan was glad to be out of the boat. He stretched his cramped legs and then glanced up the muddy hill towards the rambling wooden house overlooking the river. A soldier who was sitting on the porch watching them got up, opened the front door, and yelled to someone inside. A minute later, a heavyset man appeared at the door and stared down at them.

When Luis saw him, he waved and shouted in Spanish, "It's us—Luis Romero and the medical team from Managua."

The man waved back in acknowledgement and immediately started down the porch stairs to the stone-and-dirt path that led to the river dock.

Meanwhile, Chino handed up to Stan and Luis their personal gear from the boat.

"What about the medical supplies?" Stan asked Luis. "Are we going to unload them, too?"

Luis shook his head. "No, we'll leave them in the *panga*. That way we can get an early start in the morning for La Esperanza."

"Do you think it's safe?" Stan asked. He had spent a full day at customs in Managua filling out forms for the release of the supplies, and he did not want anything to happen to them.

"Sure. Chino and Benito both have hammocks and will sleep in the boat with them."

By then, the heavyset man had made it down the hill to the dock. "*Bienvenidos, compas*—welcome, brothers," he said, greeting them enthusiastically, his smile revealing his bad teeth. He looked to Stan to be in his late forties and had a disheveled appearance with uncombed hair, a stubbly beard, and a pocked face. His rumpled, olive green uniform bulged at his waist.

"Cesar Rodriguez, the director of the Roberto Romero State Farm," Luis said as he introduced him in English to Stan and to Clay.

Stan noticed that in contrast to his welcome, Cesar shook hands only perfunctorily and avoided eye contact. Cesar then turned to Luis and said in Spanish, "We got the message about your coming. Your rooms are ready, and after you clean up and rest a little, we'll have dinner waiting for you." He added, "*Mi casa es su casa*—my house is your house."

And indeed, the house literally was Luis's house, just as Cesar said. Stan knew the story well, and he had heard most of it again in Spanish earlier in the day on the road trip from Managua to San Carlos as Sandra interviewed Luis about his family for her articles. This was the house in which Luis had been raised—the former headquarters of his family's cattle ranch, Las Palmas, inherited through three generations from James Landers, Luis's American great-grandfather on his mother's side. In response to Sandra's questions, Luis had told her the histories of both the ranch and of his own family.

"In 1852, James Landers, my maternal great-grandfather, left Mobile, Alabama, to seek his fortune in the California gold rush," Luis began. "He booked passage on one of Cornelius Vanderbilt's steamers in New Orleans, but instead of continuing all the way to San Francisco, he decided to stay in Nicaragua."

"What made him change his mind?" Sandra asked.

"Vanderbilt's Accessory Transit Company offered him a good job, and he liked the area," Luis replied. "What happened was that the steam engine on the riverboat taking him and the other passengers up the river to El Castillo broke down. Since James was a mechanic and had worked on boats in Mobile, he volunteered to help fix it. One of the local directors of Vanderbilt's company, who happened to be traveling on the same boat, was so impressed with James's ability that he offered to hire him on the spot with a generous salary if James would agree to stay in Nicaragua and work for them. James accepted. He eventually married a girl from El Castillo and later became a river pilot for the Accessory Transit Company at a much higher salary. With his savings, he purchased two large jungle properties—one near San Juan del Norte at the bottom of the river that our family never developed but still owns, and one above El Castillo, called "Las Palmas," that the government confiscated and turned into the Roberto Romero State Farm."

"Tell me a little more about how that happened," Sandra said in Spanish. She was sitting beside Luis in the back seat taking notes as best she was able with all of the bouncing and swerving. While Stan listened as he maneuvered the ruts and holes of the dirt highway, Clay just stared out the front passenger window at the forests and farms they passed. He knew little Spanish and didn't talk much anyway.

"It's a long story," Luis replied.

"That doesn't matter," Sandra said. "We've got a lot of time until we get to San Carlos."

Through the rearview mirror, Stan saw Luis nod his head in agreement.

"I guess then that I should begin in 1968," Luis began. "That's when my father, Arturo Romero, decided to sell our family house and most of our ranch near El Castillo to Anastasio Somoza Debayle. Somoza had long pressured him because he wanted to have a place on the Río San Juan where he could fish river tarpon with his friends and raise more cattle. Anyway, both my father and my mother felt that it was time to move back from the river to Father's childhood home in Granada so that Elena, Jorge, Roberto, and I could continue our education. With the proceeds from the sale, Father was able to fix up his Granada house, pay for our schooling, open a G.M. dealership in Managua, and later build a new house on the 1,000 hectares of Las Palmas that we kept for our family next to the property that we had sold to Somoza."

"So your family was actually friends with the Somoza family?!" Sandra asked, astonished.

"My father and mother were," Luis answered.

"How did you ever decide to become a Sandinista then?"

"It happened gradually. I wanted to become a priest, but when I was in my last year of seminary training, the earthquake occurred in Managua. I dropped out of seminary to help, but then I became so involved in relief programs that I never went back. The truth is that the more I got into the aid effort, the more disgusted I became with what I saw. Much of the foreign assistance money for the earthquake victims ended up in the pockets of Somoza and his friends instead of helping those who needed it most. When I saw that protests did no good, I finally decided to join the Sandinistas. To me, there was no other viable alternative at the time. I then convinced my younger brother, Roberto, to drop out of school and join the Sandinistas as well."

"Did the rest of your family know that you had joined the Sandinistas?" Sandra asked.

"At first, no," Luis replied. "They knew that Roberto and I often disagreed with them but not that we were Sandinistas. The party was illegal at the time, and we didn't want to hurt them. The truth is that we saw a different Nicaragua from the one they saw. To my parents and to Jorge and Elena, Nicaragua was a benign, prosperous, and politically stable Catholic nation, and Somoza was both their friend and a good leader."

"And to you?"

"To Roberto and me, Nicaragua was a small fiefdom where corruption and torture were the norm and where wealth was concentrated in the hands of a few, while the vast majority of the urban and rural masses lived in abject poverty.

"Did you ever take up arms like your brother Roberto did?" Sandra asked.

"No," Luis replied. "Unlike Roberto, I just wrote articles, recruited new members, and tried to find safe houses for Sandinista sympathizers who were being hunted by the government. At first, Roberto wasn't involved directly in the armed struggle either. It's true that he smuggled guns into the country from Costa Rica, but it was only in 1977 that he made the decision to take up arms himself. He took part in a dawn attack on a National Guard garrison in San Carlos with some of his young friends from Solentiname. In the assault, they killed a half-dozen *Guardia* soldiers, and several of Roberto's Sandinista companions also were killed. Roberto was wounded, but he managed to escape by dugout to the forests and marshes on the other side of the Río San Juan before government reinforcements arrived by helicopter from Managua. During the next three days, he eluded capture, making his way through the swamps to Las Palmas. I guess that he hoped to get help there and to cross over to safety in Costa Rica."

"Las Palmas is where he was killed, wasn't it?" Sandra asked.

"It was. Members of the Guardia were waiting for him in ambush. Unfortunately, one of Roberto's companions in the attack was captured and betrayed Roberto under torture. According to the Guardia's account, Roberto died resisting arrest. But according to one of our workers at Las

Palmas who witnessed the whole thing, he was executed in cold blood after he surrendered. He's buried not far from where he fell."

"Your brother is one of the true heroes of the Revolution!" Sandra exclaimed.

"Maybe so, but he is also dead!" Luis replied.

Sandra was silent for a moment and then continued her questioning in Spanish. "How did your family react when they heard that Roberto was involved in the San Carlos attack and was dead?"

"They were stunned and devastated, just as I was." Luis paused and then added, "I personally felt tremendous guilt for his death because I was the one who had recruited Roberto to the cause in the first place. Still, I didn't have much time to grieve as I had to flee Managua for Costa Rica to escape being arrested myself. I lived in exile in San José until Somoza's overthrow in 1979."

Luis's voice cracked with deep sadness, "My family still blames me for all that has happened—not only for Roberto's death, but also for their later loss of Las Palmas and the rest of their property in Nicaragua."

"Why do they blame you for that?" Sandra asked.

"Because it probably wouldn't have happened if I hadn't agreed to it," Luis answered.

"Go on," Sandra said. "I need to understand for the article."

"What happened is that once Somoza was deposed, the *Comandantes* took over all of his property in the country. Of course, that included the ranch that my father had sold him on the Río San Juan. They made it into a state farm, named the farm in honor of my brother Roberto, and then asked my brother Jorge to be its director. Jorge, who had finished his agricultural studies and moved back to the Río San Juan to administer our 1,000 hectare ranch next door, refused. He, as well as my sister, Elena, and my parents, believed that the Sandinista Revolution would only bring heartache and economic destitution to the country, and he didn't want to be any part of it. As a second choice, the government selected Cesar Rodrigues, a cattleman from Chontales, as director. Living next to each other, Cesar and Jorge never got along."

"Any specific reasons?" Sandra wanted to know.

"There were the problems of the boundaries between the two ranches," Luis answered. "There were also questions about ownership of straying cattle, the fact of Cesar's jealousy that he was a second choice to Jorge as director, and the political differences between the two. For example, Jorge didn't like the new government telling him to whom he could sell his cattle and for how much. As he could get much more for them in Costa Rica, only a few kilometers away from Las Palmas, Jorge often used the dirt road through the forest on the property to smuggle his cattle out to sell. It was the same road that Roberto had used to smuggle arms into Nicaragua from Costa Rica for the Revolution. Cesar learned of one such planned trip from a disgruntled employee of Las Palmas, and he immediately informed the Sandinista military commander at La Esperanza about it. As a result, a trap was set, and Jorge's foreman and another employee were arrested just as they were getting ready to cross the border with the cattle. The soldiers confiscated both the truck and the cattle in it and turned them over to Cesar at the state farm."

"Was Jorge arrested, too?" Sandra asked.

"No. They didn't detain him because of his relationship to Roberto and me, but the government kept his truck and cattle. Jorge was furious and finally packed up his family and crossed over the border to Costa Rica and joined the resistance. A few months later, my parents and my sister, Elena, followed him out of the country, eventually ending up in Miami with many of their friends. But by choosing to do so, they lost everything—their home in Granada, their car business in Managua, and their land and cattle on the Río San Juan."

Sandra looked quizzically at Luis. "But isn't that the way it should have been?" she asked. "The fact is, your parents and brother and sister were enemies of the Revolution and the law stipulated that if friends and supporters of Somoza abandoned the country, that they would lose their property, and that it would be used for the benefit of the poor."

"That's true. They were enemies, and that was the law," Luis acknowledged. "I even agreed at first to the confiscation, despite my family's astonishment that I would do such a thing. My feeling was that we all had to be equal before the law. My relatives had broken it, so our property should be confiscated to help the poor.

"And that is what happened, so you should be proud," Sandra said.

"No, it is not what happened; and no, I am not proud," Luis retorted.

Stan, who was listening as he drove, was not surprised to hear the anger in Luis's voice. Luis had often expressed his shame and disgust to Stan about how his family's property had been used by the Revolution once it was confiscated.

"I agreed to the seizure of the family property if it were used to help the poor," Luis said. "The only way for the desperate poor to gain some economic justice in Nicaragua is for the wealthy to share their goods with them. When I gave my approval to the confiscation, it was for Las Palmas to be turned into an agricultural cooperative for the benefit of its former workers and for other landless persons in the region. Instead, what happened is that Cesar Rodrigues convinced the Comandantes in Managua that the land and cattle of Las Palmas should be incorporated into the state farm run by him. Furthermore, our Granada house became a vacation house for a Comandante, and my father's car business was taken over by the Sandinista Party to generate funds for its leaders. Just how did the poor benefit in all of this?" Luis asked Sandra.

There was a long silence before Sandra responded. "I don't know what the correct answer is, Luis. I guess that the lesson is that the ideals and the reality of revolutions are not always one and the same." She ended the interview there, about an hour away from San Carlos.

# CHAPTER 2

Aware of the tension existing between Luis and Cesar, Stan picked up his gray duffle bag from the dock and headed up the hill behind the two men. Stan offered to carry Sandra's army backpack and camera bag to the house as well, but she insisted on carrying her own bags, swinging them effortlessly onto her shoulders.

When Stan got to the top of the riverbank, he stopped and turned around to look at the broad river below them, admiring its beauty. Some two kilometers downstream, the barge that he had pointed out earlier was now turning a bend, heading towards La Esperanza. Looking to the right, Stan could see the muddy, littered beach from which it had embarked. An eroded dirt road, cut into the bank, connected the beach to what looked like a large barn behind the main house.

Although Stan had never before visited the state farm, he had passed by it on many occasions when he and his small brigades of international volunteers were on their way by boat to La Esperanza or to San Juan del Norte to build their simple health clinics. He was happy to have the opportunity to stop and see it, and most of all, to sleep in a real bed instead of in a hammock, as he usually did on these river trips.

Cesar was breathing heavily from climbing the steep bank when Stan caught up with him and the others at the porch stairs. Cesar then led them up the creaking wooden steps to the porch and then opened the door of the sprawling wooden structure and beckoned them to go in.

The main room of the house they entered was large and dark because of the varnished wood paneling. Quickly taking in the L-shaped room, Stan imagined that it was designed for meetings and could probably accommodate as many as thirty people easily.

When Stan asked Luis if the house had changed much since his childhood, Luis replied in English. "Basically, it's the same home that I grew up in, but Somoza put in a pool in the back and updated the plumbing and wiring. Then when the government took over, it turned everything into offices, meeting rooms, and apartments. Structurally, though, the house is the same one in which I spent my childhood."

Cesar then led them past five wooden rocking chairs to a side hallway off the main room where he said their bedrooms were located. As they passed by an open door on the left side of the hallway, Stan noticed a woman's clothes lying on an unmade double bed. Cesar hastily closed the door, explaining that these were his private quarters. He then opened the door of a room directly across the hall from it. "The men will share this room, and *Companeira* Sandra will have the room down the hall to herself. Both rooms have private bathrooms." He pointed to the key in the door. "You can lock them if you wish, but everything here is safe." He then added, "If it is all right with you, we will eat in about two hours."

"*Bueno*," Sandra said, mixing Spanish and English, "that will give us time to see a little of the farm, take a few pictures outside, and finish our interview before all of tomorrow's activities." Sandra spoke English competently since she often socialized with foreign correspondents covering the war, but her accent was strong. "Why don't we meet at the rocking chairs after we freshen up a bit?" she suggested.

Luis and Stan agreed, and as Cesar led Sandra to her room down the hall, the three men entered their own quarters.

Theirs was a room of ample size containing three single wooden beds, each neatly made-up with clean sheets and thin white bedspreads. Each bed also had a small blue towel folded at the foot with a little bar of soap on top of it and mosquito netting bunched up in a knot hanging over it. An out-of-date 1983 calendar hung on one wall, and on another was a picture of the Spanish colonial fort at El Castillo that had been built to guard the upper Río San Juan against English pirates and other invaders. A small table with a cheap wooden lamp on it separated two of the beds, and the third bed was pushed up against the wall next to the bathroom. A rusty rotating fan sat on the floor below the window.

Stan went over to the window and looked out through the bars to the grounds behind the house. There, he could see Somoza's former swimming pool of broken blue and white ceramic tiles, now empty of water. Beyond the pool was a large open space, and on the other side of the space were a barn, two wooden houses, and a corral.

Luis closed the door and put his bag on the bed by the bathroom door. "Electricity and lights come on between six and ten at night when they run the generator," Luis explained to Stan and Clay. He added, "There's a shower in the bathroom, so if you want to freshen up now, go right ahead."

Clay let out a sigh of relief. "Man, I can't wait to take a shower. I feel as if I'm caked in road dust and smell to high heaven! It's been a very long day." He rummaged through his bag and took out a monogrammed leather toilet kit. He then picked up the small towel and bar of soap from his bed and went into the bathroom, closing the door behind him.

A few minutes later, Stan heard the dripping of water on the cement floor and then a yelp and complaint. "Good night! There's no hot water!"

Stan grinned at Luis and explained. "His parents are very wealthy, and he's not used to this sort of thing."

When Clay finally emerged from the bathroom still a little wet, he was wearing only his white jockey shorts. He had a smile on his face. "The shower is just a pipe, and there is a lizard right above the soap dish. I thought President Somoza would have had better accommodations!"

Luis laughed. "Somoza's plumbing was looted years ago."

While Clay put on a clean shirt and a pair of pants, Stan undressed down to his boxer shorts for his turn at the shower. Stan was secretly pleased when he compared his own tight stomach and tanned flesh with the white, scholarly paunch of his new son-in-law. Stan took pride in his looks, and he often played tennis and lifted weights to keep in shape. He enjoyed being attractive to the opposite sex.

Returning from his shower and dressing in a clean change of clothes, Stan followed Clay's example and stretched out on the thin foam mattress to wait for Luis to finish his turn in the bathroom. Unlike Stan and Clay, Luis undressed in the bathroom and came back fully clothed. Stan imagined that Luis's modesty came from his seminary training.

It was five o'clock when the three men emerged from their room to meet Sandra and Cesar in the main room. Cesar was sitting in one of the room's five rockers waiting for them when they came out. He got up to greet them.

Stan's eyes swept over the L-shaped room and took in more of its detail this time. Four windows of the room looked out to the river in front of the house, and two windows looked out the back to Somoza's former swimming pool, a big yard, the barn, and the other buildings. Almost everything in the room was made of wood—not only the walls, the floor, and the ceiling, but also all of the furniture, including the rockers, the heavy tables, and straight-backed chairs.

"Did all this wood come from the forests around here?" Stan asked Luis.

"Most of it," Luis replied.

Stan figured that both the furniture and the room were designed to be functional instead of beautiful, as there were few decorations. The embellishments consisted of a brown cowhide rug in the middle of the floor, and on one wall between a red and black Sandinista flag and a blue and white Nicaraguan banner, hung a large picture of the Sandinista president wearing army fatigues and glasses. Mounted on the opposite wall from the picture, the enormous stuffed head of a bull stared down at them menacingly.

Stan had approached the mounted bull's head to get a closer look when he heard Sandra come out of her room and down the hallway towards them. He turned to look at her and was struck by the change in her appearance. She had let down her thick black hair from the pony tail she had used in the morning and had changed from the khaki shirt and pants she had worn to a red, flowered silk blouse and dark black skirt, showing off her firm breasts and slender waist. She looked very feminine, and Stan would never have guessed her revolutionary history had Luis not told him about it. Luis once said to him that Sandra was unlike any woman he had ever met—a mixture of beauty, cunning, courage, sensuality, and danger. And Stan agreed!

Sandra greeted them and then came over to where Stan was standing underneath the bull's head. She looked up at it and then commented ironically in Spanish, "Here's another symbol of the macho society we live in here in Nicaragua. We even put up reminders on our walls to make sure no one forgets!"

They all laughed.

"It was my brother's favorite bull, Tornado," Luis explained in English. "Jorge had his head mounted to honor his very fruitful life and the financial success he brought to Las Palmas because of it." Luis then looked around the room and commented in Spanish to Cesar. "I see that you have a lot of Jorge's things here: Tornado, the dining room table, the chairs, the rockers . . ."

"For safe-keeping," Cesar interrupted defensively. "We boarded up the house at Las Palmas and brought most of the things here to protect them from thieves."

Luis shook his head skeptically, "Take good care of them. We turned over our land and the house to the government, but the personal things inside it still belong to our family."

Stan felt the tension in the exchange, and Sandra must have felt the same thing because she quickly changed the subject. Speaking in Spanish, she suggested, "While there's still light, why don't we all go outside and take some group pictures for the newspaper article. Then maybe afterwards, I can finish my interview with Mr. Stan and Dr. Clay. Tomorrow, everyone will be so busy at the clinic, there'll be no time."

"That sounds fine to me," Luis said. "Where would you like to take the pictures?"

"What about in front of the storage building?" Cesar suggested. "It has a big sign over the entrance with 'Hacienda Estatal Roberto Romero' written on it."

Sandra concurred. "*Vamos pues!*—Let's go then."

With that, Cesar led them out the door into the backyard. Stan looked around and imagined that the yard must have been a lovely garden during the time of Somoza. Now, all that remained was a broken cement birdbath, chipped and dirty cement benches, and the empty pool with the missing tiles. At the right side of the pool, vegetables were planted, and a bamboo fence protected them from the chickens in the yard.

An open grassy area about fifty meters in width separated the backyard of the house from the farm's other wooden buildings and the corral. "When government authorities come from Managua," Cesar explained, pointing to the empty area, "that is where they land their helicopters."

Beyond the buildings and corral, Stan could see in the far distance vast pastures where hundreds of white Zebu cattle grazed.

While they walked across the grassy helicopter landing area, Sandra questioned Cesar about the state farm, and Stan translated his replies to her for Clay.

"Including Las Palmas, we have around three thousand hectares," Cesar said.

"The farm's over seven thousand acres," Stan explained to Clay.

"Most of it is still forest, but there's pasture for a thousand head of cattle," Cesar continued on. "We've also planted about a thousand citrus

16

trees and could plant many more if we had a more reliable labor force. Right now most of our workers are women and older men from La Esperanza. They complain about the wages, but they're grateful for a job."

"Is the farm lucrative?" Stan asked in Spanish.

Cesar snorted in laughter. "*Lucrativo?* How could it be! Cattle prices are at rock bottom, and our orange trees aren't old enough to produce anything. Wages, pesticides, and veterinary fees eat up everything."

"What about security?" Sandra inquired as she stopped and jotted down some notes in the small notebook she carried.

"We have five soldiers stationed here, and if there's trouble, we can always radio for help from the garrison at La Esperanza. But really, there's not much military activity at this end of the river. ARDE, the Contra branch out of Costa Rica, operates mostly below El Castillo and around San Juan del Norte. Sometimes they mount a quick raid from Costa Rica to show that they can be a nuisance, but mainly they just steal some cattle or supplies and run. We lost some fifty cattle that way a few months ago."

As they neared the barn, Stan noticed that three of those soldiers, dressed in army khaki pants and sleeveless tee shirts, watched them from one of the weathered wooden houses. Two of them lounged in olive hammocks hung from the supports of the house's front porch, and the third observed them from a pane-less window whose shutters were open. Clay waved at them, and the soldiers languidly waved back.

Sandra stopped taking notes and turned to Luis, "Was it here where your brother Roberto was assassinated by the Guardia?"

"Not exactly here. It was at Las Palmas, about a twenty minute walk from here." Luis paused a moment and then added, "Actually, if you don't need me after the picture taking, I'd like to go over and visit his grave and maybe greet some of our old employees who still live there."

"Of course," Sandra said. "You've already given me most of the information I need for the article. It's *Señor* Stan and *Doctor* Clay I have to interview now."

Stan felt bad because he would have liked to accompany Luis to visit Roberto's grave. Roberto fascinated him. From his three-week stay with the Romero family in 1973, Stan remembered the young man, who was then studying at the prestigious Central American Academy in Granada, as quiet, intelligent, and polite. Stan was astounded when he learned that this gentle Roberto had chosen to become a violent revolutionary and had died as a result of that decision. While Stan had often espoused different causes with vocal fervor throughout his life, he could never imagine one for which he would actually kill or die as had Roberto.

When the group got to the barn, Cesar called their attention to the new tractor and implements parked just outside the door. "We received them last month as a gift from the DDR, the East Germans."

While Sandra took a picture of the machinery, Stan noticed that the only other vehicle in sight was an old truck with tall wooden slats on three sides, standing abandoned by the gate of the corral. He imagined that this must be the vehicle that the soldiers had confiscated fifteen months earlier from Jorge's men when they arrested them at the Costa Rican border with the cattle. Neither he nor Luis, however, made any comment about it.

The so-called barn was actually much more of a storage and repair shop than a place for animals. Stan looked inside, and in the dim light coming through the door and the cracks in the wooden walls, he could make out several large blue plastic containers of fuel and pesticides and a wall full of tools and farm implements. There were also stacked-up boxes of veterinary supplies for the cattle. A side room of the barn housed the generator that produced the electricity for the farm, and frayed wires extended from it to a pole and then on to the roof of the main house.

"Where do you keep your arms and ammunition?" Sandra asked, as she peered inside the building.

"In the main house under lock and key," Cesar replied. "The soldiers have their own weapons and supplies with them at their houses."

Sandra nodded and then raised her eyes to the black and red sign over the door that proclaimed the farm's name and motto in Spanish: Hacienda Estatal Roberto Romero—"We plant that others may reap." She backed up and looked through the lens of her camera as if previewing a possible picture.

"This looks as good of a place as any for a group photo." She motioned for all of them to line up in front of the door under the sign, and after they had done so, she snapped a few pictures. She then gave the camera to Cesar and asked him to take one with her in it. Following her instructions, he did so somewhat clumsily. Clay then took some more pictures with his own camera.

As Cesar handed Sandra's camera back to her, Luis announced in Spanish that he would like to get going to visit Las Palmas and Roberto's grave. "I want to be back by nightfall."

"Make sure you tell the soldiers your plans, or you might be shot coming back," Cesar warned only half in jest. "And take a flashlight, just in case."

Luis nodded and pulled a small flashlight from his pants pocket. "I'm prepared."

Turning to leave, Stan touched his friend lightly on the shoulder in solidarity. "Honor your brother for me, too."

Luis smiled in appreciation. "I will." He then headed towards the watching soldiers to let them know his intent.

# CHAPTER 3

"Where would you like to do the interview with us?" Stan asked Sandra in Spanish after Luis had left them.

"What about on the front porch of the house?" she responded. "We could bring out the rockers and be comfortable there. There's still enough light and a slight breeze."

Stan agreed and then told Clay the plan.

"While you three are doing your interview," Cesar interjected in Spanish, "I'll excuse myself and check in the kitchen on the preparations for dinner. If you need anything, just let me know. You are distinguished guests, and we want to treat you well!"

Sandra and Stan thanked him, and as Cesar headed towards the back door of the house, Stan, Sandra, and Clay took the other route, walking by the open grassy area down the dirt road linking the barn to the loading beach on the river. When they got to the crest of the riverbank, they turned left towards the front of the house instead of going down to the water.

Once on the porch, Stan and Clay went inside and brought out three of the heavy rockers from the sitting room. They arranged the chairs so that they faced each other, and after Sandra had sat down, they took their seats. Brushing back her black hair with her hand, Sandra took out her notebook and pen from the side of her camera case. She then smiled at Stan and asked him in Spanish, "Why don't we start by you telling me a little about yourself and why you are in Nicaragua?"

"Of course," Stan answered. It was a question that he was often asked, so he did not have to think twice for an answer—even in Spanish.

"The short version is that I'm an only child, born in 1940 in Alexandria, Virginia. My father was a lawyer who worked for a lobbying firm in Washington D.C., and my mother was a public health consultant. They were fairly wealthy and ambitious people who divorced in 1955, sending me off to a boy's boarding school in Chattanooga, Tennessee for high school. Later, I moved to Nashville, Tennessee, to attend Vanderbilt

University. That's where I met my wife, Elizabeth, and Nashville is where we lived before moving here. I taught history in a boy's school there."

"How many children do you have?" Sandra inquired. "I know I met your daughter this morning when we picked you up at your house."

"Laura is the only one. She's newly married to Clay here and just announced to us that they are expecting their first child."

Sandra smiled at Clay and congratulated him in English. Turning back to Stan, she reverted to Spanish and asked, "And how did you become interested in Nicaragua?"

"I guess it started as a boy when my father first told me about one of my ancestors Captain George Hollins. I don't know what you know about him, but he was the commander of the U.S. warship that bombarded and destroyed San Juan del Norte in the 1850s."

"I knew about the bombardment by your government, but not the name of the captain," Sandra replied. "That's fascinating that he was a relative of yours."

Stan nodded. "My father was obviously proud of him being his ancestor, but I wasn't. It shamed me that a relative of mine would have wiped out an entire town because of some slight to national pride. And then later, when I was living in Nashville, I learned about another infamous American connected to Nicaraguan history—William Walker, who was born and raised in that city."

"One of the greatest American villains of our past," Sandra commented, dryly.

"Exactly," Stan replied. "So when the Managua earthquake happened, I figured that both the people of Nashville and I personally owed something to Nicaragua. I was in graduate school at Vanderbilt at the time, in part to escape the Vietnam draft," he added in order to stress to Sandra his political leanings. "So I used my contacts there and in the city to gather supplies and money for the victims of the earthquake. It wasn't much, but we did fill a truck that I drove down myself."

Sandra nodded appreciatively.

"When I arrived in Managua and contacted the Red Cross, they got me in touch with Luis and his family. Luis's father was on the Red Cross Board, and he invited me to stay in their home in Granada. He also offered Luis as my translator. Luis and I quickly became friends as we were the same age. Afterwards, I started coming back to Nicaragua during summer vacations bringing students with me from the school where I taught. Luis put us to work as volunteers in community development projects in Managua, Solentiname, and San Juan del Norte, and my love for the country grew. Later, when the Revolution succeeded and Luis was put in charge of coordinating help from foreign non-governmental organizations, he invited me to move here permanently. He thought that I could be of help to the country by bringing in supplies and volunteers from the U.S. on a more formal basis."

Sandra wrote some more notes in her notebook and then asked, "And your work here now? Tell me about it."

"After my family and I arrived in 1980, Luis helped us get settled and to set up a not-for-profit organization we called '*Acción para la Paz.*' Mainly what we do is bring in emergency supplies for disasters, but we also build and equip simple health clinics and schools in very poor rural areas. So far we've built two schools and three health clinics, including two here on the river—one in San Juan del Norte and the one in La Esperanza, which we'll visit tomorrow. We now have small offices in Managua and in Nashville, and more than two-hundred volunteers have come down to help. When they go back, they help educate the American public about what is really happening in Nicaragua."

Sandra turned to Clay and switched to English. "So you're one of the volunteer doctors who came down to help?"

Clay laughed. "It's hard not to volunteer when your new father-in-law asks you to."

Sandra smiled. "Have you ever been to Nicaragua before?"

"Actually, this is my first time out of the U.S., other than a family trip I took to Canada. Being a medical student, I don't have much time to travel—just to study."

"And what are your impressions of Nicaragua so far?" Sandra asked.

"Pretty much what Mr. and Mrs. Hollins and Laura told me. It's very hot and not so developed, but a beautiful place with very nice people."

Sandra jotted down some more notes and then looked penetratingly at Clay. "And what do you think about your president's support for the Contras?"

Clay visibly squirmed with the question. "I really don't know enough about it to give an opinion," he said. "All we medical students think about is medicine. I just want to be able to contribute a little to the people here."

Stan laughed and remarked, "Clay is about as apolitical a person as you can find."

"But you must have an opinion about Reagan financing the Contras, don't you?" Sandra insisted. "They are killing so many people."

*"Por supuesto*—of course, he's against the killing." Stan intervened again, and this time in Spanish. "But Clay's not a political person. He just wants to help. If you put anything in your article about him being for or against U.S. policy, it will only cause problems for us and for him in Nashville. Clay's father is a generous donor to our work, but he's also an ardent Republican."

"So where do you get the financial support for your organization?" Sandra asked Stan, now somewhat suspiciously.

"Mainly from donations from people I know, like Clay's father and former students. We also get some help from churches, from individuals who are against U.S. policy here, and also from other NGOs—non-governmental organizations. It's not a lot, but enough to get us by. People who come down and work with us on projects go home and talk to their newspapers and friends about what we're doing. A few send money. We've also gotten a lot of donated supplies, especially medical ones from hospitals and companies in Nashville."

"No U.S. Government support?"

"None—except, of course, tax exemption for our organization in the U.S."

At that moment, a young woman who looked to be in her late teens or early twenties opened the front door and came out carrying three tall glasses of water on a tray. To Stan, she appeared to have a mixture of the Indian, Spanish, and Negroid features so common to many women in this area of Nicaragua, and like many of them, was a little overweight. She offered them the glasses.

*"Gracias,"* Sandra said, taking hers. "I was just thinking about getting some." She smiled up at the young woman, "What's your name?"

"Adalina," the girl replied, somewhat ill at ease. "I help with the cleaning and the cooking here."

Stan imagined that she might also be Cesar's mistress, whose clothes he had seen on his bed.

After Adalina had gone back into the house, Sandra put her notebook and pen back into her camera case and placed the case on the floor. She then began to rock slowly and to sip from her glass of water, gazing out

23

over the river. Stan followed her eyes and saw that the sky above the dark forest was now beginning to turn red with the sunset. "Isn't it beautiful and peaceful?" Sandra said in Spanish, as if talking to herself. "So different from Managua," she added. "I've always wanted to live in a place like this."

Sandra's comment was the first personal one that Stan had heard her make on the trip, and its softness surprised him. Seeing it as an opportunity to find out more about her, he asked in Spanish, "What about you? How did you become a Sandinista and then a journalist for *La Barricada*?"

Sandra turned and looked at him for a moment and then smiled deviously. "I'm supposed to be the interviewer. Not you."

"When you put down the pen and paper, I thought the interview was over," Stan replied.

"I guess it is for now," she said and was then silent.

As she said nothing for a few more seconds, Stan was unsure if she was going to respond. He took up his glass of water and took a drink from it as he waited. As for Clay, he left his glass on the floor untouched and just slowly rocked, enjoying the view.

Then, suddenly, as if she had come to a decision, Sandra began to speak. Like Stan, she told her story quickly in Spanish in executive summary form, as if she were used to telling it. "I was born and grew up in León where my father taught economics at the university there," she began. "When I was four, Somoza Debayle's father, who was president at the time, was assassinated during a visit to the city. Immediately, the National Guard rounded up everyone in the town suspected of being a political opponent of the Somoza family, and that included my father. He was taken to Managua where he was held and tortured at the El Chipote prison for several months. When he was finally released, he lost both his teaching job and his health, and in 1962, he died a broken man. I grew up hating the Somoza family, and when I was in the University of León studying communications, I joined the Sandinistas. Much of my work was preparing pamphlets, but I also was involved in a plot that captured a prominent Guardia hostage to exchange for some of our prisoners held by them. It was after our victory that I joined the staff of *La Barricada*."

"Luis told me that you were also a poet," Stan said.

Sandra laughed. "Like all Nicaraguans, Luis included!"

"Have you ever published any of your verses?" Stan asked.

"Never in book form. Most of it is too feminist, erotic, and political for most Nicaraguans. It just wouldn't sell."

"I would love to read some of it someday, if the Spanish isn't too hard. Nicaraguans use words I can't even find in my dictionary!"

Sandra laughed again. "We have our own language."

"Like I said, I'd love to read some of it."

"Maybe when we get back to Managua, I'll give you some copies. But I warn you, it's pretty strong stuff!"

While Sandra was talking, suddenly a loud clatter and then an even faster pounding noise came from the utility building they had just visited. Clay was startled and gripped the armrests of his chair in response. Immediately afterwards, the light bulbs on the front porch and inside the living room began to flicker dimly and then with a little more strength.

"The generator has started," Sandra said. She then looked at her watch. "It's getting close to dinnertime so I guess I need to go inside and find the farm director. I want to do another article on this place, and I need to ask him a few more questions before we leave tomorrow."

"So we're finished?" Stan asked.

Sandra nodded and got up, "At least until tomorrow when we get to La Esperanza. I'll probably have more questions after I see your center and work." She switched to English and added, "Thank you both for your help to Nicaragua and for sharing your stories." She reached out and shook their hands.

"Thank you for telling your story, too," Stan replied. "And don't forget about the poetry."

Sandra smiled and went inside.

Once she had left, Stan repeated to Clay what she had told him in Spanish about herself. "A very strong woman," Clay replied, "and a little intimidating, too!"

Stan laughed. "Intimidating, but fascinating!"

They then sat in silence, mesmerized by their rocking and the slow moving river flowing beneath the tinted and darkening sky.

Down at the visitor's dock below them, the boat they had come in also rocked softly in the current. Chino and the young soldier Benito had rearranged the boxes of medical supplies and hung their hammocks to the roof supports and were now stretched out inside them.

"It really is a beautiful place," Clay said. "I wish Laura was here to enjoy it with us."

Stan smiled in self-satisfaction. "See, I told you so. All that worrying you and Laura and Elizabeth did about the Contras was for nothing. They operate near Honduras and towards the coast, not here. I've been in Nicaragua for four years and have yet to see a Contra. Anyway, they aren't going to attack Americans. We're their bread and butter."

"Thank you for saving me from her question about President Reagan and his support for the Contras," Clay said. "That was a no-winner. My family would die if I was quoted in *La Barricada* denouncing the U.S. Government. I have no desire to be a 'Hanoi Jane' or a 'Managua Clay!'" He laughed at his own joke.

"We'll convert you yet to the cause," Stan said, smiling at his son-in-law.

They continued rocking and listening to the sounds of the forest across the river as howler monkeys communicated with one another. Tiny green bugs began to gather around the lights that dimly illuminated the porch. "*Chayules*," Stan explained to Clay as he brushed some from his arm. "They aren't so bad here, but in San Carlos, they can be a plague at certain times of the year. They are a nuisance to humans, but fish and birds feast on them. That's one of the reasons this whole region is so blessed with natural abundance."

"How long do you and Mrs. Hollins plan to stay in Nicaragua?" Clay asked after another few minutes of silence. He always used "Mr." and "Mrs." when he referred to Stan and Elizabeth. That pleased Stan because of the respect shown, but it also made him feel old and uncomfortable. Stan pictured himself as a young, dynamic, progressive revolutionary—a defender of the poor—and the last thing that he wanted was to be thought of as middle-class by his son-in-law or anyone else.

"I have no idea," Stan answered, shaking his head. "Elizabeth would leave tomorrow if it weren't for me, especially now that you and Laura are going to have a baby. She likes the people, but hates the poverty, the heat, and the noise of Managua. She also feels bad that she can't communicate so well in Spanish. Still, she's a good sport!"

"But you love it here?"

"I do. I get up with enthusiasm every morning. The attention of the whole world is focused right now on whether this little country's revolution will succeed or fail. I want to help it succeed. I feel alive here, and that I'm making a difference."

"I understand," Clay said, "but we still wish you were back with us in Nashville. There's a lot of good that you could do there, too."

Before Stan could comment, he heard footsteps in the main room, and then the front door creaked and opened. It was Luis. He greeted them and then came out, taking a seat in the chair vacated by Sandra. "How did the interview with Sandra go?" he asked.

"Short but good," Stan answered. "When it was over, she even told us a little about herself." He paused for a few seconds and then shook his head. "But you know, she never even mentioned if she was married and had any kids."

Luis laughed. "Sandra's married only to the Revolution. She's had her share of affairs, even with a couple of people now in positions of power, but she has always gone her own way." Luis swatted a mosquito on his arm and then asked, "Where's she now?"

"She went inside to interview the farm director," Clay said.

"I'd like to interview him myself!" Luis noted with disgust. "He has ruined Las Palmas."

"What do you mean?" Stan asked.

"The place is a mess, and one of our former employees there made some serious charges about Cesar."

Before Luis could elaborate, the front door again opened and this time it was Adalina who appeared. She had two aluminum containers in her hands. "*La comida está en la mesa*—dinner is served," she announced pleasantly. She then came outside and went down the steps, taking the food in the containers to Chino and Benito on the boat.

Stan, Clay, and Luis got up from their chairs and went to their room to wash their hands, soon returning to the long wooden table where Cesar and Sandra were already seated and waiting for them. On the table was a plate of beef from the farm, a salad, and large bowls of rice and beans as well as glasses for beer and water. When Adalina returned from the river, she served them.

As they helped themselves to the food, Sandra asked Luis about his visit to Las Palmas and to Roberto's grave.

"The place is totally abandoned," Luis replied. "It breaks my heart to see it. Roberto's grave is overgrown, Jorge's house has been looted of everything and boarded up, the corral is broken down, and all the cattle and equipment are gone. No one takes care of anything." Luis looked straight at Cesar, and his voice betrayed his restrained but unmistakable anger. "When I gave my consent to the government's confiscation of our family's property, I did it because I understood that Las Palmas was going to be turned into a cooperative for landless farmers, including our own employees. Instead, from what I learned this afternoon, they have been shunted aside and are surviving on subsistence crops and on whatever they can fish from the river."

Cesar defended himself, "You have to be patient. Our plan one day is to use Las Palmas's pastures to plant orange trees, but things take time. We just don't have enough funds from Managua to do everything we want. And it's abandoned because we have no one to take care of it. Everyone is in the army, and anyway, we have little money."

"You could hire Pedro and Luisa. They live there and can take care of it. Or at least, give them some land to farm. They lived and worked for ten years for our family at Las Palmas, yet they told me that you now won't even let them plant a corn patch on the property."

"Pedro is untrustworthy and is a supporter of the Contras," Cesar replied.

There was a heavy silence for a few moments, and then Sandra broke it by turning to Luis and asking, "Have you heard lately from your brother, Jorge? I understand he is now a Contra."

"Personally, no," Luis replied, still angry. "All my news of him comes through my mother. Neither he nor my sister, Elena, will have anything to do with me."

Sandra nodded in sympathy. "That's the pain of any revolution, I guess. Many Nicaraguan families are experiencing the same split."

"I did what I thought was right," Luis said, justifying himself once again. "Economic justice doesn't just happen by itself. There's sacrifice involved. The poor will always be poor if the rich don't share what they have with them. What bothers me, though, is that I don't see any poor people benefitting from the confiscation of Las Palmas. I only see its ruin. That wasn't what I intended, nor what the Revolution promised."

"Like Cesar said, things take time," Sandra reasoned. "A fair society doesn't just pop-up overnight—especially when you have the most powerful nation on earth violently opposing it."

No one responded, and for the most part, they ate the rest of the meal in an uneasy silence. Stan tried to lighten things up a couple of times by asking some questions about hunting and fishing in the area. Cesar's answers, however, were short, and no one else picked up the conversation.

Finally, giving up and noticing Clay's efforts to keep his eyes open, Stan suggested that they all should go to bed. "It has been a long day," he said, "and we need to get an early start tomorrow morning."

Luis and Sandra agreed. "What time would you like breakfast?" Cesar asked as they got up from the table.

"No later than seven," Stan replied. "There's a lot of setting-up that we have to do at the clinic before the first patients get there. If we could get to La Esperanza by eight, that would give us a half-hour before the first round of consultations."

"That would be good for us, too," Luis said. "The public boat from El Castillo to San Carlos stops at La Esperanza at around ten o'clock. We need to be on it to have time to catch the afternoon flight back from San Carlos to Managua."

"That should give me sufficient time to take some pictures and interview the mayor for the article," Sandra said. She then turned to Stan and asked, "What about you and Doctor Clay? When will you return to Managua?"

"We'll stay for two days of clinics, if Clay can bear the crush of the work," Stan answered. "Chino will take us back to San Carlos, and then we'll pick up the Land Cruiser and head back to Managua on Thursday. Clay and my daughter Laura have only ten days of vacation, and we need to be back in time for their flight a week from now."

After saying goodnight to Sandra and Cesar and thanking Adalina for dinner, the three men headed to their room and got ready for bed. It was 8:30 p.m. when Stan put his flashlight on the table and climbed under the mosquito net that he had spread over the bed and tucked in under the mattress. Stan disliked sleeping under nets because they made him feel as if he were in a stifled tomb, but he disliked even more the irritating zoom-zoom of hovering and attacking mosquitoes.

By the time Stan turned out the light, Clay had already fallen asleep. Stan said goodnight to Luis and then turned on his side. The fan's hum and the steady beat of the generator drowned out most of the night sounds of the river and forest, and he quickly fell asleep.

# CHAPTER 4

At about 2:30 a.m., Stan woke to go to the bathroom. He didn't need his flashlight as the moon was almost full, and its light made it easy for him to make out the obstacles in his path to the toilet. For the umpteenth time, he realized that he should never drink beer before going to bed because doing so always caused him to get up during the night.

The generator had shut down, the fan was now silent, and every night sound was magnified. Both Clay and Luis were breathing heavily in deep sleep, and Stan could also hear the loud snoring of Cesar from his apartment across the hallway. Outside, some dogs barked at what Stan imagined must be an intruding animal.

After relieving himself, Stan quietly climbed back into his bed, readjusted the mosquito net, and turned his head towards the wall away from Clay. As he tried to go to sleep again, his mind wandered to Sandra in the next room. There was something about her that deeply attracted him to her—her mystery, her dark beauty, her strength and independence, her dedication to the Revolution. How different she was from his wife, Elizabeth. Elizabeth was the loyal Tonya in "Dr. Zhivago," one of Stan's favorite movies. Sandra was Pasternak's enticing Lara. Stan imagined himself sneaking out of his room and into hers and making love to her.

Stan then bought his mind back to Elizabeth whom he loved deeply. He valued her stability, her loyalty, her unselfishness, and her simple faith. Elizabeth's authentic unselfishness was one of the things that attracted him to her in the first place. She was so different from his own dysfunctional parents whom Stan remembered as manipulative and egotistical people who yearned for nothing but pursuing their own pleasures and personal advancement. Appearances were everything to them, and Stan was even convinced that his mother had died in a freak car accident after her divorce because she refused to use seat belts because they wrinkled her clothes. As for his now retired father, Stan could not bear to be with him for they argued constantly—mostly about politics and religion. If it were not for the efforts of Elizabeth and Laura, he would have no relationship with him.

Stan valued Elizabeth also because she tried so hard to support him in his work in Nicaragua, even though he knew that her heart and her mind were just not there. She was much more cynical about the Revolution than he was, and she sometimes wondered out loud "if the emperor had no clothes." It wasn't that Elizabeth didn't care about the poor and the injustices that they faced, for she did. She cared deeply, but not in the same way that Stan did. While Stan concentrated his thoughts and energies on changing laws, institutions, and structures in order to create a more just society, Elizabeth concentrated hers on how she could help individual people whom she knew. She cared for their gardener, Domingo, and for the children who would sometimes come to their door asking for help to buy school uniforms or supplies. She especially cared for their maid, Isabel, and her daughter, Rosa. Seeing Rosa's innate intelligence and potential, Elizabeth even suggested to Stan that they help her attend the same expensive school that Laura attended in Managua.

Stan fought the idea at first because of the cost, but he finally agreed to it. Offering Rosa a scholarship helped him soothe his own conscience about living in a comfortable house and having a maid and a gardener and a fancy Toyota Land Cruiser, while those whom he had come to serve lived in such poverty. Doing so also made him look magnanimous and equalitarian to those he sought to impress. Stan was aware of his hypocrisy and of the guilt and pride that motivated so much of the good that he did. He hated himself because he was so much like his own parents. He longed to have the genuine empathy for others that both Elizabeth and Luis seemed to have naturally. But he just didn't.

As these thoughts went through his head, Stan tried to force himself to fall asleep again. He knew that he would need all of his energy for the myriad activities of the next day. He turned back on his other side to face the window and tried to cleanse his mind of his lustful and guilty thoughts.

While he was still trying, all hell broke loose.

Abruptly, three enormous explosions rocked the room in quick succession, and the night darkness was transformed into a ball of flame that surged upwards into the sky from the barn. Stan reared up in his bed terrified. Outside, the clatter of automatic weapons punctuated the blasts, and Stan could not decide if it was some horrible nightmare or a much worse reality that he was experiencing. He knew that it was reality when he heard the crack of a door being broken, shouts in Spanish, and heavy boots running from the back door through the main room coming towards them. They were being attacked by the Contras!

Instinctively, Stan dove for the floor seeking protection. In the process, he became entangled in the mosquito net.

Luis and Clay also rolled onto the floor. A woman screamed across the hall, and outside Stan heard shouts of pain and terror mixed with orders being yelled. Automatic weapons fired everywhere, from behind the house as well as from the river.

Almost immediately the door to their room burst open, and a powerful flashlight swept over their beds and the floor. Behind the light, a commanding voice ordered, "*Levanten-se*—get up with your hands in the air. We will kill you if you try anything." As if to emphasize the seriousness of the order, the man fired several bursts into the ceiling. Luis, who was on the floor beside his bed, cried out, "*No tenemos armas*—we are unarmed. Don't shoot."

As Stan, Luis, and then finally Clay struggled to their feet and disentangled themselves from the mosquito nets, doors crashed simultaneously in Sandra's and Cesar's rooms. Men shouted, and the woman continued screaming hysterically.

"Out into the hallway," the man with the light commanded in Spanish, and Stan felt some hands grab him and push him towards the door. Clay kept repeating over and over in English, "We're Americans, we're Americans, please don't shoot!" Someone also grabbed him and pushed.

Once in the hallway, they were herded into the main sitting room and ordered to place their hands against the wall underneath Tornado's head. Stan, looking to his right, saw Cesar with his hairy belly hanging over the elastic band of his underwear and Adalina trembling in a simple nightgown beside him. On his other side, Stan glimpsed Clay, whose body was shaking as he pressed his hands against the wall. Luis was on the other side of Clay. Within a minute, Sandra, wearing a light exercise suit, joined them in the room and also was pushed against the wall.

"Is there anyone else in the house?" The man with the largest flashlight inquired in Spanish to one of the men.

"I don't think so. We checked all of the rooms."

"Frisk them to make sure they don't have any weapons."

Three men grabbed Stan and the others from behind. Even though Stan was clad only in a tee shirt and boxer shorts, he felt hands going up his sides and legs. They then swept over his chest and groin area.

"Take your dirty hands off of me," Sandra yelled in Spanish, turning to push the person behind her away.

The man slapped her and slammed her back against the wall.

When the commander seemed satisfied that they carried no hidden arms, he ordered, "Turn around, so we can see the fish that we've caught."

All but Clay turned around.

"You heard him," one of men yelled at Clay in Spanish, grabbing him by the shoulders and spinning him. "He said to turn around!"

By the light of the blaze outside, Stan could see the shapes but could not make out the features of his captors. There were at least ten of them—four with flashlights and six with rifles pointed at them. Although he wasn't sure, he thought that several were wearing army fatigues.

The man who gave most of the orders shined his light onto Adalina's and then onto Cesar's faces. He then laughed. "Well, well, look who we have here. The big fish, himself—a whale actually, Cesar Rodrigues." He lowered the long flashlight to Cesar's bulging belly and then poked the flabby protrusion with its steel case. "Look at him in all his glory, boys." They all laughed. The man then turned to Adalina who was still shaking and sobbing in fear, "How can you bear to sleep with fat scum like this?"

"Jorge! Is it you?" Luis exclaimed.

The man with the flashlight backed up and turned the light abruptly on the face of Luis. "*Mierda!* Luis! What the hell are you doing here?"

"We're on our way to La Esperanza for a medical clinic tomorrow," Luis answered. "Two Americans are with me—Stan Hollins you know. It's his clinic, and the doctor is his son-in-law."

Jorge swung the light on the faces of Stan and Clay and studied them. The light blinded Stan. *"Mierda!"* Jorge exclaimed again. "Why the hell did you bring them to a war zone? We could have killed them. We could have killed you, too!"

"It wouldn't be a war zone, if you hadn't made it into one," Luis answered. Poor people still need medical care."

"They also need protection from thieves and power-hungry hypocrites like your Sandinista friends—especially from this scum, Cesar Rodriguez!"

Jorge retorted. He then turned the light on Sandra, standing on the other side of Luis. "Who is this one?"

Before Luis could reply, Sandra answered for herself. "Sandra Espinosa. I'm a reporter for *La Barricada*.

"Sandra Espinosa. Yes, I know who you are and the rag of a paper you work for," Jorge said. "I also know that there are a lot of ex-Guardias who would like to get their hands on you for your treachery."

"There're a lot of ex-Guardias that I would like to get *my* hands on, too," she answered, her voice full of defiance.

"A lioness worthy of her reputation!" Jorge said to his companions. He then turned back to face Sandra. "Since you say that you're now a reporter, I've got a good story for you. Tell your readers how the director of your glorious state farm, Cesar Rodrigues, has gotten rich by confiscating the cattle of the brother of the hero of the Revolution, Roberto Romero. Tell them how he sold them clandestinely in Costa Rica and pocketed the money and afterwards blamed the Contras for rustling them. Make your story one of the examples of the high morality of this Revolution!"

"That's a lie," Cesar shouted.

Jorge laughed. "A lie? I suppose, then, that you also have never heard of Ricardo Mendonza, the person you sold them to."

"I don't know what you are talking about," Cesar insisted.

"I ought to shoot you right here and now," Jorge said, "and I will, if you don't hand over the keys to the safe and to the guns and ammo closet." Jorge turned to four of the soldiers behind him. "Sal, you, Carlos, Victor, and Tito go with him. The guns and ammunition should be in two metal cabinets in the office. The money is in a safe he keeps next to his desk. The keys to the truck should be hanging on the wall." He turned back to Cesar. "You see, we know all about you." He again faced his men. "Bring the truck keys and the safe contents back to me. If he gives you any trouble," Jorge said, pointing to Cesar, "shoot him."

Two of the men grabbed Cesar and pushed him towards the office. As they did so, Stan noticed that Adalina was still trembling, though now quiet. Stan felt calmer now that he realized that the Contra commander was Luis's brother, Jorge. Stan whispered to Clay in English, "It's all right. They won't hurt us."

"No talking with each other," Jorge ordered in English, his anger showing in his voice.

At that moment, the sound of boots on the porch caused the soldiers in the room to swing their flashlights and guns towards the front door. The door opened, and Chino was pushed through with his hands behind his head. Behind him, three men with guns entered—one of them in uniform. "Another prisoner," the man in uniform said. "We found him hiding in the boat behind boxes of medical supplies. The other man dove into the river and escaped."

"Line him up with the others," Jorge ordered. He then turned to the man in uniform. "Cato, what's the situation outside?"

"All of the Sandinista soldiers in the guard houses have been killed. Kojak is wounded, but I don't think too seriously. A bullet hit his right leg. The rest is going as planned. The men are now rounding up the cattle and heading to Costa Rica with them. We have some pack mules ready outside for the arms and ammunition, but if we can get your truck working, we can load them on it instead." Cato then looked at the prisoners. "What do you want us to do with them and with the medical supplies in the boat?"

"We have a major complication," Jorge said. "Two of the prisoners are *gringos,* and another one is my brother, Luis."

"*Caramba!*" Cato exclaimed. "Your brother? What's he doing here?"

"He was on his way to La Esperanza with the gringos and medical supplies and stopped here. I guess to spend the night. One of them runs a relief agency in Managua, and the other is a doctor." Jorge paused and then said, "Actually, that's good news. Bring Kojak in so the doctor can look at his leg."

Cato went to the door and yelled to someone outside. "Help Kojak get here. There's a doctor inside."

At the same time, Victor returned from the other part of the house. "We found the guns. There must be at least ten AK-47s and dozens of boxes of ammunition."

"Load them quickly on the pack mules in case the truck doesn't run," Jorge said. He then directed two more of the men behind him to go with them to the back room to help.

While the men went back and forth carrying the arms and ammunition outside, two other soldiers brought Cesar back to the main room. One of them carried several sets of keys and three bulging manila envelopes on top of a metal box. "We found these in the safe," he said.

Jorge took the metal box from the soldier and opened it up. It was stuffed with packets of Costa Rican *colones* in large denominations. "Money from the sale of my cattle, I bet."

"It's government money to pay the salaries of the workers," Cesar responded.

Jorge laughed. "Sure. That's why it's in Costa Rican *colones* and not in Nicaraguan *córdobas*!"

Jorge put the metal box and the envelopes on the dining room table and looked through the keys until he found the one that he was searching for. "This one is to my truck." He gave it to Cato, "See if you can get it started. If you can, we'll take it back over the border with us." He put the rest of the keys beside the metal box on the table.

"What about the prisoners and medical supplies?" Cato asked.

"The medical supplies we'll leave here. We haven't got time to load them, and anyway, they're donations to the people of La Esperanza. As for the prisoners, we'll take them as hostages to the border. Then we'll decide what is best. If they cooperate, we may let them go." He turned to Cesar, "But if you try anything heroic, we'll leave you here dead."

That's when Luis spoke up. "Be reasonable, Jorge. Think of the reaction of the U.S. Government and international press when they find out that you've captured two Americans who just came to Nicaragua to help poor people. You should let us all go. The army will be after you soon, and we'll just slow you down."

"Your brother is right," Sandra said. "How do you suppose that your CIA handlers in Costa Rica and Washington are going to react to finding out that you've taken two Americans prisoners. They won't be very happy!"

Jorge was quiet for a minute as if pondering what they had said. "Maybe you have a point. Maybe we *should* leave you here," Jorge said. "Not because of our CIA handlers, as you say, but just to illustrate the difference between you and us in how we treat prisoners. Maybe it will inspire you to write a truthful article for once in that propaganda rag you work for."

Jorge then turned to Cato. "We'll hold only two hostages. You take the boatman with you, but release him at the border if he cooperates." He then pointed to Cesar. "I'll take this one with me. The others we'll tie up and lock up in separate rooms." He paused and then added, "We'll need to have some rope and five horses for us to make our escape. Jacinto can stay behind with the horses, and Victor and Sal will stay here to guard the prisoners." Jorge then picked up the metal box and papers from the table and gave them to Cato. "Here, take the money and the papers along with the guns and cattle and get going. We'll follow behind you in about fifteen minutes and meet at our rendezvous spot."

Cato saluted and took the box and papers. He then went outside to get the rest of the men moving and to see if Jorge's truck was in working order. He left the back door wide open, giving Stan a view of the blazing flames shooting skyward from the barn and the wooden houses. The flames were then so bright that there was no longer a need for flashlights in the main room.

As Stan watched the horses and men moving around in the open space beyond the former pool, the wounded man they called Kojak limped through the back door groaning and leaning on the shoulders of two soldiers dressed in the simple clothes of *campesinos*. One of them also brought the coils of rope that Jorge had requested. Jorge told Kojak to lie down on the dining room table and then told Clay in English to look after him.

Stan noticed a sudden change in Clay's demeanor as he began to examine the wounded man. Now that he had work to do, his fear seemed to leave him. Clay immediately asked for a knife to cut the man's bloody trousers so he could see the wound. When Jorge handed him one from his belt, Clay cut through the cloth at the thigh and the leg was revealed—a mass of blood and torn flesh.

Clay then asked for someone to bring soap, water, and towels from the bathroom, and Jorge sent a soldier after them. When the soldier returned, Clay took them and carefully cleaned the area. Kojak cried out in pain when Clay put pressure on the wound. "The bullet probably shattered the bone inside, but it didn't slice any artery," he said. "All we can do is keep the wound clean and stable until you can get him to a hospital." Clay then asked Jorge to get someone to break the back of one of the dining room chairs for its wooden slats and to bring him some rope so that he could secure the slats to the leg to brace it.

Jorge did so, and Clay cut the rope in pieces and took the slats and tied them tightly around the leg, making sure that he didn't cut off the circulation.

As Clay worked on Kojak, one of the soldiers who had carried the weapons and ammunition outside to the mules returned through the back door. "That's it," he said to Jorge. "We've loaded it all."

"Good, then get moving. Take the boatman with you, but release him when you get to Costa Rica if he cooperates," Jorge reiterated.

Stan heard a truck motor start, and a few minutes later, Cato also came back to the room.

"Everything's ready," he reported to Jorge. "Those herding the cattle have already left, and the men with the pack mules are ready to leave. The truck is working and has enough diesel to get to Costa Rica. Kojak can go with me in the truck, and we'll put the prisoner in the back with a couple of soldiers to guard him. We're on our way."

One of the soldiers then led Chino out the door and another helped Kojak get off the table and hop on his good leg down the back steps to the waiting truck. Cato saluted again, and Jorge returned the salute. "Be careful," Cato said. "We'll see you soon in Costa Rica."

Stan glanced at his watch in the light of the flames. It was 3:50 a.m. Although it seemed an eternity had passed since the attack began, in reality, it had been less than an hour.

Jorge stood at the open back door and watched as the truck, horses, and pack animals started through the pastures heading to the dirt road that led from Las Palmas to Costa Rica. When the sound of the truck got fainter, he came back inside.

"Turn to the wall again and put your hands against it over your heads," he ordered his remaining captives. "Sal, you keep your gun on them while Victor ties them up."

"Your brother and the gringos, too?" Victor asked.

"Them, too," Jorge replied, looking straight at Luis. "But start with the thief, Rodrigues. Tie only his hands as he's going to have to ride a horse back to Costa Rica. Shoot him if he resists. I'm going outside to check on the horses and to send Jacinto to the river to watch for any activity. I'll be back in a few minutes."

As Jorge left with his AK-47 and flashlight in hand, Victor slung his own rifle over his shoulder with the barrel pointing to the floor so he could have his hands free to cut the rope and tie the prisoners. Sal maintained his automatic rifle at hip level pointed at Cesar.

Victor unsheathed the knife that he carried on his belt and cut the rope into meter-long segments. Once he had a dozen such pieces, he made small lassos with them and put all but one on the floor. He took that one to where Cesar was standing and ordered him to lower his hands and to put them behind his back so that he could tie them.

But just as Victor looped the lasso around Cesar's left wrist, Cesar suddenly spun around and hit Victor hard in the groin, doubling him over in pain. With his left arm, Cesar held him in front of him as a shield and with his right hand, he found the trigger on Victor's AK-47 and pointed the gun as best he could toward Sal and began firing.

Sal and Victor were taken utterly by surprise by the quick action. Sal reacted and fired at Cesar, but his bullets hit Victor instead. Cesar's spray of bullets, however, found their mark. Sal fell over groaning in pain and dropped his rifle. As he hit the floor, Sandra quickly pounced on the rifle and pointed it at him. But after a quick spasm, there was no more movement from Sal's body.

When Cesar saw that both of the soldiers were dead, he jerked the weapon from Victor's lifeless shoulder and ran with it to the back door. As soon as he got there, he began to fire furiously. Outside, Stan heard Jorge scream out in pain.

"I got the motherfucker," Cesar exclaimed. "He's down." Even so, Cesar kept shooting.

When Luis heard his brother's scream and saw that Cesar continued to fire at him, he rushed at Cesar in a fury, knocking him face down on to the floor. Grabbing the rifle from Cesar's hands, he pummeled him on the back of the head with its butt. Then, with the weapon in hand, he ran outside to the open space where his brother had fallen.

Stan ran to the door after him. In the light of the flames, he saw Luis bending over his brother in the open space crying, "Jorge, Jorge, where are you hit?" There was no answer, just groaning.

"Stan, Clay, help me!" Luis yelled back to the house. "Jorge's badly hurt and is losing a lot of blood."

"Let's go!" Stan yelled to Clay.

At first, Clay just stared at Stan in stunned silence but then followed him out the back door. They both ran bent over in fear of the unknown. When they got to Luis, they quickly fell on their knees beside him, and Stan saw blood all over the front of Jorge's shirt and blood coming from his mouth. Clay quickly assessed the situation and said to Luis and Stan, "We need to take him inside. The fire's too hot here to do anything. I'll get his arms, and you two get his legs."

Stan stumbled as they picked up Jorge and started to carry him through the open space to the back door of the house. They had only progressed a few meters when a barrage of bullets came from the direction of the river towards them. Immediately, Clay dropped Jorge's body and fell over him on the ground. Stan screamed as he felt a sharp pain in his thigh and then collapsed. Luis dove to the grass as well, seeking cover.

"What in God's name is happening?!" Stan yelled to anyone who could hear him. The only answers that came back were the continued clatter of automatic weapons and the shriek of bullets over his head. Stan was terrified as he had never been before in his life. He hugged the ground tightly, sweat coming out of every pore in his body, both from fear and from the intense heat of the hell-like barn fire. All that he could think about was his own survival. Hiding behind Jorge's body, Stan felt the metal of Jorge's AK-47 lying beside him. Grabbing it with his right hand, he pointed it towards the flashes coming from the river and pressed furiously on the trigger, the rifle butt pounding in rapid rhythm against his shoulder. When the clip was empty, Stan prayed and waited in despair for the inevitable—his own sure death.

# CHAPTER 5

Nine hours later on that same day in Managua, Elizabeth Hollins was hosting a small homecoming luncheon for her daughter Laura and three of her Nicaraguan friends, Rosa Guevara, Flavia Matos, and Marta Toledo. All of them were seated around the heavy wooden table in the Hollins's dining room, finishing the cold chicken salad that Elizabeth and the Hollins's cook, Isabel Guevara, had prepared. Elizabeth had insisted that Isabel join them at the table as she didn't want Isabel, or her daughter, Rosa, to feel at all uncomfortable with Laura's other two friends.

Laura had a twinkle in her eye as she reminisced with her friends. "The first time I came to Nicaragua," she said, "I came kicking and screaming. Can you imagine—Mom and Dad pulled me out of high school in my senior year where I was to be cheerleading captain and took me to a place where I didn't know a soul and couldn't even speak the language?!" She paused to let the question sink in. "Now, though, I'm really glad to be back!"

Elizabeth Hollins smiled sheepishly at her daughter as the others laughed.

"It was you who saved me," Laura said, turning to Rosa who was sitting beside her. Laura patted her on the hand. "You made me laugh, you taught me Spanish, you introduced me to all of the good things of Nicaragua." Laura then turned to Rosa's mother, Doña Isabel, across from her. "And you introduced me to all of the good food!"

"It's true," Elizabeth added, looking at Isabel and Rosa, "I don't know what Laura and I would have done without you two putting up with all of our complaining the first few months. You always had such good humor and patience. I'll always be grateful to Luis Romero for making you a part of our family."

"And we to you for treating us like family," Rosa replied. She turned to Marta and Flavia. "Mr. and Mrs. Hollins made it possible for me to go to the International School. I could never have imagined something like that when I was growing up on the Río San Juan."

Laura always wondered how anyone as self-assured, bright, pretty, funny, and caring as Rosa could come from such a humble background and be so natural about it—never boastful or ashamed. Rosa was born on a tiny subsistence farm on a tributary of the Río San Juan near the Romero family ranch Las Palmas and was the second child of Isabel and her mother's common law husband, Rodrigo Guevara. Rodrigo, a fisherman and farmer, was twelve years older than Isabel, and according to Isabel, their union was not a happy one. Isabel had gone to live with him at sixteen, and Rodrigo blamed her for the death of their first-born of malaria. He often beat her and constantly spent what little money they had on alcohol and other women. Coming home one late night in his dugout canoe from La Esperanza, he fell into the river in a drunken stupor and drowned.

Hearing of Isabel's situation, Jorge Romero hired her as a cook and cleaning woman for the new house he had just built at Las Palmas. Later, when Rosa reached high school age, Jorge arranged for Isabel to get a job in Managua at the home of a United Nations agricultural advisor from Iowa. That way, Rosa could continue her studies. During the two years that Isabel worked at the American's home, she picked up some basic English, while Rosa became fluent in the language. In 1980, after the agricultural advisor returned home to Iowa, Luis and Jorge arranged for the Hollins to inherit both the advisor's rental house and the services of Isabel.

"Isn't the Río San Juan where your father and husband are now?" Marta asked Laura. She then joked, "Actually, I'm beginning to think that you are hiding Clay from me as I am the only one here who has never met him!" Of the three Nicaraguan friends of Laura, Marta was the shortest and the least attractive physically, but she made up for her lack of looks with her brains, her caring spirit, and her confident personality.

"It's because you weren't able to come to the wedding," Laura replied, "but I promise that I will introduce you to him when he gets back from the river. He's a good man, and you two should get along well."

Along with five of her Nashville friends, Laura had asked Rosa, Marta, and Flavia to be her bridesmaids. Marta couldn't go, however, because the trip was too expensive for her and her father to manage. While he earned a decent salary as a high official in the customs department of the Sandinista government, he was stretched with his payments for Marta's nursing studies at the local university. As for Flavia, she paid for her own trip. Her family was comparatively wealthy as her father was the representative of the Texaco Oil Company in the country, and he also owned a coffee plantation outside of Managua. As for Rosa, the Hollins paid her way.

"Clay *is* a good man," Rosa agreed, "and rich, too! I never saw a wedding like that before—bagpipes, tuxedos, flowers everywhere, shrimp at the reception—it must have cost a fortune!"

"It was mostly Clay's mom's doing," Laura explained. "She wanted a large ceremony since they know half of Nashville, and she and Mr. Danforth insisted on picking up the tab!"

"We certainly could never have done it on Stan's salary," Elizabeth interjected.

"How did the Danforths get so rich?" Marta asked.

"Shoes," Laura answered. "Mr. Danforth has a factory that turns out thousands of men's shoes. Mostly dress shoes but also work shoes and boots for the military. He's done very well." She then added, almost apologetically, "But he also contributes a lot to charities in the city."

As Isabel returned to the table with a desert of mangos and ice cream, Flavia, who looked more European than Nicaraguan with her light skin and tall, thin body, remarked to Laura, "We had a large contingent of Nicaraguans there, but I was surprised that Antonio didn't go to the wedding. I guess he was heartbroken when you got married," she joked.

"He wrote and sent a gift, but he was on a study program in Germany at the time and just couldn't make it," Laura explained. "As for being heartbroken, I don't think so!" She laughed. "He only took me to the senior prom at the International School because his Uncle Luis made him invite me!"

Antonio Lopez was Luis Romero's nephew, the son of Luis's sister, Elena, and of her husband, Ricardo Lopez. Chosen by the faculty and students as the outstanding senior at the International School, he had gone on to Harvard on a full scholarship. Most of the girls at the school, including Flavia and Laura, had crushes on him. Antonio, however, was mainly interested in his studies and sports at the time and rarely went out on single dates. The senior prom had been an exception.

After the meal, while Elizabeth and Isabel cleaned up, the four girls got up and headed to the rockers and hammocks on the back veranda for their coffee. This was the nicest part of the house and looked out on a lemon tree full of fruit and on a garden bursting with exotic and colorful plants—a little place of beauty and respite from the intense heat, noise, and dirt of the city.

The Hollins's house was in the cooler, less earthquake-prone southern part of Managua, just off the Pan American Highway that headed to Costa Rica. Like most of the better houses in the area, the rental home was surrounded by a high wall that was topped with barbed wire and broken glass to discourage thieves. Stan, however, differed from most foreigners living in Managua. He had chosen not to hire an armed guard at their front gate to protect them from thieves and beggars.

Sipping the after-dinner coffee that Elizabeth had brought them, the four friends talked about their university studies and their plans for the future. They all were in their third year of university—Laura studying Romance languages; Flavia, art history; Rosa, social work; and Marta, nursing. Except for Laura, none of the other three girls had married or was even dating anyone seriously.

"When is your baby due?" Flavia asked Laura.

"In late November," Laura replied. "To tell you the truth, I didn't realize having a baby was such a big deal. Before we found out that I was pregnant, I was planning to go with Clay and Dad on this trip to the river. My doctor nixed it because of the roads and the war."

"If he hadn't, I certainly would have," Elizabeth said. "Laura and I tried to get Stan and Clay not to go, either, but Stan insisted. He said there was no danger and the people in La Esperanza needed medical help."

While they were talking, the telephone rang in the living room, and Isabel, who was clearing the table inside, answered it. She came to the sliding glass door of the porch. "It's for you, Doña Elizabeth. It's Señor Luis."

"Oh good," Elizabeth said getting up, "They must be calling from La Esperanza."

"Let me know if I can talk to Clay," Laura said to her mother. "I want to find out his impressions of the river." She then turned the conversation to what name her friends thought that she should choose for the coming baby.

When Elizabeth returned to the veranda a few minutes later, followed by Isabel, she was ashen-faced. The girls immediately noticed that something was wrong and stopped their light-hearted talk. "It was Luis," she said. "Something terrible has happened on the river. Early this morning, the Contras attacked where they were spending the night. Clay and Stan were wounded and have been flown to Managua by an army helicopter. They're at the military hospital."

"What are you saying?! Wounded?" Laura could not believe what she was hearing. "How badly are they wounded?"

"All that I know is that they are operating now. Luis said that he has sent a car from the Foreign Ministry to pick us up and take us to the hospital. We need to go immediately."

Laura jumped up from her chair, "We can't wait for the car. We'll take yours. It's the hospital on the hill near the pyramid hotel, isn't it?"

"I think so, but I'm not sure," Elizabeth said. "But we should wait for the driver. Luis said the car would be here any minute." Her voice broke, "Oh God, please let them be all right!"

As Isabel hugged her, the electric bell at the gate buzzed. Laura rushed into the living room with the others following her. When she opened the front door, she saw a young man in an army uniform standing outside the iron bar gate of the driveway looking in. Elizabeth, who was right behind her, grabbed a key off the hook by the door and headed quickly to the gate. Laura and her friends followed.

"Are you from the Foreign Ministry?" Elizabeth asked in her heavily accented Spanish as she approached him.

"*Sí, Señora*, I was instructed to take Señora Hollins and Señora Danforth to the hospital."

"We're the ones that you are looking for," Elizabeth replied.

As Elizabeth unlocked the gate, Rosa asked Laura, "Do you want me to go with you?"

"Yes, please!" Laura's voice quavered. "You can help with the Spanish."

"I know they'll be all right," Flavia said in encouragement. "We'll stay here until we hear something from you. Whatever you need us to do, we'll do." She and Marta hugged Laura, who now started to cry.

The driver opened the back door of the new Toyota for Elizabeth and Laura. As he did so, Rosa went around to the front passenger seat and let herself in. Once they were all seated, the driver quickly backed into the deserted street and turned right on the two-lane highway that would take them down the mountain to the military hospital in town. Marta, Flavia, and Isabel watched them from the gate with concerned expressions on their faces.

It was Rosa who did most of the talking as they headed towards the hospital. Elizabeth and Laura were not comfortable in Spanish, and anyway, they were lost in their own fears and thoughts.

"Are Señor Danforth and Señor Hollins OK?" Rosa asked the driver.

"All that I know is that they are wounded and are being operated. Señor Luis Romero will meet you in front of the hospital."

As he sped down the road, the driver asserted the power and prestige of his official car by frequently honking at pedestrians and slower traffic and passing when he was able. Within ten minutes, he had gotten them to the entrance of the military hospital. When the guard saw the official car approaching, he immediately raised the barrier bar so that they could enter.

The driver quickly located a parking place under a tree near the hospital's entrance, parked, and got out to open the door for Elizabeth and Laura. Before he could do so, however, all three of the women were out of the car, had thanked him, and were heading towards the main entrance. Luis Romero stood there waiting for them, unshaven, looking exhausted, and wearing muddy and blood-splotched clothes. Even so, he hugged both Elizabeth and Laura tightly.

Luis's high position in the Ministry of Foreign Relations and his friendship to them was a great comfort to Elizabeth and Laura. It was Luis who had arranged for their house, their employees, and their visas. It was Luis who got Laura and Rosa into the International School at the last minute and who helped Stan set up Acción. He was always there to help them whenever they ran into problems, and they were immensely grateful for his presence now at this new time of crisis.

Luis opened the door, and after passing through the waiting room filled with patients, he led them into an empty private office and offered them chairs. He then sat down in front of them with a pain-filled look on his gentle face. When Laura saw his expression, her body tightened, bracing herself for the coming news. "Are they going to be all right?" she asked.

Luis looked at her, and his voice broke. "Stan was shot in the thigh, but the doctor says that he will be all right."

"And my husband?" Laura asked, fear seeping through her pores.

"Clay didn't make it. He was killed," Luis said softly, tears welling in his eyes. "I'm so sorry."

Elizabeth, Laura, and Rosa sat with their faces frozen, unable to speak.

Elizabeth finally blurted out, "No, God! No, God! It can't be true!"

"You are saying that Clay is dead?" Laura asked in a lifeless voice as she looked straight at Luis.

Luis nodded. "He's dead."

Laura just stared at him, as if she still didn't understand.

"It happened at four this morning," Luis said. "Clay was a hero. He died trying to save the life of my brother."

"Your brother? Not Señor Jorge?" Rosa asked. Jorge Romero had played a prominent role in her family's life on the Río San Juan as an employer and as a friend.

Luis nodded. "Jorge was also killed during the attack."

"Oh, no!" Rosa cried.

"This is a nightmare!" Elizabeth said. "It can't be happening!"

"I wish it were a nightmare," said Luis, "then we could all wake up."

Laura gasped for breath as she sobbed, tears streaming down her face. "Oh God, it's not possible, it's not true! Why did I let him go on this insane trip?"

Elizabeth held her tightly and wept with her. Rosa also got up and put her arms around them both, and her eyes, too, filled with tears. As the women embraced, Luis stood up, opened the office door, and called for a nurse outside at the reception desk to bring some glasses of water and some sedatives.

A few minutes later, the nurse came in with the glasses and pills on a metal tray, but Laura at first refused to take them. Finally, at Elizabeth's insistence, she reached out obediently and took the pills, drinking just enough water to wash them down. After she had swallowed, Elizabeth turned to Luis and asked, "Can we see Stan?"

"Not yet. He just got out of the operating room and is drugged. But the doctor will be here soon, and you can talk to him," Luis said. "Stan's wound is not life-threatening."

"Why did I let Clay go? This is just not happening. It can't be happening!" Laura cried. "How can I tell his parents? It will kill them." Rosa hugged her tighter as tears streamed down both of their cheeks. For several minutes, no one spoke but only wept in bewilderment and grief.

There was then a knock on the glass-paneled door, and as Laura looked up, Sandra Espinosa entered. Laura recognized her from the day before when she and Luis had arrived at their house early in the morning to meet Clay and Stan for the long trip to San Carlos. Sandra now wore clean black pants and a red shirt and her hair was pulled back again in a ponytail. She was accompanied by a mustached young man dressed simply in tan pants and a white, embroidered guayabera shirt. "I'm so sorry for you. Your husband was a hero. He died trying to save the lives of others." Sandra spoke in her heavily accented English as she lightly touched Laura on her shoulder in empathy.

There was a long silence and then Elizabeth asked Luis, "Could you tell us how it happened?"

"Sandra saw it all. I didn't," Luis answered. "I dove for cover when they started shooting. I didn't see anything."

"You both understand Spanish don't you?" Sandra asked Elizabeth and Laura. "It's much easier for me."

Elizabeth nodded affirmatively, "If you speak slowly."

"We were spending the night in the guest quarters at the state farm," Sandra began, "and at about two o'clock in the morning, a force of Contras attacked. There were about twenty-five of them, mainly after money, guns, and cattle. They killed the guards, set the barn on fire, and then burst into the house where we were sleeping and took us prisoner. Afterwards, most of them left to go back to Costa Rica with what they had stolen, but several stayed behind to tie us up. The farm director managed to grab a gun from one of our captors and to kill two of them. He also wounded Luis's brother, Jorge, who had led the Contra raiding party in the attack. Luis ran outside to assist his brother, and then he called for your two husbands to help him. When they picked Jorge up in the yard to carry him inside the house, they were fired upon by the other Contras outside. I saw everything in the light of the barn fire. Señor Clay and Señor Stan were hit and fell. Soon afterwards, an army patrol from La Esperanza arrived. They had heard the grenade explosions and seen the flames in the sky and sent a patrol. They killed the Contra who shot your husbands. Unfortunately, Señor Clay was killed instantly, and one of our soldiers from the patrol was also killed in the firefight with the Contras. After routing the enemy, the commander of the patrol radioed to San Carlos for a helicopter to take your husbands and the rest of us back to Managua. It took longer than we had hoped, and we only got here at ten o'clock. Señor Stan immediately went into surgery."

"You've been here since ten?" Laura asked Luis. "Why didn't you call us sooner?" She felt terrible that she had been having fun with her friends when her husband was already dead.

"The government insisted on debriefing us before we did anything else, since the attack involved Americans," Luis said, defending himself.

Sandra reached out again and touched Laura sympathetically on the arm. "Your husband was a good man who came to our country only to help. The American government finances the killers of your husband, but Señor Clay was our friend." She turned to the man beside her in the guayabera shirt and introduced him. "Señor Pedro Bartola is an employee of the Foreign Ministry who will assist you in any way that he can to deal with this tragedy."

Pedro bowed to them and spoke in impeccable, formal English. "I, too, wish to express my personal sorrow and the sorrow of our government for this terrible event." He gave them his card. "I will be outside to help you with any arrangements or in any other way that I can."

"Thank you," Elizabeth said.

"The doctor will be there shortly and then you will be able to see Señor Stan," Sandra said. "I know how hard this is for you. We are truly sorry."

Elizabeth and Laura acknowledged her words with a dazed nod.

Sandra then excused herself saying that she needed to go to her office at *La Barricada* to write an article for the next day's paper that would tell the world what had happened. She and Pedro bowed again and left the room.

Alone once again, Elizabeth, Laura, Rosa, and Luis waited for the doctor, and the room was filled with a heavy silence of sorrow, self-recrimination, and disbelief.

Ten minutes later, the surgeon entered the room accompanied by Pedro. The doctor was a short man in his late fifties with a kindly face and was clad in a green surgical outfit. He introduced himself as Dr. Edmundo Navarro. "It's OK now to visit your husband," he said to Elizabeth in Spanish. "Only for a little, though. He's still drowsy from the operation."

"Will he be all right?" Elizabeth asked.

"He was lucky that the bullet missed the artery, but it shattered some of the bone," Dr. Navarro replied. "We were able to repair most of the damage, but he may walk with a limp for some time."

Dr. Navarro opened the office door for them and led them through the waiting room and down several corridors. They passed crowded rooms where wounded and sick soldiers lay in beds or sat in rusty wheelchairs in the hallway, their bandaged stumps showing. Stan, however, had a private room with a uniformed guard at the door. When they entered, they saw that he was partially propped up on a hospital bed and hooked up to clear bags from which blood, sedatives, and nutrients dripped slowly into his veins. He had a half-cast on his leg.

Elizabeth immediately went over to the bed and kissed him on his forehead. Stan's hair was uncombed, and beard stubble sprouted from his haggard face. "Thank God, you'll be all right," Elizabeth said.

Stan hugged his wife with his free arm, and then his eyes filled with tears when he saw Laura. "I'm so sorry, so sorry," he repeated, his speech slurred, his eyes avoiding her eyes.

Laura cried again and came over to kiss her father on the top of the head, unable to speak. Luis patted Stan's good leg and asked the doctor in Spanish when he could go home.

"Maybe in two or three days. It's not such a serious wound, but he will need some physical therapy." He then turned to Elizabeth, "He'll be fine, but he does need some rest right now."

"Can I see my husband's body?" Laura asked the doctor, speaking slowly and almost inaudibly.

Before the doctor was able to respond, Luis answered. "Laura, I don't think that's a good idea. Clay was shot in the back of the head. You don't want to remember him that way."

Laura nodded like a zombie. The sedatives that she had taken in the waiting room had started to have their effect.

"I think that it is best now that everyone go home and get some rest," Luis said. "Stan's going to be OK." He then added, "I suggest that Pedro go with you and help you in any way he can. The Foreign Ministry will take care of all of the details and costs once you decide on Clay's funeral arrangements. I'll also be there to help, but right now they are insisting that I stay here in the hospital."

The doctor nodded, supporting what Luis had said.

Pedro, who had hardly spoken, now took charge. "The Ministry car will take you back to your house so that you can get some rest, like Señor Luis suggested," he said in English. "When you are ready to think through what you want to do, I will be there to help you with any arrangements that you want to make. Whatever you need, we are at your orders."

"Thank you," Elizabeth said again.

She and Laura went over to kiss Stan once more, and Rosa touched him affectionately on his shoulder. "When can we visit for a longer time?" Elizabeth asked the doctor.

"Probably tomorrow afternoon," Dr. Navarro replied. "Don't worry. We'll take good care of him."

They said goodbye, and with Pedro accompanying them, they went back to the parking lot to where the Ministry car was parked. Pedro joined the driver in the front seat and the three women got into the back.

When the car delivered them back to the Hollins's house, Isabel, Marta, and Flavia came out to meet them in the driveway. With them were the Hollins's pastor and friend, Richard Johnson, and his wife, Suzanne. Isabel had called them, and they had immediately dropped everything to come over to be with Elizabeth and Laura. Richard was in his early sixties and had been in Managua now for eight years, preaching every Sunday at the two churches that he had founded. One was a small, informal gathering for English speakers that met early Sunday morning at 8:00 a.m. The other was a much larger congregation of Spanish-speaking Nicaraguans meeting at 10:30 a.m. Elizabeth attended the international service in English, and Stan sometimes went to the Spanish service by himself.

Elizabeth told them the terrible news—not only had Stan and Clay been wounded, Clay was dead. They were all shocked, and Richard and Suzanne hugged Elizabeth and Laura tightly. Elizabeth then introduced Pedro Bartola. As Isabel closed the gate, they all slowly walked towards the house with Suzanne holding Elizabeth's hand and Richard putting his arm around Laura.

"What can we do to help?" Suzanne asked.

"I don't know," Elizabeth answered. "Maybe you can notify the others in the church and have them pray for Stan and Laura and for Clay's parents." When they got to the door, she added, "The hardest task is going to fall to Laura to tell Clay's parents what has happened. Pray that she will have the strength to do it."

"I just can't do it, Mother," Laura said, shaking her head and crying again. "You have no idea how they loved him. It will kill them to hear this news."

"It's all right, honey. I can do it for you," Elizabeth offered, hugging her daughter.

When they were inside the house, Laura rethought what she had just said and slowly shook her head. "No, it's something I'm going to have to face up to and do myself. I just can't call them right now. This is all so unbelievable."

"Why don't you go into your room and be alone for awhile?" Elizabeth suggested. "I'll talk with Señor Bartola and the others, and we'll try to come up with some ideas as to what we need to do. Maybe we should all sit around the dining room table and make a list of what we need to do and who should do it."

Laura agreed to the plan, and after thanking each of them for their support, she headed towards her room at the end of the hall. When she got there, she closed the door behind her and leaned against it for support. Seeing Clay's suitcase open at the foot of the twin bed just as he had left it, she bent over, picked up the green shirt on top, and held it to her face, trying to smell his life and feel his touch. Still holding the shirt to her cheek, she sat down on her bed, hoping against hope that somehow he would come walking into the room and that none of what they said had happened was true.

The room fan was on, and it blew cool air against Laura's body, reminding her of Clay's thoughtfulness in turning off the rotation so that it would blow only on her bed and not on his. As she sat in a daze, images of Clay's face and scenes of their days of courtship at Vanderbilt darted through her mind—the football games they had gone to, the walks holding hands, the short visits between classes, the fun surprise gifts he would bring her, the little notes he would leave in her books. She could not imagine that it was now over—in an instant, just like that!

Laura put her hand to her stomach and thought of their child. She was thankful that she had something of Clay still alive in her, but that sense of gratitude quickly turned to deeper feelings of despair, terror, and anger at now having to confront life without a husband and without a father for their child. Self-recrimination filled her, pounding against her brain. *Why did I allow my father to convince Clay to go with him into a war zone? Why hadn't I been more firm? It was all so unnecessary!*

Laura stretched out on her bed face down and buried her head in her pillow to muffle her sobs. The pain was too great for her to bear.

When she could weep no more, she turned on her side and looked at Clay's bed, imagining him there, trying to comfort her. She thought of his goodness to her and of his love for his parents. *How can I call them and tell them that their son, their only son, is dead? What will I say to them?*

Finally, realizing that she had to do it, Laura forced herself up from the bed. She walked over to her old study desk and opened the top drawer. She took out a piece of paper and a pen and began to write out two lists. The first was her thoughts on what kind of funeral arrangements she felt that Clay would have chosen. The other was a list of what she would say when she called her in-laws.

Laura decided that, before anything else, she should call their pastor, Dr. Bill Edmonds, at the Eastminister Presbyterian Church in Nashville. It was important that he be there with the Danforths when she telephoned to tell them the news. Besides being the church that the Danforths attended, Eastminister also was one of the main financial supporters of Stan's work in Nicaragua. It was at Eastminister where she and Clay had met and married, and it should be at Eastminister that his funeral service should be held.

Having a plan and something to do gave Laura new strength. After less than half an hour alone in her room, and with her lists in hand, she opened the door and went out to discuss her thoughts with her mother and then to make the dreaded calls.

# CHAPTER 6

Through the week following Clay's death, Laura felt like an actress playing the lead role in a tragedy. In order to get herself through the performances in Managua and then in Nashville, she tied her emotions inside a package and then put the package aside until she could open it later in private. Her life had been irrevocably changed—first, by Clay's death, and second, by the front page article that Sandra Espinosa published the next day in *La Barricada*.

Entitled, "*El asasinato de un yanqui bueno*—The Murder of a Good Yankee," Sandra's article portrayed Clay and Stan as "Heroes of the Revolution"—Americans who had come to Nicaragua not to kill but to help the poor. It spoke of the work of Acción para la Paz and of Clay Danforth's volunteering as a doctor to treat those in the impoverished riverside community of La Esperanza. The article had two pictures: one of Clay and the rest of the group smiling under the sign of the Roberto Romero State Farm; the second of Clay's body lying dead, face down on the ground. Sandra told of the surprise attack at night, the slaughtering of the young Sandinista soldiers at the farm, of how Clay and Stan had run out to help a wounded enemy, and of how they were ambushed by the Contras. Sandra laid the blame for the tragedy on Reagan and the CIA who supported the Contra bandits who had attacked, set fire to buildings, stolen cattle meant to feed the poor of Nicaragua, and killed the young soldiers and this good man. The article also detailed how a military contingent from La Esperanza had heard the explosions, had seen the fire, and had arrived in time to retake the farm—killing the remaining Contra attackers. Sandra grieved that they had lost one of their own in the return fire of the Contras. She ended the piece with a revolutionary salute to Clay and with the eternal thanks of the Nicaraguan people—to him, to his wife, and to his unborn child. In the article, no mention was made by name of Cesar Rodriguez, Luis Romero, or Luis's brother, Jorge Romero.

After the article's publication and the picking up of the story by other media, there was no rest for Laura, Stan, and Elizabeth, or for Clay's parents, Charles and Linda Danforth. Both of Clay's parents had flown to Managua from Nashville as soon as they heard from Laura what had happened. Reporters from local papers, radio stations, and TV channels, as well as from the international media, sought interviews and followed them all around the city. It was a circus of pushing and shoving photographers and film crews, and the government tried to protect them as best it was able.

When the Danforths arrived at the international airport, the police whisked them away to the hotel where they stayed as the government's official guests. During their stay, Pedro Bartola accompanied them as well as the Hollins family on their outings, which were mostly to the hospital to see Stan, and often Pedro served as their spokesperson to the press. The U.S. Embassy in Managua also was solicitous and offered the Hollins and Danforths their condolences and their services in facilitating the return of Clay's body to Nashville.

Stan stayed for a few more days in the hospital. At first, he was not allowed to give interviews because of his medical situation, but the doctors did nothing to stop a steady stream of prominent government officials who came to visit him and pay their respects at the hospital. As they left, they denounced to the press the Contras and their American supporters.

But it was the common people who overwhelmed Laura, Elizabeth, and the Danforths with their concern and kindnesses. Strangers with tears in their eyes left flowers at the gate of their house or at the Danforth's hotel. Many others applauded when they saw them on their sorties to the hospital to visit Stan. In the notes and poetry that they pressed into their hands or left at the gate, they thanked the Danforths for their great sacrifice, and they commiserated with Laura and her unborn child for their terrible loss. Both the Hollins and the Danforths were immensely moved, and they responded graciously.

Finally, four days after the attack, Stan was discharged from the military hospital, and Clay's body was released from the morgue and delivered by the military to a funeral home for embalming and for shipment back to the U.S. It was then placed in a coffin provided by the American Embassy and taken to the little international church for a memorial service.

Along with Stan, Elizabeth, Laura, and the Danforths, the church was packed with hundreds of friends and representatives from the government, the American Embassy, and international development agencies. Because of lack of space, many of those who attended had to sit outside and listen by loudspeaker to the service conducted by Pastor Johnson in both English and Spanish. Along the road by the church, dozens of ordinary Nicaraguans stood in respect as the body and the family entered and left the small building. Alongside these, a much smaller but more vocal group of ardent Sandinista sympathizers held up banners and shouted slogans against the murderous Contras and their U.S. sponsors. TV cameras and news photographers registered it all.

As soon as the memorial service ended, the coffin was taken to the airport in a hearse, and the Danforths, Laura, Elizabeth, and Stan followed in a Foreign Ministry van with a police escort. High-ranking government officials came to the airport to pay their respects to the Danforths and the Hollins as they left for Miami and then to Nashville. The next day in newspapers all over the world there was a picture of Stan in a wheelchair shaking hands with the president.

In Nashville, the funeral service at the Eastminister Presbyterian Church was equally emotional. The church was filled with flowers, and the pews were packed with Clay's and Laura's many childhood, college, and medical school friends, as well as friends of the Danforths and of Stan and Elizabeth. It was a service of music and of admiring testimonies about Clay's short life and about his positive impact on others. When Stan was wheeled to the front to pay a short but beautiful tribute to his son-in-law, he was given a standing ovation. After the service, Clay was buried in the cemetery plot that his grieving parents had previously purchased for themselves.

# PART II

# 1990

# CHAPTER 7

"I love you, Mommy!"

It was 1:30 p.m. and Laura Danforth put down the phone in her motel room in Miami, Florida. She had just called Nashville to talk with Charles and Linda Danforth and with her five-year-old daughter, Allison. Her in-laws were taking care of Allison while Laura and Elizabeth were in Miami for a few days to see Stan and to attend Laura's dear friend Flavia's wedding. Laura was also there for a meeting of Acción para la Paz. Laura smiled to herself as she remembered Linda's recounting of some of Allison's funny remarks about the Danforth's dog.

Like the Danforths, Laura's mother, Elizabeth, had also been a tremendous help to her with Allison during the previous six years. After Clay's funeral and Stan's recuperation, Elizabeth and Stan struggled with the dilemma as to whether Elizabeth should stay with Laura in Nashville or return to Managua with Stan. Finally, both her mother and her father agreed that it would be best for her to stay in Nashville, at least for the next year or two. That way she could help when the baby was born, and Laura would have time to finish her studies and graduate from college.

As for her father, he resisted their pressure for him to remain with them in the U.S. "You know that I can't do that," he said, defending his position. "With all the new donations and press coverage, Acción is just starting to take off. It would be irresponsible to leave it now." As a compromise, he agreed to structure his work so that he could return often to Nashville to see his family and to use his time in the States to raise money, supplies, and volunteers for Acción's expanding work in Nicaragua.

This arrangement had now extended to six years, but neither Stan nor Elizabeth was happy with it. While Stan spent several months in the States each year, a lot of it was outside of Nashville giving talks and interviews about Acción's work in Nicaragua and about the political situation there. In the process, he quickly became a "darling" of the political left and was once even invited to testify at a Congressional committee meeting in

Washington against U.S. support for the Contras. The fact that Stan's son-in-law had been killed by Contra bullets and Stan himself had been wounded by them gave his arguments great force.

In Nicaragua, too, Stan enjoyed a certain level of fame as *"el gringo bueno,"* the title with which he was introduced in Sandinista rallies in Managua, Esteli, and San Carlos. Representatives of the national and international media often requested interviews with him, and in 1987, he had returned with Sandra to the Roberto Romero State Farm for the filming of a documentary about the attack. Luis, who was also invited to participate in the documentary, declined.

Laura had mixed feelings towards her father. She loved him and admired him for his work with Acción, but as much as she tried, she could not stop blaming him in her heart for the loss of her husband. If her father hadn't insisted so much that Clay accompany him to the river clinic against all of their wishes, Clay would still be alive. She also had different views from her father politically. Laura despised the Contras because of the attack that killed Clay, but she also had a much more critical view of the Sandinistas than did Stan who always defended them even when some of their actions seemed to Laura indefensible. Laura was grateful for the support she and the Danforths had received after Clay's death from the Sandinista government, but she had also heard many heart-wrenching stories from friends who had been terribly hurt by their economic and social policies.

Laura also worried about her father—not so much about his physical safety, now that the war was over—but much more for his ability to withstand the many temptations that she knew faced him alone in Nicaragua. After all, he was still handsome and a relatively well-known and prosperous *gringo* in a poor country far from his wife. She was concerned that many women would see him as fair game.

One of those women was Sandra Espinosa. Laura knew that her father and Sandra were friends and political allies from the time of the attack, but that fact did little to reassure her when David Johnson, a classmate and the son of their former pastor, mentioned to her in a letter that he had run into Stan and Sandra Espinosa one night at a popular steak house in Managua. When Laura read the letter, she was careful not to say anything to her mother, as she didn't want to raise any suspicions. However, she could not easily get rid of her own.

Because of her concerns, Laura was glad that her father had come up from Nicaragua two days before the wedding and before the Acción meeting to spend personal time with her and her mother. Although she had not yet had the chance to have a one-on-one conversation with him, they had a good time together as a family. But tonight, after a final family dinner together, he would return by direct flight to Managua for another long separation. Laura was sad, too, that on this trip he didn't even have a chance to see his granddaughter.

After putting down the phone, Laura looked at the two pictures of Allison and of Clay by her bed, and she touched them affectionately. Whenever she traveled, she took the pictures with her and often talked to them about her day or asked Clay for advice about her work. She then went over to the chair and table by the window, pulled out some papers from her briefcase, and tried to gather her thoughts before the Acción meeting.

Although Laura still missed Clay greatly, she was generally content with her life. Allison's birth in November of 1984 brought new joy to her and to all four of the little girl's grandparents. Charles and Linda Danforth especially doted on Allison, showering her with gifts and fighting good-naturedly with Elizabeth for the right to take care of her when Laura had to travel in her work.

Laura's work also brought purpose and satisfaction to her life. A year after Clay's death, Charles Danforth sold his shoe business and set up a sizable trust for both Laura and their granddaughter, Allison. The bulk of the multi-million dollar profit from the sale, however, he used to start a foundation in memory of Clay. The Danforths insisted that Laura, whom they loved as their own daughter, become its executive director. To overcome Laura's protests that she had only just graduated from college and had no administrative experience, they arranged for her to be mentored by the CPA from Charles's former shoe company for the first three years.

One of the reasons Laura was now in Miami was in her role as director of the Clay Danforth Foundation. She had scheduled to meet with her father and other representatives of Acción to discuss with them their proposed projects and their budget for the coming year because the foundation was now Acción's principal source of financial support.

The other reason Laura was in Miami was to be a bridesmaid in the wedding of her close friends from the International School in Managua, Flavia Matos and Antonio Lopez. Since both the bride's and groom's parents now lived in the Sweetwater section of Miami, the couple decided that Miami was the best place to hold the wedding ceremony. The wedding had taken place the night before.

Although they and their families had long known each other, Flavia and Antonio had only started dating two years before when Antonio left Boston to come back to Managua to spend six months teaching and doing research at INCAE (a business school serving Central America) for his economics doctorate at Harvard. Flavia was teaching Fine Arts at the International School at the time, and Antonio had gotten back in touch with her.

While Laura was happy for both of her friends in their decision to marry, she also felt a twinge of regret at what might have been. At the International School, she, like most of the girls in her class, had a crush on Antonio, and he seemed to like her, as well. But after he went to Harvard and she entered Vanderbilt, they wrote each other only once or twice, so busy were they with their new lives.

A year and a half after Clay's death, however, Antonio had called Laura out-of-the-blue in Nashville and asked if he could come visit her sometime. Laura was polite and friendly in the conversation, but made it clear to him, as she had to other suitors in Nashville, that she wasn't interested yet in dating as her life was so full with Allison, her new job, and her memories of Clay. Antonio never called her back after that.

Looking at her watch, Laura saw that it was now 1:45 p.m., the agreed upon time to meet her parents in their room. She stood up, put her papers and notes for the Acción meeting back in her briefcase, and then stopped in front of the mirror to straighten her short blond hair before leaving. Very pretty and slim, as she took exercising seriously, she was now a professional woman, and she dressed in simple, classic clothes to reflect that role. Closing the door, she walked to the end of the carpeted hall to room 202 where her parents were staying and knocked.

"See, I'm not always late," Elizabeth said smiling at Laura as she opened the door. "I'm ready to go." In her early fifties, Elizabeth was a little overweight and with a few gray hairs but still attractive. She was informally dressed in khaki pants and in a blue blouse.

Laura looked inside the room. "Where's Dad?"

"Luis called earlier and invited him to have lunch with him before your meeting. I think they're downstairs in the restaurant."

"Are we still planning to have dinner together tonight before his COPA flight back to Managua?" Laura asked.

"As far as I know," Elizabeth replied.

"It's a shame he has to go back so soon. Maybe now that the Sandinistas lost the election, he'll spend more time in Nashville. Then, we can be a normal family again."

Elizabeth sighed. "I certainly hope so. It has been a difficult six years." She closed the door, and they walked together down the hall to the elevator. They were to meet Elena Lopez, Antonio's mother, in the lobby.

"It was a lovely wedding, wasn't it?" Elizabeth remarked to Laura as they waited for the elevator.

"It was," Laura replied. "And it looked like most of the Nicaraguans in Miami were there!"

The marriage of Antonio Lopez and Flavia Matos was a major social event for the Miami Nicaraguan community, which was already celebrating the surprising defeat of the Sandinistas in the Nicaraguan presidential elections earlier in the year. With this unexpected turnabout in Nicaraguan politics, many of the exiles, including the Romero and Lopez families, contemplated returning to their homeland and recuperating the houses and businesses that had been confiscated when they left. The destruction of the war and the confiscation of property had caused much bitterness and division within the nation and within individual families, including the Romeros.

While most members of the Romero family had since reconciled with Luis about his active support of the Revolution and the Sandinistas, Jorge Romero's widow, Inés, had not. She said that she could never forgive Luis for agreeing to the confiscation of Las Palmas or for his continuing support of the Sandinistas even after they had killed her husband. At first, she had refused to come to Antonio's wedding, knowing that Luis was also going to be there. She relented only after Arturo and María Romero, the patriarchs of the family, insisted. They wanted to heal the wounds. They also needed her there for an important family meeting scheduled before the wedding with Antonio's friend and groomsman Felipe Gonzales, who wanted to talk with them about a business deal involving Las Palmas. As an incentive, they mailed her airline tickets and even tickets to Disney World for her and her two children who were now adolescents.

When the elevator door opened on the ground floor of the motel, Laura and Elizabeth emerged and walked through the small reception area to where Elena Lopez awaited them by a rack with tourist pamphlets. As always, Elena was tastefully dressed.

"Elena, you still look like a million dollars, even after the wedding when you don't even have to!" Elizabeth said as she touched her arm. "Congratulations. It was so beautiful and fun!"

Elena smiled and brushed her hand across her forehead, wiping off imaginary perspiration. She then hugged both of the women. "Thank you both for coming."

"We wouldn't have missed it! Have Antonio and Flavia left yet for Paris?" Laura asked.

"About two hours ago. Now all we have to do is pack up all their gifts and ship them to Boston. After that, the wedding will *really* be over." Elena turned to Elizabeth. "I appreciate so much your volunteering to help me with that this afternoon."

"My pleasure! Laura and Stan will be meeting about Acción, so I have nothing better to do. It will be fun to have you all to myself."

Elena smiled in appreciation and then turned to Laura. "I will get your mom back here by four at the latest."

"And we should be finished with the Acción meeting about five o'clock," Laura said to her mother. "I'll call you when I get back to my room."

They hugged each other again, and after Elizabeth and Elena had left through the motel's front door to Elena's car in the parking lot, Laura headed to the small conference room that she had reserved for the Clay Danforth Foundation meeting with Acción.

# CHAPTER 8

Laura had chosen a nice but inexpensive motel for their stay and for the meeting, as she was always careful about how foundation money was spent. While Acción para la Paz was the principal recipient of funds from the Clay Danforth Foundation, the foundation also sponsored other projects, like the travel of medical students to developing countries to provide free treatment to the poor. She wanted as much foundation money to go to such programs as possible, and not to her own comforts.

As for Acción, its programs and expenses had markedly increased in the last six years. Now operating in over thirty rural communities, Acción had expanded its office space by turning the two empty bedrooms and the living room of Stan's house into workspace. After Elizabeth had returned to Nashville, Stan kept Isabel on to cook and clean for him, and at Laura's urging, he also hired her close friends Rosa and Marta to help him with the growth of Acción's programs. Despite their youth and lack of experience, they quickly became indispensable to Stan as they both spoke fluent Spanish and English and were quick learners. Rosa was Stan's assistant for administration and finances, and Marta was his second-in-command for training and programs. It was Marta who now did most of the orientation of the volunteer teams. These paid their own way to come down to Nicaragua to build latrines, dig wells, construct schools and health centers, and to provide basic dental and medical services. Some of the volunteer brigades also helped in harvesting coffee in zones near Honduras that were then under threat from the Contras.

Rosa and Marta were in the conference room when Laura arrived. They had already ordered a pitcher of water and some glasses and were busy setting up a projector and screen for their presentations to Laura.

Laura surveyed the room and then smiled roguishly at Rosa. "Hmmm, Rosa, where's Felipe?" she commented. As soon as she said it, Marta laughed and Rosa blushed.

Ever since being introduced to each other at the rehearsal dinner two nights before, Felipe Gonzales had not let Rosa out of his sight. The night before at the wedding reception, he sat by her at the dinner table, danced with her most of the evening, and brought her back to the hotel in his car.

"She only got back to the room after midnight," Marta interjected. "She didn't even have to turn on the lights, her face was glowing so much," she added, laughing at her own joke.

Laura continued the teasing. "Your charm hit him like a truck!"

"I don't know about that," Rosa replied. "We just sat in his car talking. I asked him a lot of questions about his work, and he had a lot to talk about—especially about his new joint venture with the Romero family on the Río San Juan."

"What kind of joint venture?" Laura asked. Like Rosa, she had just met Felipe for the first time at the wedding. He was one of Antonio's groomsmen, and from what she gathered from Antonio and Luis, he was not only affable, but also an astute businessman who had maintained good relations with the Sandinistas and members of the Nicaraguan exile community during the war.

"It involves Las Palmas," Rosa explained. "Right after the election, Felipe purchased the Roberto Romero State Farm from the Sandinistas. Evidently, they have been selling off or giving away to loyalists many of the properties that they confiscated during their time in power. Felipe plans to develop it as an orange plantation called El Futuro."

"How can a political party like the Sandinistas sell a state farm that is government-owned?" Laura asked surprised.

"I don't know, but Felipe told me that he got a bargain price," Rosa responded.

"Won't former owners try to recoup their property now that the Sandinistas are out of power?"

"Probably," Rosa said. "That's why Felipe said he scheduled the meeting with the Romeros. Even though Las Palmas is considered a part of the Roberto Romero State Farm, he offered the family a 20 percent stake in El Futuro if they agreed not to litigate in the future. He said that he also received assurances from the incoming government that they would not try to recuperate the property either."

"And the Romeros agreed?" Laura asked.

"They did," Rosa answered. "Las Palmas is no longer under their control, anyway, and both of the businessmen in the Romero family—Arturo and Antonio—agreed that the citrus project has an excellent chance of success. The soil and climate of the area are suitable for citrus growing, and a major processing plant for orange juice is located less than fifty kilometers away from their land in Costa Rica. With the war over and the Sandinistas out of power, the borders are open. Access to the plant will be easy."

"It sounds like a win-win situation for everyone," Marta said.

Rosa nodded in agreement. "And best of all," she added, "peace has returned to the Romero family. Felipe said that once they all had agreed to the deal, Luis stunned everyone by offering his own personal share in El Futuro to Inés and her children in honor of his brother, Jorge. Inés ended up embracing him in front of the rest of the family, and María Romero cried she was so pleased!

"Wow!" Marta exclaimed.

"A lot of good things came out of that meeting," Laura exclaimed. "This Felipe of yours sounds not only rich but also smart!"

"And he also has excellent taste in women," Marta added with a grin on her face.

Rosa blushed.

Laura then looked at her watch. It was past time for the meeting to start, so she changed the subject. "Have either of you seen Luis and Dad?"

"I saw them at the hotel restaurant about a half-hour ago," Marta answered. "To tell you the truth, they looked as if they were arguing about something."

"Arguing? About what?" Laura asked. Stan and Luis had always been the best of friends, and she had never seen them fight over anything before.

Before Marta could answer, Stan showed up at the door of the meeting room, followed by Luis. They both appeared tense, but Laura greeted them as if all were normal. After a few minutes of small talk about the wedding and the reception, Laura suggested that they begin as they had a lot to cover. As the convener of the meeting, she took her seat at the head of the conference table and invited the others to sit down in one of the other eight executive chairs in the room. Luis sat by Laura, and Stan took a chair at the other end of the table next to Rosa. Marta continued standing and handed out folders to each person.

"Dad, why don't you start by giving us a report on what Acción has accomplished this past year and what your plans and needs are for the future. Then we can see how our foundation can best be of help."

Stan opened his folder and then looked at Laura, "First of all, please pass on to the Danforths the gratitude of thousands of poor Nicaraguans and my own thanks for their generous assistance. They are truly making a difference."

"Of course," Laura said.

"Last year was a great year for Acción," he continued. "We were able to directly or indirectly assist over forty thousand poor people with our programs. The one dark cloud on the horizon is our uncertainty as to what is going to happen politically now that the Sandinistas have lost power. The party not only gave us tax exemptions, but they opened all kinds of doors for us to work in rural communities. I just hope that the new government will continue the same policies so that we can expand to even more municipalities."

Stan then turned to Marta who had now taken her seat at the table. "I asked Marta to prepare a written report and a set of slides that you can take back to the Danforths to show them the progress we have made. We can start with that, and then you can ask any questions that you might have."

Marta turned on the projector and began with the first slide, which she had already focused on the screen. "I'll start with what we have done in the program area this past year, and then Rosa will talk about the financial side of Acción," Marta began. "Like Stan said, it has been an exciting year."

Marta took about a half an hour going through the fifty or so slides that she had selected to help explain the activities of the year. Eight different teams had come down from the States, mostly from churches and schools in Tennessee. They had paid their own way, and each had stayed for a week to ten days. A few individuals had stayed even longer. Three of the teams had gone south to the Río San Juan and Solentiname, three had gone north to the mountains near Honduras, and two had gone east to towns in Chontales. Acción was not yet involved much in the Atlantic area, as the Miskito Indians and the Caribbean blacks who lived there distrusted the Sandinistas and their allies.

Four simple health centers had been built by the volunteers, two of them bearing the name of Clay Danforth. In the slides, international volunteers of widely different ages stood or crouched with their Nicaraguan hosts in front of the four centers, smiling and grasping the shovels, wheelbarrows, and other tools that they had used to build the facilities.

Laura was impressed with the buildings, with the number of children the teams had vaccinated, and with the local health councils that had been formed in the thirty communities. Each community health council elected a health worker who was trained in Managua by Marta in basic public health practices and emergency medicine, and then he or she became the basic health provider for the community. Acción also helped the communities evaluate their needs—such as access to clean water supplies, latrines, and mosquito nets—and then worked with the community to resolve them. While Acción offered its support free of charge, each community agreed to financially support its own health coordinator. All in all, it was an unusually empowering, grass-roots project. "This next year is going to be a year of consolidation as we wait and see what the position of the new government will be," Marta concluded.

Rosa, when it was her turn, also thanked Laura and the Danforths and reported that, excluding the expenses of the volunteer work teams, the Danforth Foundation's contributions to Acción accounted for sixty-five percent of their total budget in the previous year. The rest of Acción's resources came from small donations of money from churches and volunteers, as well as gifts in kind from U.S. firms and from the Nicaraguan Ministry of Health. She then showed a few pie charts and bar grafts that explained how much of the total funds went to administration, medicines, building supplies, training, and health education materials.

When Rosa mentioned the educational materials, Luis, who was chairman of the board of Acción, spoke up for the first time. "Laura, these past three years, Acción has been able to grow from a small organization to a major player in rural health in Nicaragua because of the financial assistance of the Danforth Foundation. Stan, Rosa, Marta, and the rest of the team have done an extraordinary job and have used your donations wisely."

"You certainly have," Laura said appreciatively, nodding to each of them.

"Also," Luis continued, "we value tremendously the transparent partnership that we have with you and the Danforths." He paused and took a drink of water from his glass and then added, "It's because of that transparency that I feel that I need to bring to your attention a disagreement that some of us on the board have had with Stan about the allocation of part of the money for education that you approved last year."

At this point, Stan stared at the table and shook his head slowly in anger. Luis, however, fixed his eyes on Laura and continued, "Most of the seventy-five thousand dollars we budgeted last year for training and education went to providing school supplies for poor children, to teacher training materials, and to health education posters, just as we had agreed. But without our board's approval, Stan decided to allocate fifteen thousand dollars of Danforth funds for Sandra Espinosa's electoral campaign for *deputada* for congress from León."

Luis paused for a few seconds and then continued, "Now, while I personally believe Sandra would be an excellent deputada for the National Assembly, none of us on the board thought that this was a legitimate use of foundation money. Stan strongly disagrees with us, but our board wanted you and the Danforths to know what was done, as well as the board's position on the matter."

Laura was confused, but before she could respond, Stan spoke up forcefully. "I stand behind the donation. Sandra is a great friend to Acción. She has written several very positive articles in *La Barricada* about our work. She has used her influence to get the government to open all sorts of doors for us so that we don't have to pay import or visa fees and other taxes. She also was the one who arranged for us to have a close relationship with the Ministry of Health and with the Sandinista mayors of so many communities around the country. Of course, we wanted her to win the election. That's why we gave her the money. To me, it is more than a legitimate expense. The only bad thing is that she lost."

The room fell silent as Luis, Stan, Rosa, and Marta looked at Laura to measure her response. As the implications of what was being said slowly sunk in, Laura's face turned pale and reflected many of the fears welling up inside her. It wasn't just the unacceptable donation of foundation money to a political campaign that concerned her, but it was the giving of that money to Sandra Espinosa in particular. Stan's action strongly reinforced her suspicion that her father might be unfaithful to her mother.

Looking directly at her father, Laura spoke with an anger that surprised both herself and the others in the room. "I'm sure that Ms. Espinosa's help has meant a lot to Acción. But the bottom line is that Acción has no right to use foundation money in a political campaign of either the left or right. It is meant only to help the poor. By giving to her campaign, you have jeopardized our standing as a tax-exempt foundation with the U.S. Government. I can only imagine their horror if they ever find out that you have given charity money to the Sandinistas. I guarantee you that the Danforths will also be appalled. The money you gave has to be paid back immediately."

Stan was surprised at Laura's response and spoke in a conciliatory tone. "I think that you're making a mountain out of a mole hill. I believe that it was a legitimate Acción expense because one of the main platforms of Sandra's campaign was to promote rural health and educational programs like ours. As for paying it back, there's no way that Sandra can pay back the money. If you and the Danforths insist on it being repaid, it can only come out of my own salary."

Laura was unsure what to reply. She knew that her father and mother already had a hard time financially on his rather meager salary that came from the donations from about twenty individuals and churches. Even though she had helped them decrease their expenses by providing them free room and board at her home while they were in Nashville, Laura knew that any cut in her father's salary or savings would seriously impact her mother.

In the few seconds of silence that followed, Laura decided what she needed to do. She turned to Marta and Rosa. "I think the meeting is over for right now. If you don't mind, I would like to talk privately with my father and with Luis. Thank you both for your great reports and for the tremendous work that you have done. I will certainly share your reports with the Danforths."

Both Rosa and Marta looked at each other nervously and got up from their chairs. They then quickly gathered their folders and notes from the conference table and started to leave. As they closed the door behind them, Rosa turned and said to Laura, "If you need us, we will be up in our room."

Laura nodded and thanked her.

# CHAPTER 9

After the two women had left, Laura, still angry, faced her father. "You've certainly put us all in a difficult situation with your actions. I'm amazed that you did it without first checking with Luis, your board, and with us."

"Why is it such a difficult situation?" Stan asked. "It's a relatively small amount of money in the big scheme of things. I felt the donation was legitimate, and like I said, I can pay it back out of my salary if you don't agree with it. No one else has to know anything about it."

"The Danforths and I don't operate that way. They trust me, and I don't want to lose their trust," Laura replied. "I will have to share what you have done with both them and with Mother."

"Why bring Elizabeth into it?"

"Why?!" Laura exclaimed. "Because she is your wife! The money that you have to pay back is her money, too. She already has to depend on me and on her relatives because you earn so little. Now she'll have to cut back even further." Laura paused, and then the worst of her fears surged upward into her mouth. "Just what is your relationship to Sandra Espinosa anyway?" she asked.

"What do you mean?"

"You know what I mean," Laura answered. "I've heard reports that the two of you have been dining together alone at night."

"Who told you that?" Stan asked, his anger turning his face red. He glared at Luis. "Did you tell her that?"

"No, it wasn't Luis," Laura retorted. "But you didn't answer my question. What is your relationship to Sandra Espinosa?"

"My relationship is what I've always said it was," he shot back. "She is a friend who has helped me and Acción tremendously in these past five years with her contacts and support. She is someone I enjoy being with and talking to."

"Is there any sexual involvement?" Laura blurted out, horrified to hear herself asking such a question to her father. "Have you been unfaithful to Mother?"

Stan was taken back at the directness of the question. "I can't believe that you are asking me such things."

"Have you been unfaithful to Mother?!" Laura insisted, pronouncing each word slowly.

"I refuse to answer such a question!"

"So you have been unfaithful."

Stan stood up abruptly. "I love Elizabeth, and I will not continue this conversation. My relationship to my wife and to my friends is none of your business, and I will only talk to you when you apologize and treat me with more respect!" He then left the room and slammed the door.

Laura was stunned, not only at her father's angry departure, but also at her own audacity in making such an accusation and at the implications of his lack of a direct response. She put her face in her hands, and tears began to stream down her cheeks.

Luis silently put his arm around her and squeezed her tightly. When he did so, Laura's tears turned into deep sobs like the day she had learned about Clay's death. After a few minutes, she regained some control, and Luis gave her a napkin to wipe her tears.

"I'm sorry," she said.

"It's all right."

"I just can't bear the thought of him being unfaithful to my mother."

"I understand."

Laura finished wiping her cheeks and eyes and blowing her nose and then looked straight at Luis. "I know this is uncomfortable for you, but I wanted you to be here when I confronted him. I know that you are his best friend, but I also know that you are honest. More than anyone, you would be aware of what is going on, and I know that you won't lie to me."

Luis didn't reply but looked down at the table as if he were ashamed.

Then Laura got up her courage again. "Is it true that he is having an affair with Sandra Espinosa or with anyone else?"

Luis paused a few seconds before he spoke. "Laura, you put me in a very difficult situation, but I will try to be honest with you. Before anything else, it's important for you to remember that your dad truly loves you and your mother and that this separation from both of you and from little Allison has been very hard for him. He is a good man." Luis was quiet again for a few seconds and then resumed, "As to whether he is having an affair with Sandra, I honestly don't know for sure. I know that they frequently see each other, especially since the TV documentary that they did together on the river. I know that she fascinates him as a revolutionary, a feminist, a poet, and as a beautiful woman. But I also know that he misses your mom terribly because he has often told me that he does."

"Why does he insist on staying in Nicaragua and not coming home then?" Laura asked.

"Acción is his life's work—something that he created and is proud of," Luis answered. "It's making a difference in the lives of many poor people." He took another drink of water. "You also have to realize that he is something of a hero among the Sandinistas—'*el gringo bueno*,' as they call him. That would inflate any man's ego, especially when he is introduced as such at large rallies with flags waving. What would he be in Nashville? A high school teacher with only a few students to impact. He doesn't want to give up what he has accomplished."

"Nor give up Sandra Espinosa?"

"Nor give up Sandra Espinosa. She has a very strong hold on him."

Luis paused again as if struggling as to what to say next. He then looked Laura straight in the eye. "Laura, you said a minute ago that you wanted me here because you thought that I was an honest person."

Laura nodded.

"The sad truth is that I haven't been totally honest with you, with my family, or with anyone these past six years. I want desperately to change that. I can't call myself a Christian and continue to live the lie that I've been living." He took a deep breath. "Stan has been living the same lie. It is partially because of that lie that Sandra has such a hold on him."

"What lie?" Laura asked confused. "What are you talking about?"

"The Contra attack on the river that killed Clay didn't happen exactly as we said that it did or as Sandra reported it in the press. Most of it did, but some crucial facts were changed in order to avoid an international embarrassment for the Sandinistas. Stan and I went along with Sandra's story, even though we knew that it wasn't totally true."

"Go on."

"The truth is that your husband, Clay, was shot and killed by our own soldiers and not by the Contras."

Laura's face froze.

74

"Clay and Stan were helping me carry Jorge to the house when a barrage of bullets hit them. But it wasn't the Contras who fired at us; it was a contingent of our own soldiers coming up the road from the river. They were dispatched from La Esperanza after they heard the first explosion, and they got to the barge landing just as Cesar Rodriguez shot Jorge. When they heard me yelling in English for help, they thought that we were Contras. Clay was killed by their bullets. Jorge's lookout was also shot in the back as he ran up the road to warn Jorge of their approach."

"But it doesn't make any sense. Why would Father lie about what had happened? I can maybe understand that you and the others lied because you were Sandinistas and part of the government. But why would Father lie?"

"He was blackmailed," Luis said. "When Stan fell to the ground wounded, he was able to grab Jorge's weapon and fire at the rifle flashes. One of his bullets killed an attacking government soldier. Sandra told him that if news got out that an American had killed a young Sandinista soldier in a firefight, many would want revenge, and he might go to prison. That frightened him."

"Father killed someone?!"

Luis nodded. "But there were other reasons, too, for his agreeing to Sandra's account."

"What other reasons?"

"He felt guilty about having insisted on Clay's coming despite yours and Elizabeth's fears about the Contras and your protests. He also wanted to protect the Revolution and me," Luis said. "Afterwards, while we were waiting for the rescue helicopter, Sandra called the captain of the Sandinista patrol and Cesar into the room where I was trying to treat Stan's wound. Clay had already died. Stan was in pain but was fully conscious. She said that all of us—the captain, Stan, Cesar, myself, the country, and the Revolution—were in a very difficult situation because of what happened that night. Cesar was in serious trouble because of Jorge's accusations that he stole money from the state farm; I was in trouble because I tried to save the life of a Contra leader whose raiders had just killed five of our soldiers, robbed the state farm of arms and property, and set fire to its barn and houses. The Sandinista captain was in trouble because his men had killed an American volunteer helping our people—a mistake that could cause an international incident with terrible consequences for the government.

75

Stan was in trouble because he had both killed a government soldier and also tried to save the life of an enemy combatant."

Luis took another drink of water and continued. "Sandra said that the best way to save all of our skins and to protect the international reputation of the Revolution was to blame Clay's death on ARDE—the Contra attackers. She explained that none of the Contras could say that our story was untrue because the ones who were there when the army patrol arrived from La Esperanza were now dead. The others, who left with the stolen arms and the cattle for Costa Rica, had no way of knowing what happened. As for the regular soldiers in the army patrol, they were all country boys and would believe their captain if he said that both the American and their comrade were killed by the Contras. She added that the story was not even really a lie. If the Contras had not attacked, Clay would not have been killed. So they were the real guilty ones."

Laura didn't say anything but just listened.

"Sandra said that it was imperative for the greater good of the Revolution that we all have the same story. It was also imperative for our own good. Nothing would be mentioned about my actions, or Cesar's corruption, or of Stan's killing a soldier. We just had to stick to the story that she would write up later that day for *La Barricada.*"

"And you all agreed?" Laura asked.

"We all agreed. When we got to the military hospital, they held us *incommunicado* for several hours while government intelligence tried to understand what had happened and to decide what to do. Only when they were sure that we had all committed to the same story did they allow me to call you from the hospital."

"So all of these articles and Father's speeches and testimonies about what happened have been lies?"

"They were half-truths," Luis corrected. "In one sense the Contras were ultimately responsible for what happened. It was because of their attack that Clay and all of the soldiers were killed—including the one that Stan shot."

"But I still don't understand. Once Dad was out of Nicaragua, he was safe. Why did he insist on going back?"

"Because Sandra and the Sandinistas and their U.S. supporters made him into a hero and opened all kinds of doors for him. They invited him to give interviews and to speak at rallies. Acción prospered. Stan came to believe—to really believe—Sandra's tale. It was just too painful and disadvantageous for him to admit the full truth."

Laura was silent as she tried to digest these revelations.

"Why after so many years are you telling me this now?"

"I just can't continue to live a lie. Before, I justified myself because I didn't want to jeopardize the Revolution. I worked hard for its success, and my brother Roberto even gave his life for it. And despite its flaws, I still believed in it. It seemed to me that it was the only way that we could change an immoral system that had kept so many people in abject poverty. For me, the end justified the means."

"What changed that?"

"A lot. The hypocrisy of our leaders who enriched themselves in the *piñata*—taking for themselves the expropriated property of others, their saying one thing and doing another, and their manipulating statistics and the truth so much of the time. Some good was achieved by the Revolution, but it has certainly not been worth the economic destruction and the pain caused to my family and to the country."

"To your family? What about mine?"

Luis nodded. "To your family, too! To you and Clay. To the Danforths. To Elizabeth and Stan. I don't want to be a part of these lies and cover-ups anymore, even though Sandra and Stan are both still my friends."

Laura thought a moment and then said, "I don't know whether to thank you or curse you for telling me this. You've put me into the very painful position of having to decide what to say to Mother, to the Danforths, and to my father's supporters. It is so hurtful. Why couldn't you have just told the truth at first? Unwinding a lie is so much worse."

"You're absolutely right, and I'm truly sorry," Luis said.

"Marta said that she saw you and father arguing at lunch. You told him that you were going to tell me this, didn't you?"

"I did. He was furious because he felt that I had no right. He didn't want to hurt you or your mother. Like I said, he loves you a lot."

"He has a strange way of showing that love."

As Laura got up from the table, her eyes were still red. "I need to go to my room and think about what I'm going to do, both as my mother's daughter and as director of the Clay Danforth Foundation." She nodded goodbye to Luis and then left the conference room, heading upstairs to be alone. Her head was reeling, and her heart was heavy with pain.

When she got to her room, the message light on her telephone was flashing red. She picked up the phone and pressed the button, and the voice in the recording was that of her mother. "Laura dear, your dad says that he has some things to talk over with me before his flight tonight for Managua. He says that he wants just the two of us to go out alone. He will bring me back to the hotel before leaving off the rental car and catching his plane. I'm sorry about the change in plans. Maybe you can eat with Rosa and Marta. I hope your meeting went well. I love you."

# CHAPTER 10

A half-hour before Laura received the telephone message, Stan had already packed his bags, checked out of the hotel, and left with Elizabeth in the rental car to a nearby public park where they could be alone. Elizabeth was surprised by the sudden change in plans, but seeing Stan's agitation, she agreed to it. Before heading down to the lobby, she called Laura's room to inform her.

When Stan and Elizabeth got to the ocean park, Stan parked the car and suggested that they get out and walk over to one of the benches under the palm trees that faced the ocean. Most of the benches were empty, as no one was around except for a few joggers on the hard sand near the water.

After brushing off some leaves and sand from the cement bench, Stan motioned for Elizabeth to take a seat. He then joined her. For a moment, they sat without saying anything, just staring out at the vast ocean dotted only with a few white sails. Stan was still furious at Luis's betrayal of him and at Laura for confronting him about his relationship with Sandra. He knew that he had to tell Elizabeth what had happened in the meeting before Laura did, but he had no idea of how to begin or even what to say.

Elizabeth helped him by her prodding. "Stan, something's obviously wrong. What is it? Did something happen in your meeting?"

Stan nodded affirmatively. "I had an argument with Laura and Luis, and I wanted to tell you my side first before I had to leave for Managua."

"An argument with Laura and Luis?" she repeated. "What on earth about?" Elizabeth's tone of voice revealed her surprise and concern.

"It was about a disagreement we have on the use of some funds that the Clay Danforth Foundation gave to Acción." He paused. "Do you remember Sandra Espinosa?"

"Of course." Elizabeth looked puzzled.

"She has been a great help to Acción, and I thought that it was appropriate to give her money to help her win the León seat for the

79

National Assembly. As a *deputada*, she could be of even more help to us. Luis and Laura didn't agree."

Stan hesitated again, but he knew that he had to continue despite the dread that he felt. "Ever since the attack on the river, Sandra has been a real friend to Acción. She has helped us with customs and other government red tape. Through her intervention, we have been able to get grants from the Ministry of Health of much more than the money that I gave her."

Stan paused and looked out at the ocean, as he could not bring himself to look at his wife. He then forced himself forward in his confession. "She has also become a very good friend to me. I don't know how to say this delicately, Elizabeth, but the truth is, in your absence, we have started to have a sexual relationship as well."

Elizabeth heard Stan's words in disbelief.

"It's not that I don't still love you, Elizabeth . . . I do."

She just looked at him stunned, with no words to utter. Then tears began to appear in her eyes and slowly run down her cheeks.

"How can you say that after telling me such a thing?" Elizabeth finally said in a whisper.

"It's only a physical attraction; it's not love, just excitement. It's you I love, Elizabeth. You are the mother of my daughter, the person with whom I have shared twenty-eight years of memories and friendship. I feel comfortable with you. I admire you. I want to spend the rest of my life with you. With Sandra, it's different."

Elizabeth just stared blankly.

"Try to understand. Nicaragua is my life now, and you're not there anymore. Sandra is. She opens doors for me that you can't—to youth, to excitement, to poetry, to revolution, to influence. And you open doors for me that she can't—to stability, to kindness, to family, to comfort. You complement each other." He paused again and then added. "It's the Latino way, Elizabeth. It's not only accepted, it's even expected there. Many men have wives whom they love and mistresses whom they enjoy. It's also the Old Testament way. Abraham, Isaac, Jacob, David, Solomon—they all did it. Their marriages still worked. Ours can, too. Why not?"

"Because of trust!" Elizabeth blurted out in anger. "Because of our daughter. Because of our vows to each other. Because deep in your heart you know that while you want me to accept your being unfaithful to me, you would never accept my being unfaithful to you."

Stan knew that was true, but he didn't say anything.

"You're too selfish for that," Elizabeth added.

"How am I the only selfish one?" Stan retorted. "I'm the one in Nicaragua trying to help the poor. You're the one who chose to stay in comfortable Nashville rather than come back to Managua with me."

"I chose to stay in Nashville for Laura's and Allison's sake. You agreed with me that it was the best thing to do."

"I accepted your decision for their sake but also for yours. I know how you hated living in Managua."

"And I know how you love living in Nicaragua," Elizabeth retorted. "You adore your image there—Stan, the Revolutionary; Stan, the Good American; Stan, the Helper of the Poor. You wear many masks, but we both know that beneath those masks you really only care about your own goals, your own pleasures, and your own honors."

Stan checked himself; his strong ego wanted to lash out at Elizabeth in revenge for her attack on him. Instead, he lowered his voice and said, "I'm sorry to cause you this pain, Elizabeth. Really I am. But I've tried to be honest with you. What did you expect me to do when we live apart like this?"

"What did I expect?! I expected you to have self-control and at least enough love for me and for yourself to respect your vows. And as for being honest, you're only telling me the truth now because you were found out!"

Stan shook his head in frustration, even though he knew that what she said was true. "It's useless to talk to you now, Elizabeth. You just want to hurt me because of your own hurt. It's your middle-class morality. Just remember that having an open marriage and multiple relationships isn't such a big deal anymore to many people in the world. It's a normal part of life."

"If *normal* means lying and unfaithfulness, then I don't want anything to do with it."

Stan was silent for a long time. "I don't know what more I can say." He looked at his watch. "I've got to take the rental car back before I catch my plane."

"You mean this is it?" Elizabeth exclaimed. "You drop these bombshells on me, and then you leave on the next plane for Managua. Do you have no shame?!"

"I don't know what else to do, Elizabeth. You need time."

Elizabeth just stared back at Stan, her eyes blazing. "Are you going to break off your relationship with Sandra?" she asked.

"I don't know what I'm going to do," Stan responded.

Elizabeth shook her head angrily as she stood up.

Stan got up, too, and during the walk back to the car and the drive back to the motel, neither of them said a word. It was only after Elizabeth let herself out of the car in the hotel parking lot that she turned to Stan and said, "Stan, until you come to the end of yourself, you will never truly be good or do good, or, for that matter, have any peace. You'll only cause pain to yourself and to others."

Elizabeth then turned away with tears in her eyes and walked quickly to the front door of the motel.

# PART III
# 1990-1994

# CHAPTER 11

When Stan arrived back in Managua, he did not break off his relationship with Sandra, but he did break off with just about everyone else. First, he resigned as executive director of Acción. In the letter that he sent to each board member, he justified his decision by saying his authority as director had been undermined, and he could no longer continue to work in such a climate of mistrust. He again strongly defended his action of giving money to Sandra's campaign because of the support she and the Sandinista Party had given to Acción's programs to help the rural poor. No mention was made in the letter of his affair with Sandra or of his offer in Miami to pay back from his own pocket the misused funds. Instead, he said, "My many hours of work without pay for Acción more than compensate for the money that I gave to Sandra Espinoza." Stan also sent copies of the letter to the Clay Danforth Foundation and to Rosa and Marta.

As soon as Luis received Stan's letter, he called an emergency board meeting of Acción. In the meeting, the board accepted Stan's resignation with regret and with appreciation for his years of leadership and service. They named Rosa Guevara as the new director in his place.

When Laura and the Danforths received information about the change of leadership, they decided to continue to support Acción but with very reduced grants. Laura did not want the centers named after Clay to close or to lose the investments that they had made in the organization. She also felt that Acción was doing a good and useful work, and she did not want to undermine Rosa, Marta, and Luis in their efforts to continue it.

As for Stan, he moved out of Acción's office into Sandra's rented house near the national baseball stadium. Stan was disappointed that Sandra wasn't all that keen about the new arrangement because of the loss of some of her cherished freedom. She agreed, however, because she needed Stan's income to help pay her rent. Since the Sandinistas' fall from power, the finances of *La Barricada* were tenuous, and Sandra's salary had been greatly reduced.

Within a few months, Stan's own ability to help Sandra financially also was diminished. Most of his former supporters curtailed their help when they found out what had happened. They were kind but were clear that they could no longer justify their support of him now that he had left Acción. While nothing specific was said about his separation from Elizabeth or his dishonesty, Stan knew in his heart that these were the main reasons that influenced their decisions to abandon him. Stan was forced, therefore, to look for another job.

Through Sandra's contacts, he soon found one, although with a much smaller salary. The election defeat of the Sandinistas left many high-ranking officials without government jobs. Some of them, looking for ways to continue their work and to support themselves, started new non-governmental, community development agencies and sought funding for them from Europe and the U.S. Stan's experience, international contacts, fundraising and language skills, made him highly employable, and one of these new organizations, working for the protection of the environment, hired him to write grant proposals.

Stan's relationship to Sandra Espinosa started going downhill soon after he left Acción, and it ended a few months after he started his new job with the environmental agency. The truth was that Sandra often got on Stan's nerves, as unlike Elizabeth, she was extremely self-centered and selfish. Everything revolved around her—her poetry, which Stan never liked, but still falsely praised; her reputation as a militant; her job and articles; her pleasures; her freedom; and her financial needs. On top of all of this, Sandra was a terrible housekeeper and cook. Yet, even so, Stan still clung to her, and he could not bear the thought that one day she might reject him in favor of someone else.

The final breakup happened one Saturday morning. On the night before, Stan sat up late in Sandra's cramped and hot living room waiting for her to come home. He wasn't worried about her safety, as he knew that she could take care of herself. Instead, he was concerned about their weakening relationship, illustrated by her spurts of anger and long periods of coldness to him.

When Sandra finally got in at one o'clock in the morning, Stan confronted her, more hurt than angry. "Where have you been?" he asked. "I've been waiting up for you since nine."

As if a switch had been turned on, Sandra's face immediately turned red, and she shouted at him, "It's none of your business where I've been! You don't own me, Stan. Nobody owns me. I do what I please."

Stan was taken back both by the intensity and by the quickness of her anger, and he backed off. "I'm not trying to control you. I was just worried about you."

"Well, stop it!" She then went into the bedroom and slammed the door, locking it from the inside. "You sleep somewhere else!"

Stan knew it was best not to argue with her when she was angry. At times, she shouted profanities, waking up the neighbors, and they gave him questioning looks the next day. Instead, he went to the small couch, took the cushions off the seat, and made himself a bed on the tile floor of the living room. That night he slept fitfully.

When morning came, Stan heard Sandra in the other room opening and closing drawers, and he waited for her to come out to use their one bathroom. When she finally did appear at the bedroom door, she was fully dressed with an armful of his clothes. She put them on the couch. "I want you out of the house," she said. "Our relationship is over."

Stan was stunned. While they had had their fights before, never before had she gone to this extreme. "I don't understand," he said. "You are kicking me out because I was worried about you last night?"

"No," she replied. "I'm kicking you out because you want to control me and because I'm tired of you! You've become a burden to me." She went into her bedroom again and returned with another armful of his clothes on hangers.

"This is ridiculous. Can't we talk about it?"

"It's over, Stan," she repeated, now matter-of-factly without anger. She then paused and added the *coup de grâce,* "I've taken another lover."

"So that's it!" Stan said. What he always feared had finally happened. "Who is he?"

"It's none of your business, and I don't want to talk about it anymore. When I get back at noon, I want you and all of your stuff out of my house." Sandra then went to the front door and opened it. "By noon," she repeated as she walked out, closing the door after her.

Stan was angry and humiliated, but he moved out that same day and settled into a cheap hotel in the Belo Horizonte area of Managua not far from where he was working. He called Sandra several times, but she told him to stop bothering her. He then made some inquiries among mutual friends as to whom she was seeing. One of them told him that it was a French reporter assigned by *Le Monde* to Managua. A few months later, the same friend informed Stan that Sandra had gone with the reporter to Paris after he relocated there.

Like his relationship to Sandra, Stan's relationship to his new employer did not last long either. Stan was not good at taking orders from someone he felt was less competent than he was and who paid him such a measly salary to boot. From then on, Stan frequently changed jobs—partly because NGOs opened and closed regularly in Managua, and partly because he was unable to find any job that paid as well or was as fulfilling as his former position with Acción. Stan also frequently changed girlfriends, having one short affair after another, mostly with much younger Nicaraguan women who were impressed with his notoriety and the fact that he was a foreigner.

As for Acción, it survived for only three more years after Stan resigned. International funds and volunteers began to dry up now that the war was over, and when Rosa and Marta decided to leave in order to marry, Luis and the board finally decided to close it.

Rosa was the first to leave, marrying Felipe Gonzales, the dynamic and successful businessman she had met at Antonio and Flavia's wedding in Miami. For her part, Marta married a sociology professor at her former university, a well-known advisor to the leaders of the Sandinista Party.

Before the members of the board pulled the plug on Acción, Luis consulted Stan. Stan vehemently opposed the closure, but as he had no other viable alternatives to offer, the board decided to turn its programs and remaining resources over to another rural health organization headquartered in Managua.

Soon after this bad news about the dismantling of the organization that had been his chief achievement in life, Stan received one more humiliating blow to his self-esteem—Sandra Espinosa had written and published simultaneously in Paris and in Managua her memoir, *Amor a la Revolución.* The book recounted in detail Sandra's exploits and love affairs during the war, and in it, she laid out her own strong feminist and political opinions. Her depiction of her relationship to Stan in the book was not flattering, nor was it flattering to many other better-known leaders of the Revolution. She blamed the Revolution's failure not only on the U.S. Government's meddling, but also on the inexperience, machismo, and lust for personal position, power, and financial gain of many of its leaders. Because of Sandra's notoriety in Nicaragua for her exploits during the Sandinista revolution and for her access to top officials, the book's "tell-all" nature made it a big success throughout the country.

One whole chapter of her book was dedicated to the Contra attack on the river when Clay was killed. After recounting what really happened that night, Sandra proudly defended the cover-up that she had initiated as a means of protecting the Revolution. She also presented her own theory as to the unsolved murder in 1986 of Cesar Rodriguez, the former director of the Roberto Romero State Farm. She was convinced that it had not been a botched robbery, as the police had stated in the newspapers, but that Cesar had been assassinated by a government intelligence officer as a means of settling accounts with him for his stealing of cattle from the state farm.

What was especially devastating to Stan about the book, however, was Sandra's claim that she first became Stan's lover, not out of any great attraction for him, but as a means of making sure that he didn't diverge from the storyline that she had concocted. She added that she had found him to be a poor lover and that she had stuck with him for almost a year after the fall of the Sandinistas only because of her own financial needs.

Almost overnight, Stan became the butt of jokes. One newspaper reviewer of Sandra's book wrote that Stan's image had fallen from being "the Good Yankee" to that of a "Yankee Doodle"—a simpleton and cuckolded lover who had been manipulated by both Sandra and the Sandinistas.

Stan could face many things, but he could not face being mocked. Once that review appeared and his friends started to make jokes, Stan decided that he could take no more. He had to leave Managua because his life there had become hell. *But where should I go? Back to Nashville? Never! To do so would be to admit failure,* he reasoned, and his ego rebelled against that humiliation. Anyway, Elizabeth and Laura probably wouldn't want him back, and he could not take another rejection.

Stan had not seen Elizabeth or Laura since their Miami encounter three years earlier. He had not returned to the U.S., nor had they come to Nicaragua. Rosa had invited Laura to be her maid of honor in her wedding to Felipe, but Laura declined the offer once she found out that Rosa had also invited her father. "It would be too painful for me," she told Rosa. "I can't forgive him for his lies, his affairs, his treatment of Mother, his role in Clay's death, and his lack of repentance."

Given Stan's unwillingness to show any remorse for his actions, Laura and some of Elizabeth's friends advised her to divorce him and to move on with her life. Elizabeth refused, however, saying that she took seriously her wedding vows despite her deep hurt and anger. She told Laura that as long as Stan never asked her for a divorce, she would remain as she was—Mrs. Stan Hollins. She still hoped that one day the man she continued to love would come to his senses and return to her.

Elizabeth even wrote Stan from time to time with news of Laura and Allison and of his ailing father in the nursing home in Virginia. Unlike Stan, Elizabeth often spoke with Stan's father by telephone and visited him when possible, as did Laura and Allison. When he died of pneumonia in July of 1994 at the age of 82, it was Elizabeth who relayed that information to Stan. Six weeks later, it was also Elizabeth who sent Stan the news that his father had left in his will a hundred and fifty thousand dollars apiece for him, Laura, and Allison—his father's only surviving relatives.

To Stan, the news of his unexpected inheritance burst like cool rain on the barren soil of the last two years of his life and gave him a new sense of liberty and enthusiasm. The money, he felt, was his key to leaving the emptiness and humiliation of his life in Managua for a new start somewhere else. As he considered where he should go and what he should do, Stan recalled his original reason for coming to Nicaragua—to make amends for the wrongs done to Nicaragua by his own ancestor, Captain George Hollins, in bombarding San Juan del Norte. A eureka moment came to him one night as sat alone in his room. *What I need to do is go to San Juan del Norte and leave something of value by trying to help the people of that town.*

The tiny town at the end of the San Juan River was as far as one could get from Managua and still stay in Nicaragua, and its people were as poor as any population in the country. Stan felt that with the unexpected hundred and fifty thousand dollar inheritance from his father and the twenty thousand dollars that he still had in savings he could begin life again in San Juan del Norte, help the people of the town, and redeem his family's history and his own life.

Excited and with a sense of new direction, Stan decided that he would open a small eco-friendly backpacker hotel in San Juan del Norte. There he could live cheaply and simply and escape the noise and painful memories of his life in Managua. There he could indulge his love for fishing and the outdoors as well as use the hotel as a base for helping the town and its citizens.

This time, Stan was determined to do things right, and the more he thought about it, doing things right meant that he needed to get back in touch with Luis Romero and his family. They were the largest land owners in San Juan del Norte and would be important allies for the fulfillment of his plans. Swallowing his pride, Stan called Luis on the telephone and invited him to lunch at his favorite restaurant, Los Ranchos.

# CHAPTER 12

Stan had run into Luis a half-dozen times in Managua since their angry encounter in Miami—once at Rosa's wedding, once to discuss the closing of Acción, and several times in restaurants or at parties for mutual friends. Except for the heated meetings about Acción, they had always been *correctos* with each other, but the camaraderie of their former relationship was no more.

From these encounters, Stan learned that Luis had resigned as a member of the Sandinista Party—the FSLN—and was now working for the United Nations Development Program in Nicaragua. His main task was to head up an effort for the resettlement of ex-Contras and other war refugees in the Río San Juan region—including in the town of San Juan del Norte.

During the war, the town had been totally destroyed in a siege by the Contras, and most of its former inhabitants had sought refuge over the border in Costa Rica. Now that peace had returned, they had come back to the region to try to rebuild their lives. Most of them were desperately poor, and the new Nicaraguan government, with the help of Luis and the UN, had built a new town for them in a higher area, about three kilometers away from the former town.

Luis also gave Stan news about Elizabeth, Laura, and Allison. When Luis had flown to Nashville to discuss with Laura and the Danforths the closing of Acción, he had dinner with Stan's family at their home. Luis's description of Elizabeth was so full of warmth and admiration that Stan wondered if he might secretly be in love with her. The thought provoked in him a twinge of jealousy but also a flood of shame as to how much better a husband and father Luis would have been to his family than he had been.

Stan got to Los Ranchos early so that he had a choice of tables before the business crowd came in. He always liked sitting near the inside stone waterfall, surrounded by green tropical plants, as the sound of gently falling water helped mute the other noises of the restaurant. When Luis entered soon afterwards, Stan stood up and welcomed him.

"I don't know how you do it," Luis said good-naturedly. "You're as slim, tan, and youthful-looking as you always were."

"You don't look too bad yourself," Stan said. "A little grayer and heavier maybe, but the same open, optimistic face. It must be because you never married."

Luis laughed as he sat down. "Must be. No wife and children could ever take my simple life style."

"I probably should have followed your example. My own track record with women has not been good!" Stan said. He added, "You would have been a much better husband to Elizabeth and father to Laura than I have been."

Luis said nothing in reply as they both sat down.

Overcoming the awkwardness, Stan asked, "What did you think of Sandra's new book? To me, it was devastating!"

Luis nodded. "I felt bad for you when I read it. But if it's any compensation, she also spoke condescendingly about a lot of others, including a lot of important politicians."

"She spoke highly of you, though," Stan said. "'A true Sandinista,' she called you."

Luis laughed. "Whatever that means! I guess she said positive things because we were never lovers. I was surprised to get off so easily."

"Have you seen her or heard from her lately?"

"No, but I understand that she has made quite a name for herself in Paris among the left, and also that she's unattached again!" He smiled ironically. "Who would have imagined?!"

It was then that the middle-aged waiter came to the table, greeted them politely, and took their orders. Stan didn't even have to look at the menu as he already knew what he wanted—his usual *churrasco, salada, tajadas, and queso frito* with a cold Victoria beer. Luis ordered the same. When the waiter left, Stan got straight to the point.

"Luis, you must be wondering why I invited you to lunch after all that has happened."

Luis nodded. "I am curious but very pleased."

"The bottom line is that I've had enough of living here in Managua. I'm embarrassed by Sandra's book and that I was manipulated by her. I'm also tired of jumping from job to job, from relationship to relationship, and of having no real purpose in my life anymore. To tell you the truth, I'm getting old with little to show for my life. I want to make a radical change, and I need your help."

Luis's eyes sparkled expectantly. "Have you finally decided to go back to Elizabeth and your family?"

"No, not that," Stan answered, surprised at Luis's question. "I've treated her too badly for that. Even if Elizabeth took me back, she doesn't need an unhappy husband. I just can't bring myself to return to Nashville as a failure. I still want to make a significant and positive difference in the lives of others here in Nicaragua before I die."

"Then what do you want to do?"

"That's what I wanted to talk to you about," Stan said.

At that moment, the waiter returned with two cold bottles of beer and poured them into glasses for both Stan and Luis.

"I want to move to San Juan del Norte, open a small backpacker and sportfishing hotel and use that as a base from which to help the people there," Stan explained.

"You're kidding!" Luis said, genuinely surprised. "There's nothing there—just some poor fishermen, a few government workers, and several highly primitive commercial establishments. It's nine hours by boat from San Carlos, and boats only go there twice a week. There's not even a telephone or post office yet, and they have electricity only a few hours each night. You would be bored to death. It's a beautiful place, but there is nothing for someone like you to do except fish."

"But all that you just said are reasons that make me want to move there. I think it's small enough, poor enough, and new enough that I can make a positive difference. As you know, my ancestor George Hollins destroyed it once; maybe I could help bring it back to life again."

Luis took a sip of his beer and thought about what Stan had said.

"I'd start a small eco-lodge for backpackers and fishermen. The place is teeming with natural beauty, tarpon, and history, and I'm sure I could support myself that way. Just look at the success Costa Rica is having with eco-tourism. We're right across the border on land that's at least as beautiful and certainly many times cheaper."

"But their infrastructure is much better than ours, and San Juan del Norte has even less than most other towns in Nicaragua."

"Maybe remedying that isolation is one of the contributions I could make," Stan said.

"Well, it's true that the people of San Juan del Norte need all the help they can get right now," Luis said. "But where would you get the money? Wouldn't it require a lot to purchase land, build a hotel, and buy the fishing boats you would need?"

"I have about a hundred and seventy thousand dollars between what my father left me when he died and the money that I have saved. I figure that by doing a lot of the construction myself, using local materials and labor, and buying second-hand boats, it would be more than enough to get started."

Luis thought a minute. "Maybe, but it would really have to be a simple construction. Have you prepared a business plan yet?"

"Not yet. First, I plan on spending a few weeks visiting some eco-lodges in Costa Rica to get some ideas," Stan said. "But before even doing that, I wanted to bounce my ideas off of you and talk with you about the possibilities of you and your family going in with me on the venture. The perfect place for the hotel would be on a tiny section of your family's property at the juncture of the river and the ocean. You showed me the spot when we inaugurated the health center in the old San Juan del Norte."

"But everything is just jungle there," Luis said. "There's no electricity or anything. Why don't you buy a lot in the new town? They are cheap, and there is drinking water and access to electricity for a few hours a day from the town generator."

"But that's the point of eco-tourism, Luis. I don't want to be in the town. I want to live off the land and show others how to do it. The idea is to get our building materials from the property, use wind and solar power when possible, and raise or grow most of our own food."

"Well, I guess I could talk to our family about it once you are further along with your ideas and have a business plan. For sure, developing some of the land is in our interest. It has just sat there for decades and has been a financial drain rather than a resource for the family. Maybe something could be worked out." Luis then added, "But I warn you. We don't have any cash to invest. Our investment in El Futuro won't begin giving a return for a few more years, and between getting the family's businesses operational again now that my father has died, taking care of Mother and Jorge's family, and with Flavia's medical treatment, we are all stretched for cash."

"What's wrong with Flavia?" Stan asked.

Luis shook his head sorrowfully. "Just a few months ago, she discovered that she has advanced ovarian cancer."

"I'm so sorry," Stan said. "It's only been four years since she and Antonio married."

"That's what makes it doubly sad," Luis said. "They thought that she was pregnant when they went in for the exam. They had been trying so hard to have a baby. Antonio, of course, is devastated."

"Is there anything they can do?"

"She's got the best doctors possible in Boston, but survival rates for her stage aren't good. We can just pray," Luis said. He then added, "Antonio wrote that Laura flew up to be with Flavia for a weekend when she heard the news. She's been such a dear friend to her."

The waiter returned to the table with a large round platter and served them each their *churrascos*. Stan took the opportunity to ordered another beer for himself and for Luis. Then, cutting his steak, Stan addressed Luis's comment about the Romero family not having cash to invest.

"I don't expect you to put up any cash for the venture—just your land. I would be the one responsible for putting up all of the cash for the building of the lodge and for its management, although I may ask you for advice and contacts."

"Do you have any idea yet of what you would offer the family in exchange for the land?" Luis asked.

"My first guess is that it would be a twenty-five to thirty percent share in the venture. It depends on how much land you put up, its location, and its appraised value."

"Well, like I said, everything is possible," Luis reiterated. "Once you've finished your trip to Costa Rica and have come up with a business plan and a concrete proposal, I will share it with the rest of the family."

Stan agreed.

After commenting on the tastiness of the meal, Stan turned their conversation to another subject. "I need your help on something else, too."

Luis nodded.

"Sandra's memoir has forced me to relive what happened that night on the river, and my old guilt has resurged with a vengeance."

Luis nodded. "I know what you mean. Mine too!"

"I'm not talking about the cover-up so much, or even about my having insisted so hard that Clay come with us. It's true, I do feel bad about those decisions, but not nearly as bad as I do about my having killed someone."

Luis nodded again in sympathy.

"I know that it was self-defense in a wartime situation," Stan continued, "but the fact is that I took a life and caused immense sorrow to that soldier's family. And worst of all, it has been ten years since it happened, and I have done absolutely nothing to ask for forgiveness or to try to remedy the situation as best I can. I don't even know the soldier's name, where he was from, if he was married, or if he had children—nothing about him." He paused and looked at Luis with hope. "Can you, with your contacts, help me find out about him?"

"I don't know, Stan. Like you say, it's been ten years, and the government has changed."

"Would you be willing to try?" Stan pleaded. "It is very important to me."

"Of course," Luis replied. "I still have some good friends in high places in the army, and I'm sure that we can at least discover the man's name. What may be more difficult will be tracing his family's whereabouts, as so much time has passed."

"But you will try?"

"I'd be happy to try," Luis said. "I tell you what. Two months from now, you invite me again to lunch, and I will bring whatever information I have gathered, and you will bring the business plan for your venture in San Juan del Norte."

Stan reached across the table and shook Luis's hand. "Agreed!" He then ordered some coffee for them both, and as the two of them sipped it, they talked and joked as if their split had never happened. When they finished and Stan had paid the bill, they both stood up to leave. Stan reached out and patted Luis on the shoulder in an affectionate half-embrace. "You're a good man, Luis Romero," he said. "I'll see you in two months."

# CHAPTER 13

After that meeting with Luis, Stan was a transformed man—full of gratitude to Luis and full of new energy and resolve. First, Stan resigned from his two current jobs as an English teacher and as a local point-person for a U.S. university sending students each year to Nicaragua. Next, he began to do all the research that he needed to do before presenting the Romero family with a business plan.

Two days after their meeting, Stan went by bus to Costa Rica and spent ten days there visiting eco-lodges in the mountains and on the coasts. Then crossing back into Nicaragua through Los Chiles, he took the public boat from San Carlos all the way to the bottom of the San Juan River to San Juan del Norte. There he stayed for a week in the rustic three bedroom hotel of Enrique Faris, gathering information on land prices and the availability of skilled labor and supplies. He also surveyed possible sites for his eco-lodge.

Enrique, a jack-of-all-trades who also owned the only private telephone in the town and knew more about San Juan del Norte's history and inhabitants than anyone else, promised to help Stan with his project. Together they spent three days exploring the Romero property with machetes in hand. As he looked for where to place his hotel, Stan paid special attention to beauty, elevation, access, soil conditions, and sources of lumber, energy, and fresh water.

When Stan returned to San Carlos and Managua, he obtained aerial maps and property plats of the area from government offices and drew up some rough plans for his hotel and other projected economic activities. He showed them to a friend who was an architect and to another who taught entrepreneurship at INCAE, the business school where Stan often played tennis. Finally, when he was ready with his documents and proposal, he telephoned Luis to confirm their next meeting at Los Ranchos on the day they had determined previously.

Luis was ready as well with the results of his research from army contacts, town records, and telephone calls to various people. "The soldier you killed was named Samuel Pinto," he said. "He was born in 1955 and came from the town of San Miguelito."

Stan knew of the town on Lake Nicaragua off the road between Managua and San Carlos, as he had visited it once on an excursion to the Solentiname Islands. He did some quick calculations in his head. "That means Samuel was about 29 years old when he died."

Luis nodded in confirmation. "I found out also that he was married at the time to a woman called Carmen Vergueiro whose family was also from San Miguelito. She and Samuel had one child when he was killed, a son named Marcos Pinto who was born in 1976."

"Fantastic!" Stan exclaimed. "Were you able to find out how I can get in touch with them?"

"I did," Luis said. "Three years after Samuel's death, Carmen married a small businessman named Vinicio Paredes who owns a *pulpería*—a small general store in San Carlos. It's called Santo Antonio and is located right near the bus station. Besides Marcos, they now have two other children of their own—a five-year-old son and a two-year-old daughter. From what I understand, Marcos still lives with them."

"I don't know how to thank you, Luis," Stan said.

"I'm glad that I could help," Luis replied. He then asked curiously, "What do you plan to do with the information?"

"I'm not totally sure," Stan said. "I guess that I just feel that I need to get in touch with them, ask for their forgiveness, and see if there is some way that I can help Marcos. It would be a way of trying to make amends."

During the rest of the meal, Stan talked about the other main agenda item—his hotel project. Taking out a bundle of papers from the briefcase by his chair, he presented Luis with the project—a thirty-five page business plan with accompanying building sketches and aerial maps of the Romero property. He had inked in the small area by the river and coast that he wanted to use for his lodge and for other economic activities. The plan was neatly typed and presented in a plastic folder with the title "Rainbow's End Lodge." As he handed it to Luis, Stan explained, "These are the most recent topographical images that I could find of the property. They seemed accurate to me on the ground, but who knows, given the way that the rivers constantly change course down there."

Luis laughed. "That's for sure. Silt and storms are always creating and destroying property near the coast." He then looked carefully at the aerial map of the area that Stan wanted for his hotel. "The land area that you want is definitely ours and is on all of the early maps."

Luis flipped through the plan, asked a few questions, and then agreed to take the partnership proposal to discuss with his sister, Elena, and her husband, Ricardo Lopez. They both were now running the family car business, which they had recuperated from the Sandinistas. Luis and Elena had legal authority to make any decision about the land, as Luis had a power of attorney from his aging mother and he and Elena were the only two surviving children of his parents. "I will also talk it over as a courtesy with Antonio and Jorge's wife, Inés."

Two weeks later, Luis called Stan to say that while the family was in agreement with the venture, Ricardo wanted Luis to hold out for a thirty percent instead of a twenty-five percent stake. Stan immediately agreed provided that the Romeros would pay for all of the legal costs in setting up the partnership.

Two months later, the agreement was formalized. For a thirty percent participation in Stan's projected hotel, the Rainbow's End Lodge, the Romeros ceded thirty *manzanas* (about fifty acres) of their property on the Río San Juan. Now with everything legalized, Stan feverishly and enthusiastically began to work.

# PART IV
# 1995-2003

# CHAPTER 14

Stan's first purchases were in Managua—a used boat and twenty-horsepower motor, a gas generator, gasoline saws, and other basic tools that he would need to fell trees, make planks, and build the simple construction that he intended. He planned to use as much as possible the wood of fallen trees found along the banks of the river and even in the water in order to reduce his imprint on the land.

Stan then moved to San Juan del Norte for good. For a month, he rented a room from Enrique and his family in the tiny town. From there, he made frequent trips back and forth to the property to identify where he would place the buildings, dock, generator, vegetable garden, and animal pens. He also located and marked trees that he would use for his planks.

Stan already knew some of the people from the San Juan del Norte community from thirteen years earlier when Acción had started its first health center in Greytown—the old site of the town. Because of Stan's past assistance and his relationship to Luis Romero, most of the inhabitants of San Juan del Norte were helpful and friendly to him. Very few of them knew the history of his ancestor's bombardment of the town, and those to whom he told his story praised him for wanting to come back to make amends.

Although one or two young women showed interest in him, Stan made a decision from the beginning that he was not going to complicate his life by becoming sexually involved with any local women. His experience with Sandra and with others in Managua, while bringing him momentary satisfaction, had caused him immense, longtime distress. Stan reasoned that if Luis could be celibate and happy, so could he. It would be a way of honoring Elizabeth and perhaps even God—if there was a God. Now that some good things were happening to him, Stan began to re-entertain the idea that a loving God might exist and care for him after all.

After deciding on a plan of action, Stan hired two men in San Juan del Norte to help him clear the land and obtain the lumber for his projects. He also hired Enrique as his master builder and carpenter. Stan then moved to the site of his future lodge two kilometers from the town. Early each morning, he would return to pick up Enrique and the other workers at the dock. Before nightfall, he would take them back.

Stan set up a large army tent on a high bank by the river where he slept on an army cot, used folding chairs and tables, cooked with a gas stove, and kept food cold in a kerosene refrigerator. While the weather could get terribly hot at times, Stan kept fresh by keeping the flaps of the tent open during the day and by taking quick dips in the river. As for drinking water, Stan set up aluminum funnels and plastic barrels to gather runoff water from the short, heavy rains that characterized the region. Every month or so, Stan would travel up the river to San Carlos to get more supplies.

On Stan's second trip to San Carlos from San Juan del Norte, he contacted Carmen Paredes, the former wife of the man he had killed.

# CHAPTER 15

Stan had been thinking about getting in touch with the Paredes family for months, but he also dreaded doing so as he didn't know how to begin the conversation. Finally, after breakfast at the Cabinas Leyko hotel in San Carlos where he was staying, he gathered up the courage to locate the Paredes's *pulpería*.

Walking up the cobblestone street from the hotel, Stan went by the Catholic church and school and the remains of the old Spanish fort on the hill. He then headed down the hill to the bus station near the river. After Stan sold his Toyota to raise cash because he was passing through a difficult time in Managua, he started using public transportation to go between San Carlos and Managua. This meant traveling in old and colorfully repainted former U.S. school buses that were hot, cramped, and noisy with blaring radios. The feeble suspensions of these buses always made for an uncomfortable trip, but at least they were inexpensive. Passing the station, Stan then followed the narrow, paved street in front of it in the direction of the *Alcaldía*—city hall.

Among the street's small restaurants and tiny stores selling shoes, clothes, watches, and radios, he caught sight of a faded sign, *Pulpería Santo Antonio*. The sign was partially hidden by a jumble of electric wires. Since it was still early in the morning and the stores were just opening, Stan decided to come back later at ten o'clock, a more appropriate hour for the conversation that he felt that he had to have.

When Stan returned to the small store later in the morning, he hesitated but then entered. As his eyes adjusted from the outside daylight to the store's dimness, he could make out two glass-door refrigerators along the wall filled with sodas, beers, and fruit drinks. In the middle of the room, three racks held a mixture of snacks, soap, shampoo, pens, notebooks, canned goods, and sacks of rice, beans, and other grocery items.

The only other person in the store was a young woman with frizzy hair who appeared to be in her mid to late thirties—a little plump perhaps, but pleasant looking. She glanced up from where she was seated behind the counter, smiled, and greeted him. Stan smiled back and then went to one of the shelves and picked up a small notebook of lined paper and a *Bic* pen from an open box full of them. He then walked over to the woman in order to pay.

Stan had made the decision to go straight to the point, so while she was giving him his change, he asked in Spanish, "Excuse me, are you Doña Carmen Paredes?"

The woman looked surprised at the question, and although she hesitated a second as if she were trying to figure out who this stranger was, she answered, "I am."

Stan introduced himself and offered his hand. "My name is Stan Hollins. I'm an American living now in San Juan del Norte." As she took his hand, Stan paused and then continued, "I know that this sounds strange, and maybe this isn't a good time to talk, but I would like to speak to you about a personal matter involving your first husband, Samuel Pinto."

"About Samuel?" the young woman asked. She looked even more dumbfounded.

Stan nodded. "About Samuel and his death at the Roberto Romero State Farm."

"I don't understand," Carmen responded.

"I was there, and I wanted to share with you some information about his death."

She looked at Stan bewildered, but Stan took her nod to mean that he should continue.

"This is very difficult for me to say to you, but I was the one who shot and killed your husband. It was not intentional but by chance. I was wounded and terrified at the time and just shot back at the flashes of those who were firing at me and at my friends. My bullets killed your husband, and I just wanted to seek you out and tell you how sorry I am."

"You are the Contra who killed Samuel?" she asked incredulously.

"I'm the person who killed your husband, but I was not a Contra," Stan explained. "My son-in-law and I just happened to be staying at the state farm that night when the Contras attacked and your husband's army unit showed up to repel them. We were caught in between. Your husband's army unit thought we were Contras and opened fire on us, and I fired back. Tragically, in the confusion, my son-in-law and your husband were both killed."

"The army told me that Samuel was killed by the Contras," Carmen said.

"That is only partially true," Stan replied.

"Why are you telling me this now?" she asked.

"Because your husband's death has been on my conscience ever since it happened. It was an accident, but I need to ask your forgiveness and see if there is any way that I can make amends."

"But it's been eleven years!"

"I know, and I'm sorry for that delay, too." Stan said.

Carmen looked carefully at Stan's eyes as if trying to assess his sincerity. She then said, "If it was an accident as you say, then you have my forgiveness. War is war." She then added, "As for amends, how do you make amends for killing someone's husband and someone's father? There's not enough money in the world for that, is there?"

"No, there isn't," Stan replied. "But I feel I need to do something, particularly for your son Marcos who lost his father. I don't have much money or influence, but I would like to help him in some way get started in his life—maybe a scholarship or something to the university. I understand he is nineteen and that he lives with you."

"You certainly seem to know a lot about us," Carmen said.

"I have a friend who has contacts in the government and army," Stan explained. "He helped me find out the name of your husband and to trace you and your son Marcos."

"Marcos is a fine young man, but he doesn't like book-learning much."

"Is he working now?"

"Sometimes he helps out in the store, but it's not a real job, as we can't afford to pay him anything," Carmen said. "He's a good worker, but there are few jobs here in San Carlos. He'll probably end up sneaking over to Costa Rica to look for work. Lots of his friends are doing it, but there's no future there as it's so hard to get papers now."

"Maybe that's how I could try to make amends," Stan said, as much to himself as to Carmen. "If he is a good worker as you say, maybe he could work for me in San Juan del Norte."

"San Juan del Norte! I thought the situation there was worse than here," Carmen said. "What kind of business do you have there?"

At that moment, a customer came in to buy a soda and a bag of chips, and Doña Carmen attended him. After she had given him his change and he had left, Stan answered her question by telling her of his plans to build a simple hotel and start some other businesses. "If Marcos is willing and a quick learner, he could learn all sorts of things—building, cooking, hotel management, being a tour guide, fishing, even English. I would, of course, register him and pay him, and if he did well and we found that we got along, he could eventually become my assistant." Stan looked at Carmen in the eye. "But I have to be frank with you. I am starting from scratch. I'm living in a tent right now by the edge of the river, and probably I will continue to do so for another six months. It's terribly hard and dirty work—certainly not for everyone. But for the right person, it is a unique adventure and opportunity to create something of value and to learn a lot by doing so."

Carmen listened carefully, and then she turned to an empty page in her notebook and asked Stan to write down his name and how she could get in touch with him. "Of course, I will have to talk with Marcos and my husband about all of this. This is all so strange and unexpected."

Stan wrote his name and Enrique's name and his telephone number in San Juan del Norte. "I'm leaving tomorrow morning on the boat with my supplies, but tonight I will be at the Cabinas Leyko. If Marcos wants to talk with me tonight about this, then leave a message for me there. Otherwise, he can leave a message at this number in San Juan del Norte. I should be back in San Carlos sometime next month." Stan then shook Carmen's hand, thanked her, and left.

After making purchases and calls to Managua during the rest of the day, Stan returned to his hotel close to 6:00 p.m. and got a message—not from Marcos but from his step-father, Vinicio Paredes. In the message, the step-father invited Stan to come by their store after it closed at six o'clock. He and Marcos wanted to learn more about him and his offer. As soon as Stan had washed his face and put on a clean shirt, he headed over to the pulpería.

When Stan got there, Carmen opened the door for him, holding on her hip her young daughter Natasha whom she introduced to Stan. She welcomed him into the store, now lit with a florescent tube lamp, and then excused herself to go back to their private quarters to call her husband and eldest son.

Within less than a minute, she reappeared with them and introduced them to Stan. Vinicio, a slender, mild-looking man wearing glasses, who appeared to Stan to be about ten years older than Carmen, shook his hand perfunctorily and thanked him for coming. Marcos, a well-built, handsome young man of medium height, just acknowledged the introduction with a nod. He did not look at Stan in the eyes, nor shake his hand.

After the introduction, Vinicio asked Marcos to go back to their kitchen and get some chairs for them to sit on. Marcos obeyed immediately and soon returned in two trips with four straight-backed chairs. Vinicio arranged them facing each other and offered Stan a seat. Once everyone was sitting, he asked Stan to repeat what he had told Carmen that morning so that they could better understand his offer.

Stan did so and said again how sorry that he was for what had happened and how grateful he was for their willingness to receive him and hear him out.

"War is a terrible thing and unfortunate things happen. The truth is, though, that good things can come out of evil," Vinicio philosophized. "As tragic as Samuel's death was, it made it possible for me to marry Carmen and have Marcos as my son."

Carmen smiled at her husband, but Marcos continued staring at the floor. Until now he had said nothing.

Stan, noticing Marcos's silence, directed his attention to him and tried to draw him out. "You were about seven or eight years old when your father died, weren't you?"

Marcos nodded affirmatively but didn't look up at Stan.

"I know it must be very hard for you now to meet the man who shot your father," Stan said sympathetically. "My granddaughter lost her father that night, too. Someone in your father's patrol killed him, thinking wrongly that he was a Contra. A lot of people have suffered because of that night, and I know a little of how you must feel towards me. I am so sorry."

As no one said anything, Stan continued, still addressing Marcos. "I know I can never make amends to you for the death of your father, but I would like to help you get started in life in some way—like your own father would have tried to do." He paused to see if there was any reaction, but there wasn't. "Your mother said that you don't want to go to the university but that you are looking for a job." Stan looked at Carmen, "Did you share with him my offer?"

Carmen nodded affirmatively.

Turning back to Marcos, Stan said, "I need someone young, strong, and a good learner and worker to help me build and run a small eco-lodge in San Juan del Norte. It is going to be hard work, especially at first, but it is also exciting work, as we will be creating something new. I would like to offer you the chance, Marcos, partially to make amends in some way for what I did, and partially because I need someone reliable to help me. Your mother says that you are a good worker."

"How much would you pay him?" Vinicio asked.

"Starting out, two minimum salaries plus food and lodging, which would be basic at first. He would hardly have any expenses. For six months, he would be living in a large tent with me, but after the structures are ready, he would have his own room. Like all things in life, it may work out and it may not. But for a young person, it would be an adventure—a chance to save money and an opportunity to learn a lot of new things."

"But San Juan del Norte is so far away," Carmen said.

"It's closer than San José and Managua," Stan countered. "And he could return often to San Carlos to get supplies for me."

Stan could see that they were thinking about his proposal, but he didn't want to pressure them for a "yes" or "no" answer. "I tell you what," Stan said to Marcos, who was now looking him in the eye, "You think about it for a few days and let me know your decision by Friday. You can leave a message for me at the number in San Juan del Norte that I gave your mother. If you want to accept the offer and try it, you can come down on next Tuesday's boat with some basic things, and I will take care of the rest down there."

Marcos nodded and said, "Thank you."

Stan then got up and expressed his gratitude to them again for receiving him so graciously. As he left, he shook Marcos's hand. "I really hope to have a positive reply from you."

The next morning Stan left with his supplies on the public boat to San Juan del Norte, pleased that he had finally made contact with Marcos and his family. Then, two days later in San Juan del Norte, his pleasure increased when Enrique told Stan that Marcos had called and left word that he was accepting Stan's offer and would be on the Tuesday boat from San Carlos.

Tuesday evening, Stan was waiting on the dock for Marcos when the boat arrived. After putting him up the first night in Enrique's small hotel, the next morning Stan showed Marcos the small settlement of San Juan del Norte and introduced him to some of his friends and workers. He also explained in more detail his plans for the hotel. After eating lunch in a small restaurant and buying some extra supplies he needed now that Marcos would be living in the tent with him, they both left in Stan's boat for the building site on the river.

From then on and throughout the many months of building the lodge, Stan's relationship to Marcos progressed from initial wariness to warmth and mutual trust. Marcos showed himself to be a quick and enthusiastic learner and a reliable helper. He also picked up considerable English from working with Stan and from Stan teaching him at night when there was nothing much else to do. On a personal level, within a few weeks, Marcos felt comfortable enough with Stan to share some of his feelings about their first meeting.

"When my mother told me about your offer to help me, I had such mixed emotions," he confessed. "On the one hand, I didn't want to have anything to do with you. You were the person who had killed my father, and I thought that it would be disloyal to him for me to receive a gift or accept a job from you. I felt it would be 'blood money.'"

Stan nodded. "I understand."

"*Por otro lado*—on the other hand," Marcos continued, "I needed a job, and you had killed my father accidentally. As my step-father pointed out, you didn't know him, and your bullets could have just as easily hit someone else in the patrol. He said also that it could even have been my father who killed your son-in-law."

Stan had never thought before of that possibility—that it had been Samuel who shot and killed Clay. "Your step-father is right," Stan said. "Both of us were shooting at *the enemy*. We weren't firing at real individuals like Samuel Pinto or Clay Danforth. I guess it's that depersonalization that makes war possible in the first place."

Marcos agreed. "Anyway, what my step-father said changed my perspective about you."

"Do you and your step-father get along well?" Stan asked.

"Now we do," Marcos said. "At first, his courting of my mother was difficult for me, as I felt I needed to be loyal to my father. But then I began to see I could respect them both. They are such different people, and that helps. My father was fun-loving, loud, and liked to fish. My step-father is quiet and serious and is involved in the Catholic Church a lot. But he

111

loves my mother and he loves me and he does his best for us. It's true what he said to you, 'good things can come out of evil.'"

Stan thought a lot about that statement and began to see its truth in Marcos's companionship, in his forgiveness, and in his help to him. Over the weeks of living and working together, Marcos became to Stan the son he never had. Stan loved his daughter, Laura, but her rejection of him had hurt him deeply. He yearned for the time when she, like Marcos, would be able to get beyond the wrong that he had done to her and to her mother. But Stan still was unable to face the humiliation of asking for forgiveness from Elizabeth and Laura as he had from Marcos and his mother.

Within a year, Stan, Enrique, Marcos, and the rest of his team had erected a quaint lodge of rustic timbers and bamboo covered with thatched roofs. The lodge consisted of a main building with a reception area, kitchen, and dining room that was linked by a raised covered walkway to his and Marcos's personal quarters and to five other guest cabins overlooking the river. As many as twenty-five individual guests paying from fifteen and thirty dollars a night apiece could sleep there. Stan also dug a well and a septic tank and installed solar panels, a wind generator on the beach, a backup gasoline generator, and a propane icemaker.

# CHAPTER 16

Rainbow's End Lodge was inaugurated in June of 1996, and among those who came to take part in the ceremonies were Luis Romero, Ricardo and Elena Lopez, and Marcos's parents, Carmen and Vinicio Paredes. It was a happy and hopeful occasion, and Stan felt that he had turned a corner in his life, and the future looked bright.

Indeed, for the first seven years after the inauguration, the small lodge's fortunes were constantly on the upward trend, and Stan proved to be a natural as a businessman. His prices were fair, his food was good, and he took a genuine interest in his guests and other customers. Guests at his lodge could fish, kayak, go horseback riding on the beach, or visit the Indio Maíz Biological Reserve and the graveyards at Greytown. Stan made money, too, by furnishing ice to fishermen and to the other restaurants in the town, by raising and selling iguanas, and by buying river shrimp and reselling them in San Carlos or in Bluefields. On his return to San Juan del Norte from delivering his products, he transported beer and gasoline and other items to sell locally. He also transported tourists for a reasonable fee.

Most tourists loved the trip down the river in Stan's *panga* or in the public boat from San Carlos to San Juan del Norte. It was a magnificent journey passing through vast forests and through several small rapids, and the boats stopped at picturesque settlements and towns along the way to pick up and leave off passengers. Some tourists, however, didn't appreciate that they had to do the same trip again, returning by the same route. As beautiful and inexpensive a trip as it was, it was also uncomfortable and tiring in the cramped quarters of a narrow public boat filled with people, bags, and cargo. In order to meet the tourist demand for an alternative route from San Juan del Norte to Managua and Costa Rica, Stan created two more options for them.

One of these was a five-hour ocean route north from San Juan del Norte to Bluefields. In Bluefields, tourists could take a commercial flight back to Managua or go to visit the most Caribbean part of Nicaragua—the Corn Islands. Since fuel was expensive and space limited in his open-sea boat, Stan usually made this trip to Bluefields only once a month when he delivered shipments of iguanas or river shrimp to his buyers there.

The other cheaper, less dangerous route was south from San Juan del Norte to Barra del Colorado in Costa Rica. Stan came up with the idea of a horseback route along the empty beach so that guests from his Rainbow's End Lodge could cross over the border to Costa Rica and take the small commercial plane that connected Barra to the Costa Rican capital, San José. Partnering with his friend Jimmy Langston, a hard-drinking and outgoing American ex-pat who owned a small sportfishing lodge in Barra del Colorado, Stan arranged with local authorities to issue special temporary tourist visas to his clients that were valid for several days in the two towns.

In all of these business activities, Marcos quickly became indispensable to Stan despite his youth. He helped Stan run the lodge, and he often would be the one to make the trips to San Carlos, Barra del Colorado, and Bluefields. On the first of his many trips to Bluefields, Marcos met his future wife, Amelia, the daughter of the Creole owner of the store where Stan sold his river shrimp. Within six months after they met, Amelia and Marcos were married, and a year after that, they had a little boy named Samuel. Just like Marcos, Amelia became a great asset to Stan with her ability in English, her good nature, hard work, and business sense.

In their early years of operation, Stan's lodge and other businesses did well enough so that Stan was considered the second richest man in the impoverished town. The richest was Stan's main customer, Adric Williams, who owned the town's main general store, which Stan supplied with goods from San Carlos and Bluefields. Two years before Stan moved to San Juan del Norte, Adric had transformed himself from one of the poorest fishermen in the tiny town into its most wealthy citizen—the proud owner of a two-story masonry house with his store on the ground floor. Adric always attributed his good fortune to the death of a relative in Limón in Costa Rica, but everyone knew that it was really because of the "white lobster" that he found floating in the water one day while fishing in the Atlantic.

The region off the coast of San Juan del Norte was an important drug route stretching from Colombia's San Andrés Island to drop-off points in Mexico. Both the Nicaraguan and U.S. Coast Guards knew the route and often stopped suspicious "go-fast" boats off the coast and boarded them looking for the drugs. When traffickers saw government boats approaching, they would throw bales of the packets into the sea, knowing that the ocean currents of the area would likely take the cocaine to unpopulated shores where some poor local beachcomber or fisherman like Adric would find them. The dealers would then buy them back through intermediaries at around four thousand dollars a kilo, and everyone would be happy. Sprinkled here and there along the Atlantic coast of Nicaragua, one could find people like Adric with new houses, boats, satellite TVs, and generators. Their lives had been transformed by "God's blessings to them from the sea."

Because of Stan's apparent prosperity and the fact that he was an outsider and supporter of the Sandinistas, a few of the desperately poor Creoles, Indians, and Mestizos who lived in San Juan del Norte were suspicious and jealous of him. Stan worked hard to reduce those negative feelings by contributing to the town in any way that he could. He bought shirts for the local baseball team and lobbied for small community development projects with some of his former non-governmental agency and foundation friends in Managua. Sometimes they helped, and among Stan's successes were a new community dock at Greytown, elevated cement sidewalks over the often marshy ground of San Juan del Norte, a small community center, and nature trails through the forest. One Christmas, Stan even got Samaritan's Purse, an international Christian agency, to distribute shoeboxes full of presents to the numerous barefooted children of the town—an act that especially endeared him to many mothers.

Stan batted zero, however, in getting outside help for his most important community project—the building of a landing strip so that the Cessna Grand Caravans that flew between Managua and San Carlos could also land in San Juan del Norte and bring in the tourists and sportfishermen who were the lifeblood of the community.

A major airport behind the town had been promised by a former Nicaraguan president who loved to fish there, but after some clearing had been done, the work was stopped for lack of money. Later the ex-president was tried for pocketing the funds that were budgeted for that and other projects. Stan, accompanied by the mayor of San Juan del Norte, had travelled twice to Managua to lobby the new government to reinitiate the work, but each time the answer was the same: "We don't have the money, and there is not enough demand to make the flights profitable."

Given the necessity of some sort of airport for the future prosperity of San Juan del Norte, Stan began to look into the possibilities of an alternative—building a simple and inexpensive dirt landing strip near the town where small planes could safely land and take off. Having heard stories from Enrique and others of how light planes and helicopters once landed on the main street of Greytown—the former site of San Juan del Norte before it was destroyed in the war—Stan believed that this was where the landing strip should be. The location was only a few kilometers from the new town, and all that was needed was to clear the new jungle growth from the area, fill in former battle trenches, compact the soil, and plant grass to hold it in place.

Stan talked with an engineering friend in Managua and a former pilot who knew the old landing strip, and they both calculated that a runway at Greytown would not only be viable, but it would cost only a tiny fraction of the proposed multi-million dollar airport behind the town—perhaps as little as fifty thousand dollars. Greytown's main advantages were that the landing strip could be built without draining swamps and without bringing in big earth-moving machines. Everything could be done with local labor and hand tools.

With the approval of the town council and their promise to share revenues with him from landing fees, Stan tried to interest members of the government, owners of airlines, and his friends Antonio Lopez and Felipe and Rosa Gonzales into putting up the fifty thousand dollars. Although expressing admiration for his efforts, they all declined his request.

Given the importance of the landing strip to his hotel and to the town, Stan, therefore, decided to finance the Greytown project himself. He would cash in the twenty thousand dollars that he still had in investments for his retirement, and then he would take out a low-interest loan for the rest of the amount from a small foundation named Adelante, which promoted eco-tourism in the region. His idea would be to repay the loan with future revenue from landing fees. Stan presented his plan to Adelante, and they agreed to the loan on the condition that Stan's investment in Rainbow's End Lodge would serve as collateral.

Once Stan had the money he needed in hand, he hired thirty of the unemployed of San Juan del Norte to begin the clearing of the location and Enrique Faris to coordinate the project. For several months, they worked steadily—felling trees, burning logs, filling in battle trenches from the war, shifting dirt—all by hand. While there was always progress, it was much slower than Stan first imagined. The three months that he had calculated for finishing the project now looked as if it would extend to six, and the situation was becoming ominous as Stan was quickly running out of cash.

Not only did Stan have to pay the workers every two weeks, but he also had to pay back his loan and maintain his businesses. His transportation business was suffering because of a huge rise in the price of boat fuel and his inability to pass the costs on to his customers. Worst of all, Stan's income from the hotel was the lowest it had been since its inauguration seven years earlier because of the unexpected drop in the number of tourists to the region. None of the promises of the government to promote tourism by asphalting the highway from Managua to San Carlos, dredging the river, and simplifying entry and exit requirements with Costa Rica had been fulfilled. With a world economic crisis in full swing, few tourists came.

Returning to his quarters at the end of 2003, Stan sat down at his desk with pen and paper. In the last light of the evening, he worked out financial calculations for several probable scenarios. The conclusion he came to in all of them was unmistakable. Even with the loan, he had money for only three months to pay his bills. He would have to have a fresh infusion of cash or he would have to cancel the Greytown landing strip. And even if he did call off the work, it was doubtful that he would have enough money both to maintain his hotel and pay back his loan to Adelante. With a heavy heart, Stan got up from his desk to go to bed. His only consolation was the feeling that things could not get worse.

# PART V
# 2004

# CHAPTER 17

Two months later, in February of 2004, things did get worse for Stan. One morning when he woke up and went to the bathroom, he looked at his stream of urine and saw that it had blood in it.

"You have to see a urologist immediately," Dr. Eduardo Castillo advised Stan when he saw him that same day at the government health center in town. The young doctor had just been assigned to the newly opened San Juan del Norte government health center as part of his national service requirement. "Your symptoms could be a sign of something very serious," he added.

Leaving the health center, Stan immediately went to Enrique's house and called Luis Romero at El Futuro, where he was now living in his old family house at Las Palmas. Luis had long proposed a special economic development project for the Río San Juan, and Felipe and Rosa Gonzales had hired him to put together the project at El Futuro. Stan told Luis what the doctor said, and asked him for his recommendation of a urologist in Managua or San José.

After hearing him out and commiserating with him, Luis advised, "My best choice is Dr. Benedicto Arvelo, a friend I met in Costa Rica when I lived there. He has an office at the Clínica Bíblica in downtown San José, and everybody respects him. I'll be glad to call him and set up an appointment for you." He paused and then asked, "Could you go next week?"

"I guess that I've got to do it, so my answer is yes," Stan replied. "Marcos and Amelia can take care of things here while I am gone."

"OK," Luis said. "I'll call him right now and then get back to you at Enrique's. Give me up to an hour in case he's busy with a patient."

"I'll wait," Stan said.

Within twenty minutes, Luis called back, and Enrique's wife, Myra, handed Stan the telephone.

"The appointment is set for next Tuesday at ten o'clock in the morning at his offices in the Clínica Bíblica," Luis said. "Benedicto said that you should be ready to stay for as much as two weeks, as they will probably have to do some tests, given your symptoms."

"Two weeks!" Stan exclaimed, thinking about his financial situation and duties. He then added in resignation, "I guess I have no alternative but to do it."

"Let me know what happens, and if I can help in some other way," Luis replied. "I'll be praying for you," he added.

Stan thanked Luis for his friendship and help, paid Myra for the use of the phone, and then left for his lodge. He had a lot to do before leaving.

A few days later, after making arrangements with Marcos and Amelia, Stan set out at dawn for Barra del Colorado on horseback, accompanied by a British couple staying at Rainbow's End Lodge who were also heading to San José. With the money that he had reserved to pay the workers at Greytown at the end of the month, he bought a ticket on the daily Cessna flight from Barra to San José and then rented an inexpensive room in a simple hotel near the bus station and the Clínica Bíblica.

The next morning Stan went to the hospital where Luis's friend Dr. Benedicto Arvelo worked. The doctor was cordial and received him warmly. They both talked of their respect for Luis, and when the doctor saw Stan's thigh wound in the course of his examination, they talked of the war and of its consequences to both Nicaragua and Costa Rica. Dr. Benedicto, however, was reluctant to answer Stan's questions and make any preliminary diagnosis until he saw the results of the tests that he had ordered.

A week later, after those tests and a biopsy of his prostate had been completed, the doctor confirmed the bad news that Stan already suspected. "I'll be frank with you," he said. "I'm afraid you have a very serious case of prostate cancer, and it looks as if it may have spread into your lymphatic system. You will have to have an operation to take it out. If the cancer has spread, as I suspect it has, then you will need to start chemotherapy immediately."

Stan was expecting bad news but was still devastated at the diagnosis and prognosis. "I just don't have the time or the money for this sort of thing right now."

"If you do nothing," Dr. Benedicto warned, "the cancer will surely spread and you might not live long. If it gets to the bones, it can be very painful."

"It couldn't happen at a worse time," Stan exclaimed. "I'm short on cash and have a lot of projects up in the air." He was silent for few seconds and then said, "I'll have to return to San Juan del Norte and think through my options."

"I understand," Dr. Benedicto said kindly. "My advice to you, though, is to take it out as soon as possible."

Stan nodded and thanked the doctor and then said, "I'll let you know what I decide to do as soon as I can."

On his way out, Stan paid a small part of his bill, and he then went back to the hotel to call Luis. He had promised to do so as soon as he knew the final results of the tests.

"You need to call Elizabeth and Laura immediately," Luis advised when he heard the bad news about Stan's medical and financial situations. "They will want to know, and they'll be able to help you."

"I just can't, not yet," Stan replied. "I guess I still have too much pride in me. I have to think things through first."

The next morning, with his last remaining cash, Stan paid his hotel bill, took a taxi to the airport, and bought a SANSA air ticket back to Barra del Colorado. When he arrived in the small town at eleven o'clock, he walked over to his partner Jimmy Langston's fishing lodge on the Colorado River and told him where he had been and what had happened. Jimmy commiserated with him and tried to persuade him to stay at least one night at his lodge to rest and talk over what he was going to do. He could then head back to San Juan del Norte in the early morning when it was much cooler.

Stan, however, was adamant about leaving right away, so Jimmy offered to take him to the corral on the coast where they kept the horses for their joint venture. Letting his assistant know his plans, Jimmy went to one of his four fishing craft tied up in front of the lodge and helped Stan climb in with his knapsack. He then started the motor and headed up the Colorado River, turning off after a short while into a channel that paralleled the ocean. Fifteen minutes later, they arrived at the dock and small house of Jimmy's employee Manuel Verde. The house was on an isolated beach at the end of the channel, and next to it was a fenced-in area for four of the eight horses that the two friends used for their tourist route.

Getting out of the boat, Jimmy and Stan walked the short distance to the wooden house just as Manuel came outside to greet them. They then went to the corral, and as Manuel picked out and saddled the best of the scrawny-looking animals, Jimmy told Stan stories of some of his other friends who had battled cancer and had survived. "Everything will be OK, you'll see," he said as he gave Stan a strong bear hug.

After Stan had mounted the emaciated mare and was settled in the saddle, he turned to Manuel to get his knapsack, now full of dirty clothes. He adjusted it on his back and then turned the horse's head towards the gate of the corral to begin his twenty-five kilometer journey up the deserted beach to San Juan del Norte.

"I'll be thinking of you," Jimmy said as Stan rode the horse through the gate. Stan thanked them both and waved goodbye.

About five minutes later, Stan heard the shrill scream of Jimmy's outboard motor as he returned down the river channel to Barra del Colorado. Its irritating sound contrasted sharply with the deep bass rhythm of the Atlantic waters pounding the Costa Rican shore. It was close to noon, and the sun was almost at its peak over Stan's head—a hot and humid afternoon.

As he headed back to San Juan del Norte, Stan felt as alone and despairing as he ever had in his life. His spirit was reflected in the scrawny animal under him, slowly plodding forward in a stupor. Everything had gone wrong in his life. His parents had died estranged from him. Because of him, his son-in-law Clay had been killed, and Stan himself had killed a young man. His marriage had failed, and he had no contact with his daughter or his granddaughter. The Revolution that he believed in and had lied to protect, had brought ruin to Nicaragua and had succumbed to corruption, just like the regime it had replaced. He had been betrayed by Sandra and held up by her for public ridicule. His life's work, Acción, was no more, and the eco-lodge that he had created might soon go under, as well. Cancer loomed before him as a death sentence, and he had no money for treatment. Even the small benefits that he had helped bring to San Juan del Norte were unknown by most and unappreciated by those who envied him. All of his dreams and his accomplishments and perhaps even his life would soon disappear like the old town of Greytown—destroyed by warfare, encroaching jungle, and shifting rivers.

As Stan often did when he was depressed, he turned his attention outward to his immediate surroundings and to the tasks at hand. He swiveled in the leather saddle and looked behind him, but he could no longer see Manuel's house and corral. Squinting in the sunlight, he then scanned the ocean to see if he could spot any local fishermen. There were no boats in sight. He was totally alone in this isolated section of the planet. His only companions for the next hours were the sounds of the ocean breeze, the harsh regular beat of the waves, and the slow rhythm of his horse's hooves in the deep brown sand.

This was not the Caribbean of crystal clear water and white beaches of the islands. Instead, the pounding surf was dirty brown and speckled by foam, and its undertow was treacherous. Just the year before, a French tourist staying at Stan's hotel had gone walking on the beach in his bathing suit to look for the nests of giant sea turtles. Two days later his drowned body washed up on the shore three kilometers away. The ocean pulled objects out to sea in one section of the coast and deposited them back in another.

Sometimes these objects were little treasures. When Stan traveled on foot or by horseback along the strand, he always looked for unusual objects amid the coconuts, broken tree trunks, and man-made debris that littered the empty beaches. When he found something, like a beautiful shell or colored glass bottle from another era, he would take them to his hotel to sell or to decorate his restaurant tables.

While these objects were always fun to find, what he and just about everyone else along the coast actually looked for was something much more valuable and life-changing. They all searched for "white lobster." Finding these floating packets of cocaine was the coastal equivalent to winning the lottery. It happened rarely, but it did happen. And such a discovery, Stan knew, could help turn him from failure to success. So Stan always looked.

At 3:26 p.m., Wednesday, February 18, 2004, the miracle happened. On a deserted beach, three-quarters of the way between Barra del Colorado and San Juan del Norte, Stan saw the bale tumbling in the surf about fifty meters in front of him. It was as if it had its own mind and was trying to decide whether to remain on the shore or to return to the ocean. When Stan saw it, he pulled on the reins of his horse and stopped abruptly. He stood up in his stirrups and refocused his eyes until he was sure of what he saw. Then filled with a mixture of fear and expectation, he looked out to sea to see if any boats were near. He stared up the beach and down it, and then he perused the lagoon and trees on his left for any sign of people. There was none.

Stan excitedly dismounted from the horse and with reins in hand, pulled the animal to the half-trunk of a coconut tree lying splintered on the beach. There he tied the horse and took off the bulky knapsack from his back, laying it by the log. He then walked quickly to the water's edge, and just as the next wave pushed the bale forward, he grabbed the plastic covering and pulled with all of his might. The effort ripped the plastic but released the bale from the grip of the undertow. Stan fell back with it onto the hot sand. He then stood up, panting from exertion and excitement, and looked around him again to see if anyone was in sight. There was still no one.

Stan carefully examined his treasure to make sure it was real. In the bale were bricks of white powder tightly wrapped in brown, waterproof plastic. He dragged the bale nearer to where his backpack lay, pushed his fingers deep into the plastic that held all of the bricks together, and tore open the clear outer covering. He then took out twenty separate packets of powder. These he wrapped one by one in the dirty clothes that he removed from his knapsack. As many of these as he was able, he tightly repacked in his knapsack. The ones that wouldn't fit he took over to one of the coconut trees at the edge of a lagoon. There with his hands and broken branches, he dug a ditch about a meter in length and twenty-five centimeters deep in the sand. He then carefully placed the remaining packets in the trench, covered them up, spread branches and debris on top as camouflage, and lastly, cut a cross on the trunk of the coconut tree with his pocketknife. Backing up from the spot and looking at the surrounding geography, he fixed it in his memory, satisfied that his cache was well hidden.

Returning to the horse, Stan tied his remaining clothes into a bundle and attached them to the back of his saddle. He then put on his now much heavier pack and remounted. All the way back to the Rainbow's End Lodge, Stan carefully watched for any beachcombers, but he didn't see any. All the way back, he rejoiced in his good fortune, and he planned how he would use this gift from the sea.

# CHAPTER 18

"*Señores y señoras,* we will be landing in the Augusto C. Sandino International Airport in ten minutes. Please fasten your seatbelts, and put your chairs in an upright position."

As the TACA Airlines plane circled over the center of Managua and the lake as it lined up for the descent into the airport on its outskirts, Laura Danforth leaned over and pointed out familiar sights to her nineteen-year-old daughter, Allison, who was sitting by the window.

"I didn't realize it was so beautiful!" Allison exclaimed, as she looked out the porthole.

Laura's mother Elizabeth also tried to see from her aisle seat when the plane dipped its wing as it maneuvered for a landing. She then sat back with her eyes closed as if in prayer.

The sight was indeed lovely from the air. Set between mountains and two vast lakes, Managua sparkled in the late afternoon sun. It would be paradise were it not for the fact that the lakes were polluted, the sparkles came from the galvanized metal roofs of poor houses, the mountains could erupt in volcanoes, and the land could shake from earthquakes.

Flying over the city, Laura could see changes that had been made during the twenty years that she had been away. She could make out what looked like new avenues and roundabouts, as well as hotels and shopping centers. But the same landmarks that she remembered were also still there—the small crater lakes dotting the city, the National Theatre, the pyramid hotel where Howard Hughes had once lived in the penthouse, the baseball stadium, and the ruins of the cathedral. Laura also recognized the roofs of the military hospital near "the Bunker"—the former presidential headquarters of Somoza.

"That's the hospital where your daddy was taken," she said.

Smoldering embers of the pain associated with Clay's death flamed up anew as Laura saw the hospital. They also reignited the anger that she had long felt at her father. If it had been left to Laura, they would never have come on this trip. When Luis called to inform them in late February about Stan's cancer and his precarious financial predicament, it was Allison who had insisted that they come and try to help him.

Although Stan had held her often as a baby and toddler, Allison knew her grandfather only through a few letters, some pictures that she had of him holding her, and things others told her about him. Still, she told her mother, she could not bear the idea of not helping him in such a time of need. She insisted that they all go down to Nicaragua during her spring vacation from Davidson College where she was a sophomore, and visit Stan and try to bring him back for treatment to Nashville. The trip would also be an opportunity for her to learn more about her own father and a chance for Laura and Elizabeth to visit friends whom they hadn't seen in many years.

At first Laura resisted Allison's proposal, but then Rosa called at Luis's instigation and pressed them to come and to stay at their house. Rosa even offered to lend them her husband's helicopter and pilot and to accompany them to San Juan del Norte to see Stan.

"Mother hasn't seen you in twenty years," Rosa added, "and it's also a great opportunity to get together with some of your old school friends. I'll give a big party for you."

Once Elizabeth joined Allison in insisting that the trip was the right thing to do, Laura finally relented. She purchased airline tickets for all three of them and accepted Rosa's generous invitation. She asked, however, that the party be small and that only a few of her close friends be invited so that they could talk more easily. As for Elizabeth's former friends, all except for Rosa's mother, Isabel, had either died or retired to the U.S.

The plane jolted and shivered when it touched down on the runway and then sped past the old cement bunkers that were reminders of the 1980's war. As the plane taxied to the terminal, Laura noticed construction everywhere, and when they finally deplaned and entered the modern, air-conditioned arrival area, she knew that a new era had arrived in Nicaragua. The glistening blue tiles and blasts of cold air in the airport were a total contrast to the hot, crowded, and dirty arrival room she remembered from the past.

At the passport checkpoint the line was long, and Laura and Allison struck up a conversation with a young woman in front of them. She was part of a mission group of some fifteen excited Americans who had come down on the same flight, all wearing blue tee shirts proclaiming

"Nicaragua 2004, Christ's Love in Word and Deed." The young woman said her name was Lisa and that she and the others had volunteered to help build a local Pentecostal church and provide dental services in a rural community near the border with Honduras. Lisa reminded Laura of the many *brigada* volunteers who had come to help Acción in its work many years before.

Since Clay's death, Laura had mostly abandoned her Christian faith, and she had become cynical about both religion and politics. She continued to try to do good but mainly out of an inner sense of duty because it was her job as director of a foundation. As she explained to her mother, part of her attitude was tied to the early death of her husband; the other part was tied to the actions of her supposedly "Christian" father who had hurt her and her mother in such an unforgivable way. Unlike Laura, Elizabeth and Allison were strong and active believers.

After the friendly immigration official stamped their passports and waved them on, the three women entered the baggage retrieval area. There Laura and Elizabeth scanned the dozens of faces pressed against the big window panes that separated the incoming international passengers from those waiting for them outside. Laura picked out her friend Rosa in the crowd, and she was waving enthusiastically at them with a huge smile on her face. She was a little plumper than Laura would have guessed, but her warm smile and enthusiasm identified her right away. Laura pointed her out to her mother and Allison, and all three waved back. Once they got their two bags off the conveyer belt, they quickly passed through customs and entered into the reception area and into Rosa's waiting arms.

"You're finally here!" Rosa gushed in her endearing way. After she had politely shooed off the baggage handlers and taxi drivers offering their services, Rosa introduced the three women to her own chauffeur, *Don* Angel Martínez, who had driven her to the airport. Don Angel welcomed them to Managua and immediately took their bags from them and started to lead them to the car.

Laura still considered Rosa one of her best friends, and even though she had not seen her in years, they had kept up with correspondence and telephone calls on birthdays and at Christmas. In those conversations, Rosa had shared with Laura her appreciation for Felipe but also some of the difficulties that they had in adjusting to each other. While both Rosa and Felipe were alike in that they were well-educated, had strong social consciences, and were nonpolitical, in most other ways, they were opposites. Rosa, like her mother, was an ardent Christian who came from a very poor background. Felipe, on the other hand, came from a superficially religious background and from a wealthy Nicaraguan family. "Despite our differences," Rosa told Laura, "we adore each other, and we try to learn from each other."

Five years older than Rosa, Felipe had gone to a university in the U.S. and worked there for a few years. He decided, however, to return to Nicaragua to run his family's business in the 1980s when the Sandinistas were in power. Highly practical, Felipe saw business and hard work—not politics or religion—as the solutions to development, and business was a game that Felipe was exceptionally adept at. He mistrusted enthusiastic political or religious do-gooders who depended on other people's money for their support and projects.

"Did you have a good trip?" Rosa asked as they passed through the crowd of porters and taxi drivers hoping for business.

"Excellent," Laura answered. "I'm amazed at how nice the airport is looking now. It's so clean and modern."

"We're trying to give Nicaragua a facelift. We want to be like Costa Rica and attract more tourists and investments," Rosa replied.

"How is Doña Isabel doing?" Elizabeth asked, as they walked across the access road to the parking lot.

"She's getting older and a little slower, but she still keeps us in line," Rosa answered. "She lives with us now and helps take care of Miguel and still loves to cook. As a matter of fact, she insisted on preparing Laura's favorite chocolate cake for the party tonight."

Rosa then turned to Allison and squeezed her elbow. "*Caramba*, Allison you've turned into such a beautiful young woman!"

"Thank you," Allison said. "And it's so good to finally meet you in person. Mom has always said that you are an amazing lady!"

Rosa blushed and shook her head. "Much of who I am today is because of the opportunities that your grandparents gave me!"

Rosa's new, silver Nissan Pathfinder was parked in the crowded airport lot, and when they arrived at it, Don Angel put the bags into the back and then opened the door for them. Laura slid onto the back seat and felt the full force of the Managua heat. It was four o'clock in the afternoon, and the car was a furnace. "Thank goodness for air-conditioning!" she said as Don Angel started the engine and directed blasts of cold air towards them. He then paid the parking fee and headed towards the center of the city.

The road into town had improved vastly in the years that Laura had been away, and within about ten minutes, they arrived at what had been the former center of the city before the 1972 earthquake. Along the route, many sights reminded her of the Managua that she had known—the old yellow U.S. school buses reincarnated now as passenger buses, cars and trucks with dents and broken bumpers spewing out diesel smoke, and buildings still in disrepair from the time of the earthquake.

At the stoplights, the car was immediately surrounded by people selling things—candy, sunglasses, cell phone covers, and plastic bags of water. Others begged. One man in a wheelchair held a hand-lettered sign saying that he was a war veteran. A young boy started washing the window with a dirty, wet rag despite Don Angel's protests. However, when he was done, Don Angel rolled down the window and gave him some small coins.

"I don't think I've ever seen so many poor people in one place," Allison whispered to her grandmother.

Elizabeth nodded. "It's heartbreaking. You just don't know what to do."

As they drove through the city, Rosa gave Allison a quick tour. She pointed out to her the old cathedral that the 1972 earthquake had left without a roof and the new one that was built with donations from the founder of Domino's Pizza. "With its multiple domes, the new cathedral looks like a mosque," Rosa complained.

"To me it looks like a pepperoni pizza!" Laura joked.

Rosa also showed Allison the downtown plazas where tens of thousands of jubilant Nicaraguans had celebrated the overthrow of Somoza, and then a few years later, where even more had gathered to hear Pope John Paul II celebrate mass in a politically-charged atmosphere.

Laura remembered some of the sights, like the dignified Palacio de la Cultura, the Teatro Ruben Darío, and the statue of the revolutionary with his gun raised high in victory. But in some areas, previously empty land was now filled with totally new avenues with roundabouts beautified by fountains and sculptures and lined with TGI Friday's, Burger King, modern filling stations, hotels, and shopping centers. Parts of the Masaya highway that took them to Rosa and Felipe's house reminded her of prosperous avenues in the U.S.

At the edge of the city, Don Angel turned off the highway into a neighborhood filled with large houses surrounded by walls or fences. Most had security guards sitting at their gates.

"Why are there so many guards everywhere?" Allison asked. "Isn't it safe here?"

"Of course," Rosa answered. "We're probably the safest country in Central America as far as violent crime is concerned. While we certainly have theft, the guards are also there to handle beggars and people selling things. People need jobs."

The Gonzales's house was surrounded by a brick wall, and when they got to the elaborate wrought iron gate, the uniformed guard stood up, greeted them with a wave, and opened it. They drove on a circular driveway into a beautifully landscaped yard dotted here and there with stone sculptures surrounded by flowers. Just as they pulled to a stop in front of the large Spanish colonial-style house, Isabel, Felipe, and young Miguel emerged from the front door. Elizabeth and Laura immediately got out of the car, and amid loud shouts of delight, they hugged Isabel, greeted Felipe and Miguel, and introduced Allison.

"What a handsome young man," Elizabeth exclaimed as she shook hands with Miguel. "How old are you?" she asked him in Spanish.

"*Siete*—seven," he responded.

"Good, you still remember some Spanish," Rosa said to Elizabeth. "Mother was a little worried."

Elizabeth hugged Isabel again and smiled. "We understand each other no matter what language we speak."

Isabel, her hair totally grey now, smiled also and returned the hug.

Entering the foyer of the house with the others, Laura was struck by the number of brightly colored, original paintings that filled its white walls. "I feel as if I'm in an art museum," she said.

"Felipe's been supporting Nicaraguan artists for years, from primitive painters on Solentiname to some modern ones in Granada," Rosa explained. "The pre-Columbian sculptures in the yard were found on Ometepe, and he will eventually turn them over to a national museum."

Rosa directed Don Angel to take the bags to the two guest rooms upstairs, and Laura and the others followed him. Rosa first led Elizabeth to her room and then Laura and Allison to the one they would share. Both rooms had double beds and balconies overlooking a swimming pool and a spacious yard full of flowers and more pre-Columbian statues. Behind the pool was a miniature soccer field with a circle in white chalk in the middle. A silver and blue helicopter was parked in the middle of the circle.

"Look Mom, they have a helicopter in their backyard!" Allison exclaimed from the balcony.

Rosa, who was behind them, was almost apologetic. "Felipe needs it for his businesses," she said. "It's just too far and takes too much time to travel by car to his farms in so many different parts of Nicaragua."

"Everything's so beautiful, Rosa," Laura said.

"God has blessed us. For sure, it's a far cry from my home on the Río San Juan and Mother's old cinderblock house that you remember." Both of them laughed.

"Our little dinner party will begin about six o'clock," Rosa said. "That gives you an hour to bathe and rest and pack for the trip tomorrow. Remember to take just the minimum because of the weight. We will be gone for only two days, and there'll be five of us in the helicopter, counting Luis and the pilot." She added, "Come down when you're ready." Rosa hugged Laura and Allison again and went downstairs, following Don Angel.

After changing clothes and preparing for the helicopter trip, Laura, Allison, and Elizabeth came down together to the spacious living room. There Felipe and Rosa were playing a game with Miguel at a table, while Isabel sat watching them from a brown leather chair next to a matching couch. Felipe got up politely when he saw them, offering them chairs. Instead of taking hers, Elizabeth went behind Isabel and put her hands affectionately on her shoulders.

"It's been way too long since we've seen each other," Elizabeth said. "How wonderful it is that you can all live together now as a family in such a beautiful home."

"Mother's a joy to have and helps us take care of our little bundle of energy," Rosa said, patting Miguel's head. "He's a handful, just like Felipe was at his age."

"I bet you're still a handful!" Laura joked, grinning at Felipe.

"Believe me, he is," Rosa replied as she reached out for his hand. "But beneath that gruff, deal-making exterior, he's a good man and very generous."

"She says that just because I finance all of her projects," Felipe said. "If it were up to her, she would give away all that we have!"

"Not the helicopter," Rosa interjected with a wink. "We need it for our trip tomorrow to the river."

"I don't know how to thank you both for offering to take us!" Laura said.

"You don't have to," Rosa replied. "Anyway, I'm looking forward to going with you. It's hard to believe, but even though I was raised on the Río San Juan, I've never been to San Juan del Norte." She turned to Elizabeth. "You're sure that you want to stay here and not go?"

"I'm sure. Going would put too much pressure on Stan," Elizabeth said. "He'll know that I'm waiting here in Managua for him, and he can return with you if he so chooses. Anyway, I'm looking forward to visiting with Isabel for a few days."

"I'd like to go with you, too," Felipe said, "but I have a meeting tomorrow that I can't postpone."

"Does Dad know that we're coming?" Laura asked.

"He does," Rosa said. "Luis saw him a few days ago in San Carlos and told him. Stan had come up the river to pick up an American travel writer doing a story about San Juan del Norte."

"And he's all right with it?"

"Luis thought so. He complained about Luis involving you in his troubles, but Luis said that he seemed secretly pleased that you still cared enough about him to come all of this way to see him."

"That's good," Laura said. "I just hope that it all works out."

"God willing, I'm sure it will," Rosa said.

Laura then turned to Felipe. "Now, I want to learn more about the man who captured my best friend Rosa's heart! All I really know is that you are a good man and a business genius!"

Felipe smiled. "Flattery will get you everywhere, but the truth is, a significant number of my brilliant ideas turn out to be flops!"

"What are you involved with now?" Laura wanted to know.

"Mainly agricultural activities, like cultivating palm oil, oranges, and coffee. Of course, I also inherited the family Caterpillar business, and I dabble in some other businesses as well—real estate, construction, automobiles. That way I can get our houses and cars more cheaply," he joked.

Laura was amazed. "How in the world did you get involved in so many things at one time?"

"When a lot of the businessmen left Nicaragua during the Sandinista years, I decided to return and stay," Felipe answered. "It was a good decision. That way I was useful to the Sandinistas, who needed people with business knowledge and contacts, and I was also useful to some of the exiles, who needed a reliable partner in the country to help them manage the investments they left behind. In the process, I became a part-owner in a number of their businesses." He grinned. "Like I said, I make the money, and Rosa here spends most of it."

"Baloney!" Rosa said. "It's not just me who spends it. One of Felipe's chief pleasures now is the little foundation that he set up to give back a little to our country."

"Actually," Felipe confessed, "I find it easier to make money than to give it away wisely."

"I find it hard to do either!" Laura replied.

"One of our biggest problems here in Nicaragua is that we're always looking for a handout from someone," Felipe complained. "First it was the U.S., then the socialist states, and now it's the European Union, United Nations, and international development organizations. Billions have been spent here, but poverty is still everywhere you look."

"Be fair, Felipe. We've also had to confront one disaster after another," Rosa interjected. "Earthquakes, volcanoes, hurricanes, war. We've needed outside help."

"Agreed, but in the process, we've become too dependent on others. We have got to get out of our victim mentality and find a better way!"

"What exactly is the focus of your foundation?" Allison asked, entering the conversation for the first time.

"It's mostly on youth," Rosa answered. "We want to train future leaders to have a servant's heart—to teach them to be the practical, knowledgeable, humble, accountable, and moral leaders that our country so desperately needs. Not like our usual egocentric and greedy *caudillos* of the left and the right."

"If you can do that, every nation in the world will be running to your door for the formula!" Laura interjected.

Rosa smiled. "Oh, I know it's pretentious, but we want to do what we can. Luis Romero is helping us establish both the vision and our first pilot training program for sustainable and ethical development. He's working out of his old house at Las Palmas and plans to start our first school somewhere on the river next year."

"What a great idea," Allison said. "I'd like to take that course, too!"

"You could probably teach it, Allison, with your brains and your heart!" Elizabeth said.

Allison blushed.

While they were speaking, a maid in uniform came out from the kitchen and announced to Rosa that their first guests had arrived at the gate.

Rosa looked at her watch. "Right on time. I told them that it had to be *hora Britannica*—punctual, as you would be tired and need to get to bed early. We have to have an early start tomorrow for the river."

# CHAPTER 19

David and Nancy Johnson were the first of the five guests to arrive. David, a classmate of Laura's at the International School and the son of friends of Stan and Elizabeth, had taken over his father's ministry at the Gloria a Dios Church when his father retired and returned to the U.S. In the five years since then, David had turned the church into one of the largest and most dynamic in Nicaragua. Isabel and Rosa now regularly attended David's services and financially supported some of the church's charities—sometimes with fundraising events at their own home.

While not always comfortable with the high decibel level of the services, Rosa highly appreciated David's sincerity, his loving and humble spirit, and his organizational ability. She especially valued the church's weekday social programs reaching out to addicts, prostitutes, prisoners, the unemployed, and to other hurting people. Raised in Nicaragua, David was totally bilingual, and Nancy made up for her heavily accented Spanish with her enthusiasm for others and with her beautiful soprano voice. They had two small children.

Marta and Geraldo García arrived fifteen minutes later. This was the first time Laura had met Geraldo who was ten years older than Marta and who had a considerable paunch and a graying beard. Geraldo had been Marta's sociology professor, and they had become close because of their work for a Sandinista candidate for the mayor of Managua. Geraldo still taught at the UCA, the University of Central America, and was a prominent advisor to the Sandinista Party. As for Marta, after leaving her job at Acción, she had returned to school to get a Masters degree in Nursing. She now taught at the Universidad Politécnica de Nicaragua. Marta and Geraldo had no children.

Antonio Lopez was the last to arrive, apologizing profusely for having been detained unexpectedly at his office to finish a report that had to be ready for the next morning. Antonio was now a widower and had no children as three years earlier his wife, Flavia, had died of ovarian cancer.

Laura had flown up to Boston to be with her friend shortly before her death and had later returned for the memorial service.

Laura was glad she had made the trip to Boston, but had often pondered a short conversation that she had with Flavia two days before she entered a coma. Antonio, with tears in his eyes, had kissed Flavia's forehead and left the hospital room to talk privately with the doctor. When Flavia saw that he was outside, she called Laura to her side and whispered weakly, "Laura, I worry about Antonio when I die. He needs a loving wife. And you need a loving husband. I want you to know that I would be truly happy if you two married one day."

"Flavia!" Laura said, flabbergasted. "You aren't going to die. You're going to get well. No one could possibly take your place in Antonio's heart. He worships you!"

Flavia smiled at her friend and squeezed her hand. "I'd be happy," she reiterated.

Laura never mentioned that conversation to anyone, nor did she have any idea if Flavia had also confided her wishes to Antonio before she died. After Flavia's death, Antonio had not been in contact with Laura except to thank her for all of her support to Flavia in her last days and to tell her of his decision to take a six-month leave of absence from his teaching duties at the Harvard Business School. It was through Rosa that Laura had learned that Antonio later resigned from his teaching and research job at Harvard and moved back to Managua, accepting the invitation of the country's new president to become his economic advisor. Antonio's main job was to help him with strategic planning and renegotiating Nicaragua's massive external debt.

Rosa said that the move had worked wonders for him. He had a new enthusiasm for life, was widely respected in the country, and as a middle-aged, handsome, powerful, and wealthy widower, he was the target of many Nicaraguan women. In her own opinion, Rosa added, Laura and Antonio were the perfect fit—they were good friends, good people, good looking, and both had lost their spouses and needed each other.

Laura wrote back that as much as she liked and admired Antonio, she was happy with her life just as it was. In fact, she had never seriously considered remarrying after losing Clay and had even discouraged several potential suitors. In her letter, she did not mention to Rosa that Antonio had been one of those potential suitors before his marriage to Flavia, nor did she mention Flavia's conversation with her in the hospital. She just said her life was already full with Allison and her foundation work, and she did not want to have to modify her lifestyle to focus on the needs of a new husband. Nor did she ever wish to go again through such a loss as the death of a beloved spouse.

The dinner that night was an elegant affair supervised by Isabel with a white-jacketed waiter serving salmon and steak prepared by the Gonzales's chef and accompanied by several choices of Chilean wines.

Laura felt a little uncomfortable when she first greeted Antonio, but later at the table, her unease disappeared as they all laughed uproariously at memories of their school days together. Then each of them, starting with Laura, shared what had happened in their lives since graduating from the International School. When it was time for dessert and coffee, they moved to the living room. While the maid served the cake that Isabel had made for Laura, the conversation turned to Stan and the trip the next day.

"We should get to San Juan del Norte before noon," Rosa said in answer to Antonio's question about their plans. "We'll leave early, pick up your Uncle Luis, refuel at El Futuro, and then fly down the Río San Juan to San Juan del Norte."

"How long do you plan to stay there?" Marta asked.

"Just a day," Laura answered. "It will be enough time to see a little of my father's lodge, the town, and to pick him up and bring him back to Managua with us. We hope to convince him to return to Nashville for treatment for his cancer."

"That may be easier said than done," Felipe remarked. "Luis tells me that Stan is obsessed with finishing that airstrip of his at Greytown. Since the government won't build it, he says that he's going to do it himself."

"But I thought he had no money?" Laura said.

"He doesn't. He has used up all that he has just to get started," Felipe answered.

"But isn't that the government's responsibility, Antonio?" Laura asked, turning to him. "Why doesn't the government build the airstrip?"

"Because the airlines don't think a route there is economically viable given the size of the town," Antonio replied. "Also, it would be inappropriate for me to suggest to the president that we support the project. Our family has large land holdings in San Juan del Norte as well as a small investment in Stan's hotel. If I pushed the airstrip, it wouldn't pass the smell test!"

"I appreciate your sensitivity," Rosa said, "but that doesn't seem fair to the rest of the town if it's a good idea."

"Maybe not, but I want to avoid any hint of corruption," Antonio replied. "Besides, there's just no government money available for such a project. We're still trying to recuperate from the disastrous Sandinista years and from an ex-president of the *Liberales* party who stole hundreds of millions from the country, including money designated for the airport in San Juan del Norte." He then added, "Thanks to them, Nicaragua is now the second poorest country in the hemisphere when once it was one of the richest in Central America."

"Being the richest didn't do the vast majority of Nicaraguans any good," Geraldo exclaimed in Spanish. "All that wealth was concentrated in the hands of Somoza and his cronies. The poor got nothing. At least with the Sandinistas, the poor got something, and they learned that they had rights."

"True," Felipe said.

"And if Reagan hadn't interfered, we would have succeeded," Geraldo added.

"If Reagan hadn't interfered *and* if the Sandinista leaders had been more competent and less greedy," Antonio said. "What toppled them was not so much Reagan but the rationing, the inflation, the forced recruitment of soldiers, the cooperatives that weren't suitable for individualistic Nicaraguan farmers, and most of all, the hypocrisy. Your party wrecked our country. Even today, investors still shy away because of the Sandinista legacy of nationalizations, the *piñata*, and corruption of our legal system."

"Granted, a lot of mistakes were made, but we've learned from them," Marta said in a conciliatory tone, bringing the discussion back to English so that Allison, with her limited Spanish, could understand better. "And don't forget, those Sandinista years were a time of idealism, too. People who had no voice discovered that they had one. And for all of its failings, the government cared about the education, health care, and housing of all Nicaraguans, not just a few elite."

"You're right, Marta," Rosa interjected, supporting her friend and wanting to reduce some of the harsh tone of the conversation. "Initially, there was so much hope. For example, I never felt so fulfilled in my life as when I went out into the countryside as a volunteer teacher in the national literacy campaign!"

"That's exactly what makes everything so tragic," Antonio said. "So much good will was turned into cynicism. Greed and incompetence do that."

"Those aren't just defects of the Sandinistas," Geraldo commented, dryly. "I seem to read in the papers a lot about scandals in this government, too, and especially in the business community that supports it."

"*Touché*," Antonio answered, smiling. "That's why we need a free press and democratic system to keep us all in check."

"Will things ever change?" Marta asked, sighing.

"Yes!" Rosa answered. "It did in South Africa with Nelson Mandela, and it could happen here. We just need the right leader who combines idealism with practical good sense and a servant's heart."

"What you are saying is that we need a saint and a miracle worker, not merely a competent politician," Marta answered, laughing. "There are not many of those around."

"What about you, Antonio?" Rosa asked, turning to him. "Have you ever thought about running for president?"

"Me?!" Antonio exclaimed. "I'm not a saint or a miracle worker! Anyway, I really have no great political ambitions and certainly no political base."

"Maybe that's one of the qualities that would make you a good leader," Felipe said in Spanish. "I'd support you. You're competent, honest, caring, and fair."

"*Gracias,* Felipe. But independents like me wouldn't stand a chance. The Sandinistas and the Liberales would eat me alive. They may be bitter enemies, but they agree on one thing—on dividing the spoils of power among themselves and keeping everyone else out."

"Then there's little hope for Nicaragua," David said.

"I disagree," Rosa said, shaking her head. "There's always hope! David, as a preacher, you should know that!" She smiled at him.

David smiled back, sheepishly.

"Of course, there's hope," Antonio said. "The fact is that we've got a lot going for us as a country. Nicaragua is fruitful, beautiful, and relatively safe. It's sparsely populated, inexpensive, and has a privileged location for exporting products. It's also full of good people."

Rosa nodded in agreement, "We just need to learn to fight less among ourselves and cooperate more."

"That and break our addiction to outside aid," Felipe added. "Maybe Luis Romero's school will help show us the way."

Geraldo was curious, "What school are you talking about?"

"We're only in the beginning stages of planning," Rosa said, "but Luis's idea is to found a school for leaders in the Río San Juan to help the region develop. The aim is to teach them how to identify and solve problems in a cooperative, practical, and efficient fashion without all of the politics, ego, and power grabbing. The region has so much potential and so many challenges."

"Who would be the students?" David asked.

"We would choose about twenty of them from different towns along the river," Felipe answered. "Candidates would have to have a basic education, show strong potential as community leaders, and be willing to spend six months living together in the school. They would also all have to pitch in and work, too. We want to train servant leaders."

"And what will happen to them when they finish the course?" David asked.

"Our foundation will sponsor the best of them to either go on to further education or to serve locally in a type of Río San Juan peace and development corps. The idea is to try to solve our own problems instead of waiting for others to do it for us."

"I hope you don't take offense," Geraldo said, shaking his head, "but it sounds hopelessly idealistic to me."

"But so was the National Literacy Campaign under the Sandinistas," Rosa answered, "yet it worked!"

"But this is such a small project," Geraldo argued. "Only a strong government with resources and laws can really bring change to such a large region."

"Geraldo, you know and I know that we've had strong governments on the right and on the left throughout our history," Rosa countered. "Have any of them really changed things for the better? We've spent billions of outside money on so many top-down strategies that haven't worked either. We're still as poor as ever. Why not give a bottom-up strategy like this a try, too?"

"Why not indeed?" asked Antonio. "And my uncle Luis is the ideal person to set it up with his love for the Río San Juan and with all of his practical experience in relief and development."

"It sounds fascinating," David said with enthusiasm. "I would love to hear what you learn from the experience. Our own church programs could benefit enormously."

"Actually, I'm sure Luis could learn something from your programs, as well," Rosa said. They seem to work!"

David smiled appreciatively at Rosa and then turned to look at his wife, Nancy, who had been quiet most of the evening. She nodded back to him, which Laura interpreted correctly as a signal between them that it was time to go.

"I'm really sorry to end this, but we need to leave," David said. "We've got a babysitter at home, and anyway, I know that you are all tired from traveling and have an early departure tomorrow for the river. It's been a delightful evening in every way. I'm just sad Mother and Dad aren't still here to see you."

He got up from his chair and came over to kiss Laura and Allison on the cheek and to shake hands with Elizabeth. "I can't tell you how delightful it is to see you again after so long. I just wish you would spend more time here and visit our church."

"Maybe I can in the next few days with Isabel," Elizabeth replied. "And you come visit us in Nashville when you go see your parents. Texas isn't so far away from Nashville, you know."

Geraldo and Marta also got up to leave. "I hope very much that you can help your father," Marta said to Laura. "He's a good man and has done a lot for Nicaragua."

Finally, Antonio stood up, though reluctantly. Laura had watched him out of the corner of her eye during the evening, curious to see if he would show any interest in her. She wasn't sure, but he *had* praised her during the dinner. At the table, after Marta had offered a toast to the memory of Flavia, Antonio thanked all of them. He then shared with them how hard Flavia's death had been for him and how grateful he and Flavia had been for Laura's visit before she entered into a coma. Laura appreciated the vulnerability that he showed in revealing his pain, his loneliness, and his gratitude—so different from the rock-like certitude he had always exhibited in his youth. As a student, that extreme self-confidence had always made her feel a little uncomfortable around him.

As they all said goodbye at the door, they thanked Felipe, Rosa, and Isabel for the invitation and the meal and expressed their happiness in being together again. Antonio was the last to leave. At the door, he kissed Laura on both cheeks and squeezed her hand. He asked if he could see her again when she and Allison got back from the river trip.

"Of course," Laura said.

"Then I'll call."

After Rosa had closed the door, she gave a knowing smile to Laura and Laura blushed. Rosa then said, "We had all better turn in so we are fresh in the morning. It will be a big day. Breakfast will be served at seven."

Laura, Elizabeth, and Allison hugged their hosts and thanked them for the delightful meal and evening. Laura's step was light as they went upstairs to go to bed.

# CHAPTER 20

The next morning after a quick breakfast of eggs, toast, fruit, and coffee, everyone went out to the silver and blue five-seat Bell helicopter in the backyard. Waiting for them by the craft was the pilot, Fernando Sacasa—a thin, middle-aged man with a mustache and friendly smile. After Fernando had stowed their small bags in an underneath compartment, he explained to Allison and Laura in a mixture of Spanish and English how to strap themselves into their brown leather seats and use the earphones and attached microphones to communicate to each other over the din of the rotating blades. Rosa sat in the front with Fernando, while Allison and Laura sat in the back.

At seven-thirty, Fernando started the motor, and after a few minutes of checking his instruments, he slowly lifted the machine into the air. As they rose, Laura and Allison waved to Elizabeth and the others standing at the back door.

From above the gated dwellings in the expensive Colinas district of Managua, Laura could see the crowded metal roofs of the poorer sections of the city and beyond them, the cone of the Momotombo Volcano on the other side of Lake Managua. The helicopter climbed higher and turned, facing southeast in the direction of Lake Nicaragua, also called Cocibolca, the second largest lake of Latin America.

Flying across the fields, heading towards the colonial city of Granada, Fernando and Rosa gave an audio tour, explaining to Allison and Laura what they were seeing. Fernando pointed out the barren slopes of the Masaya Volcano right outside Managua, with its thin plumes of smoke emerging from its crater. A few kilometers farther on, he turned the helicopter towards the right so that they could fly above the blue waters of Lake Apoyo, set in an inactive volcanic crater in the midst of forested slopes. As Laura looked down, she remembered swimming in its chilly, clean waters on a weekend excursion with her parents, and she felt a pang of longing for this other time in her life when she so admired and trusted her father.

The small city of Granada on the edge of Lake Nicaragua was the next sight to which Fernando drew their attention. At Rosa's request, Fernando flew lower so that Allison and Laura could see the colonial city of churches, monasteries, and houses with courtyards filled with greenery. "It's one of the oldest, continually inhabited cities in the Americas," Rosa noted to Allison with pride. West of the city, Rosa pointed out dozens of tiny islands near the shore of the lake. "Most of them are now owned by private individuals who have built houses on them."

As they flew above Lake Nicaragua, it seemed like an ocean to Laura in its vastness and with its white breaking waves and patches of cloud shadows on its waters. Remembering that the lake was once famous for its freshwater sharks, she wondered what they would do if a mechanical problem occurred in the helicopter and an emergency landing became necessary. She scanned the water but could see few fishing boats that might save them. In the distance and to their right, Rosa pointed out the island of Ometepe, the world's largest freshwater island, where she said Felipe's pre-Columbian stone carvings were excavated. Ometepe's two volcano cones, crowned by white clouds, pointed up into the blue sky.

Ten minutes later, Rosa drew their attention to Solentiname, an archipelago of twenty-two forested islands made famous by the great poet, social activist, and Catholic priest *Padre* Ernesto Cardenal. "Many of the primitive paintings on our wall at home were done by Solentiname natives taught by the Padre," Rosa explained.

At the end of the largest island, Fernando turned the helicopter towards the eastern shore of the vast lake. His voice crackled through the earphones. "In a few minutes, we will pass over San Carlos. Then, we'll follow the river for about ten minutes before landing at El Futuro to refuel and pick up Señor Luis."

Laura looked down and was surprised at how small and poor San Carlos looked, even though it was the capital of such a large region. Houses with rusty metal roofs were packed closely together, and small fishing and passenger boats were tied up to piers along the lake and river. On one hill outside the town, some steel communication towers stuck up into the air and on another there was a small airport with dirt and gravel landing strip and a Cessna Caravan parked on it. Across the river from the town was a vast green nature preserve.

While San Carlos itself was poor, its location was magnificent. A privileged transportation hub, the town jutted out into Lake Nicaragua at the junction of the Río San Juan and the Río Frío, which flowed in from Costa Rica.

Continuing their flight down the Río San Juan towards El Futuro, Laura observed several long, narrow boats slowly heading down the river towards the few isolated towns along its banks. Dozens of white egrets perched in the palms along the green banks and on floating bunches of vegetation in the river, and immense flocks of waterfowl scared by the helicopter's noise took off from the water, leaving white trails as their feet broke the surface.

After ten minutes of flight from San Carlos, Fernando alerted them. "El Futuro is ahead on the right." He gradually slowed the helicopter until they hovered above a cluster of buildings between the river and seemingly endless rows of orange trees. Two people came out the back door of one of the buildings into the yard as Fernando expertly lowered the helicopter onto a cement landing pad in an open area between the buildings. When the rotors ceased turning, he got out and opened the doors for the women to emerge.

Waiting for them in the yard was Luis Romero who embraced each of the women warmly, welcoming them. He looked so much older than Laura remembered him from his last visit to Nashville, but his face was still full of goodwill and peace. With him was another man whom Rosa introduced as Alfonso Borges, the director of the farm and of the orange orchards. Young and friendly, Alfonso also welcomed them and invited them into the house to use the facilities and to have some refreshments. Fernando, in the meantime, headed towards a new metal storage barn where two farm employees stood next to several plastic barrels of fuel on a cart.

Rosa and Allison followed Alfonso towards the house, but Laura stayed behind taking in the scene and trying to visualize in her mind the place where her husband, Clay, had died. As she did so, an almost holy sadness welled up from deep within her, and it started to seep out slowly from her eyes in tears. Luis, who had also paused with her, noticed and put his arm around her. With the other hand, he pointed to a spot. "It was right there that Clay fell. I know how painful this must be for you, Laura."

Laura nodded, brushed the tears from her eyes, and then smiled. "Even after all of these years," she said, "I still cry."

Once inside the office building, Laura was surprised that the main room was totally different from what she had imagined. Instead of a dark and heavy place, it was freshly painted and light and even beautiful. The furniture in the room consisted of white wicker chairs set around three small, round tables. On each table were embroidered white doilies with vases of freshly cut flowers. Colorful paintings and balsa sculptures of birds and fish decorated the white walls, just as they did at Rosa and Felipe's home.

The guest bathroom was also beautiful and modern. Laura commented on the fact to Luis and Rosa when she returned with Allison.

"It's way more sophisticated and welcoming than a few years ago," Luis said. "That's what a woman's touch will do," he said, pointing to Rosa. "Now, we even have hot water."

Alfonso called someone from the kitchen, and a pretty young woman came out with glasses full of cold orange juice. She wore a yellow blouse with the El Futuro logo—a green tree whose branches were heavy with oranges.

Laura took a drink from her. "It is so refreshing!" she exclaimed, as she sat down. *"Muchas gracias!"*

Allison also sat down in a wicker chair next to her mother. "Is this the house where you and my father were held hostage by the Contras?" she asked Luis.

Luis nodded and pointed to one of the walls. "They were tying us up by that wall when the farm director broke away, grabbed a gun, and killed one of the men guarding us. He then ran over to the door and shot my brother, who was returning from checking on the horses in the backyard."

"Where we landed?" Allison asked.

"Where you landed," Luis confirmed.

Allison got up from her chair and walked back to the door that they had come in and stared out in silence at the area. Laura got up and walked over to her, putting her arm around her shoulder. Tears came again to Laura's eyes.

"There's a memorial here, isn't there?" Laura asked. "Can we see it?"

"It's in the garden outside where the pool used to be." Luis got up and led the three women outside to a well-kept flower garden behind a white picket fence. He then opened a gate, and they all walked down a short path to a two-meter high white marble stone and a white marble bench that faced it. Attached to the stone were three polished bronze plaques of the same size, each engraved in Spanish.

"Felipe and Rosa were kind enough to fill in the pool and to put up the memorial," Luis said. He added, "They brought my mother here, as well as Inés and her children, for the dedication." He hugged Rosa. "It meant so much to them."

Luis invited Laura and Allison to sit on the bench, and then he went over to the monument and translated for Allison what was written on the three plaques. He started with the top plaque: "Dedicated to the memory of Jorge Romero Landers and of Roberto Romero Landers, two brothers who loved each other and who loved their country." The plaque below it said, "In memory of Clay Danforth, an unselfish American who gave his life trying to save the life of another." He didn't translate the third plaque, but he said that on it were engraved the names of the five Sandinista soldiers and of the three Contras other than Jorge who also died that night.

Allison and Laura got up and rubbed their hands over the plaque dedicated to their father and husband. Tears now came to Allison's eyes as well as to Laura's. Laura gave Rosa her camera and asked if she would take a picture of them standing on each side of the memorial stone. Rosa did.

"It makes me so angry still," Laura said to Allison, shaking her head. "We lost your father for nothing!"

"Not for nothing, Mother," Allison said. "There's always a reason. We just may not understand it right now. A lot of good came out of Father's death. For one thing, a wonderful foundation was created that has helped thousands of people here in Nicaragua and in Africa. We all have to die someday, and he died helping others. That's an inspiring legacy for us."

"Allison, you have maturity and wisdom beyond your years," Luis noted.

Allison blushed.

At that moment, Fernando came over from the helicopter and announced, "We've finished refueling. We're ready to go any time that you are."

"I guess we'd better get going if we plan to arrive at the time I told Stan," Luis said. "I'll get my bag and join you at the helicopter." When he came back from the house, he put his bag underneath with the others. They all then thanked Alfonso and got into the helicopter—the three women in the back and Luis up front with Fernando.

Before restarting the motor, Fernando explained that the rest of the trip would take about half an hour. First, they would fly over the town of El Castillo and the Spanish fort built there in the 1700s to protect Granada from pirates and from the British Navy. "It was there that Lord Nelson, leading a combined force of Indians and British soldiers, won his first battle as a young officer," he explained. Next he told them that they would continue following the river downstream with the vast Indio Maíz Biological Preserve to their left and Costa Rica to their right. When they got to San Juan del Norte, they would land at the ruins of Greytown on the strip that Stan was clearing. Luis added that Stan would be waiting for them there and would take them by boat to his lodge.

After they had put on their earphones again, Fernando warmed up the engines and took the helicopter straight up into the air. As the helicopter turned eastward towards the ocean, Luis pointed out to them the family house at Las Palmas where he was now living.

The rest of the trip was especially fascinating to Allison and Laura. Within a few minutes of taking off and heading down the river, they passed over what Luis said was the "jewel" of the Río San Juan—the small river town of El Castillo. Laura looked down and saw colorful, stilted houses alongside river rapids. There were no signs of any vehicles on the narrow walkways of the town. Perched on the grassy hill above the town with a commanding view of the river was the imposing black stone fort of the Immaculate Conception of María. An enormous blue and white Nicaraguan flag flapped proudly over its battlements.

After hovering for a few seconds over the town for Laura and Allison to see it and to take pictures, they continued to follow the river's curves as it wound for kilometers and kilometers to the coast. The vast, dense forests of the Indio Maíz Biological Preserve, with its towering trees, spread north and east from the river, while on the other side of it were the emerald green pastures of Costa Rica. Ten minutes later, Fernando's voice crackled over the earphones again as he pointed out the junction where the main flow of the river turned right into Costa Rica, becoming the Río Colorado as it headed to the sea. They, however, continued left to follow the now smaller flow of the Río San Juan.

In another ten minutes, Laura saw one of the loveliest natural views that she had ever seen in her life. At the point where the Río San Juan ended at the Atlantic Ocean, another river cut perpendicular to it. With only about a hundred meters of forest separating it from the empty beaches, the river ran north parallel to the coastline for some twenty kilometers. Luis said it was the Río Indio and pointed out the new town of San Juan del Norte on its banks, surrounded by forests.

At Rosa's request, Fernando flew over the small town to the edge of the ocean and then made a curve to come back so that Laura could take some pictures of the extraordinary sight. He then turned up the river and over a lagoon until he was above a narrow clearing of some two football fields in length in the middle of the jungle. At both ends of the clearing, a half-dozen men and women stood around piles of burning trunks and bushes, and black smoke wafted up into the air. Two men were in the middle of the clearing, and one of them was waving at them.

"There's Stan," Luis said.

Fernando slowed the helicopter to a hover and then began to descend to a spot on the grass and dirt not far from the two men.

Luis turned to Laura in the back seat and said encouragingly, "You'll see, it's all going to work out."

# CHAPTER 21

Laura was taken aback when she first saw Stan close up. Although he was still as tan as she remembered him, he was now slimmer, his skin much more wrinkled, and his hair now totally white and pulled back in a pony tail. His black rubber boots squeaked as he came towards her with outstretched arms. While Laura felt awkward as he hugged her, Allison's face erupted into a wide smile when he included her in his embrace. "Finally, finally!" she said.

Stan backed up and looked at Allison and Laura. "You're both so beautiful!" He shook his head in admiration. "And you're actually here in San Juan del Norte!" His eyes swept the helicopter behind them, and he asked with a tone of resignation, "Elizabeth didn't come, did she?"

"There just wasn't enough room in the helicopter," Laura replied. "It only holds five. But she's anxious to see you tomorrow in Managua."

Stan shook his head. "I'm sorry, but tomorrow's impossible."

Laura was astonished. "But that was the reason we came! To take you back, so Mother could see you and then return together to Nashville for your treatment."

"Don't worry. I'll still see your mother in Managua, and we'll talk about the treatment, but it'll have to be a day later," Stan explained. "Tomorrow morning I have to take some passengers to Bluefields, and I have an important meeting there with an investor late in the afternoon. I'll catch the flight to Managua the next day. I promise."

As Laura pondered this unexpected news, Luis and Rosa approached and greeted Stan warmly.

"You got here right on time," Stan said. "Amazing!"

"Thanks to our great pilot, Fernando," Rosa said. She introduced the two. "Did you get the message about needing a guard for the helicopter?"

"I did." Stan called over the man who stood waiting some ten meters away. "Danilo here will guard it." The man looked to Laura to be an

Indian about forty years old. He wore blue jeans, a tee shirt, and a faded New York Yankees baseball cap. "Do you have any special instructions for him?"

"Just to make sure that no one comes closer than ten meters to the helicopter," Fernando said. "After we get our bags, I'll leave it secured and locked. It's not to be touched by anyone," he reiterated to Danilo.

Danilo shook his head in acknowledgement.

"What about his food and shelter in case it rains?" Rosa asked, looking up at the sky for signs of a storm.

"Don't worry. He has a tarp, and he brought food and a hammock." Stan pointed to a blue plastic sheet folded on top of a bundle at the forest edge. "He'll be fine."

Stan then took charge. "OK, once we get your bags, we have about a two-hundred meter walk through the woods to the boat." He looked down at their white tennis shoes. "I probably should have told you to bring some rubber boots, as we have to pass through some puddles. It's low here and rains a lot."

Fernando went back to the helicopter and opened the baggage compartments. He then pulled out the five backpacks one by one. He also took out a mallet and some cables and stakes that were stored there. After hooking the cables to the helicopter and stakes, he drove the latter into the ground in order to secure the helicopter. When he was finished, he put the mallet back underneath and went around locking all of the doors and compartments. He then walked over to Danilo and gave him some last minute instructions.

In the meantime, Stan picked up Allison's and Laura's bags by their straps, and Luis grabbed Rosa's and his own. "We'd better get going as we've got a lot for you to see in an afternoon," Stan said.

When Stan grabbed her bag, Allison protested. "You shouldn't be carrying our bags. You're supposed to be sick!"

"Don't worry, I feel fine," he replied, as he headed towards the end of the clearing. The ground was rough with mud furrows and gaping holes where tree trunks had been dug out. They all followed.

"You're making remarkable progress on the landing strip, Stan," Luis noted. "When I was here three months ago, all this was trees and brush and old battle trenches."

Stan smiled in satisfaction. "Everyone said that it couldn't be done without heavy machinery, but we're doing it."

"Why not use bulldozers?" Laura asked.

"It's impossible to get the machines here because of the river rapids and the sand barriers in the ocean channel. It's also too expensive. Our main problem now will be smoothing and packing the soil hard enough so that small planes can land and take off safely."

"How will you do that without heavy machinery?" Fernando asked in Spanish.

"We'll mix the soil with gravel and grass seeds and then use cement pounders and hand rollers. It should work and not be too expensive. So far, I'm out about forty thousand dollars for what we've already done, and I reckon by the time the field is ready for light planes, it will cost me another twenty or so."

"I didn't know that you had that kind of money," Laura said, before realizing how tactless she was being.

"Now who told you that?" Stan asked, looking back with a smile at Luis as they walked. Before Laura could answer, Stan acknowledged the truth of her remark. "The truth is I *don't* have that kind of money. Right now, I owe the workers for this past month's work, but I have to do what I have to do. The airstrip is essential for San Juan del Norte's survival."

"I'm surprised that you can do it for so little," Rosa interjected, partly defensively. She and Felipe had denied Stan's earlier request for assistance from their foundation. "Antonio told us that it would cost several million dollars to build an airport here, and there wasn't nearly enough demand to make it worthwhile!"

"That's because the government's plan was to build it behind the new town and not here," Stan replied. "Their calculations are based on a landing strip for much bigger planes than we plan for. They would first have to drain the swamps, then bring in tons and tons of dirt and gravel, and use expensive, heavy machinery in the process. While that might be the best long-term solution, the town might die before that project is finally implemented."

Stan stopped walking as did the others. "Our strategy here is much simpler. You can't tell it now, but this used to be the main street of Greytown. Small planes landed here, and they will again."

"This was a main street?!" Laura was amazed. "But there's absolutely nothing here!"

154

"That's because a Contra attack destroyed everything," Stan explained. "All the inhabitants fled for Costa Rica. When they came back after the war, they chose another site for the town."

"The forest retook what was left," Luis added. "All that remains are a few bricks and small graveyards—including the British cemetery over there." He pointed to a spot under the trees about fifty meters away. Laura could make out a half-dozen metal crosses and broken cement memorial stones.

"Why British?" Allison asked.

"The town was a British protectorate and a thriving port in the 1850's when my great-grandfather lived here," Luis explained.

They started to walk again and soon passed by a group of three black men and two Mestizo women who were piling up logs and brush to burn. The workers stopped what they were doing and smiled. One of them greeted them in English with a Creole accent. "Welcome to Greytown."

Rosa thanked them and told them how impressed she was with their work. They seemed pleased. When one of the men in the group recognized Luis, he came over and shook his hand with affection.

When they got to the clearing's edge, Stan led them single file on a trail through the canopy of tall trees towards the lagoon where his boat was tied. Several times they had to get off the path to avoid puddles of muddy water.

"Once the landing strip is finished," Stan explained, "we plan to build an elevated walkway from the boat dock to the field, which is on higher ground. That way, tourists won't have to get their feet wet." He turned around to Rosa and said, "Your foundation's help with the walkways at San Juan del Norte has made a enormous difference. You'll see them after lunch."

"We were glad we were able to help," Rosa replied.

At the end of the muddy trail, they came to a wide lagoon with a short wooden pier sticking out from the thick lake reeds and water hyacinths. Tied to the pier was a fifteen-seat fiberglass boat covered by a blue canopy.

Stan took their bags and put them into the stern of the boat. He then helped the women climb in. After everyone was seated, he untied the securing rope, climbed into the stern, and started the motor, slowly backing away from the dock through a path that had been cut in the reeds.

Laura looked around them. The large lagoon was surrounded entirely by thick jungle vegetation. Far off in the distance in the lagoon, she spotted what looked like a large metal tower sticking out of the water. "What's an oil rig doing here?" she asked Luis, who was sitting in front of her.

"It's actually an old dredge." Seeing Laura's quizzical expression, he explained, "Back in the 1890s, this was to be the beginning of an American canal linking the Atlantic to the Pacific. Then, after they had completed about three kilometers of the canal, Teddy Roosevelt and the U.S. Congress changed their minds and opted for the Panama route. But at the turn of the century, this was a bustling place."

"It's hard to imagine," Laura said.

A few moments later, Luis pointed to the right bank of the lagoon at the rusty carcass of a riverboat wedged on its side and covered with vines. "My great-grandfather might have been the captain of that steamboat," Luis said. He added philosophically, "The Río San Juan is a place full of dashed dreams, but we still keep on dreaming!"

Once Stan maneuvered the boat into the deeper water of the lagoon, he increased the speed and entered the channel that headed east towards the sea. Within a few minutes, he yelled above the sound of the motor, "The Rainbow's End Lodge is up ahead on the right."

Seven peaked thatch roofs rising out of the thick foliage along the riverbank came into view. Allison cried out in delight when she saw it, and the others chimed in their approval. Stan grinned with pleasure.

Getting closer, they saw solar panels glinting on the thatched roofs, absorbing the sun's hot rays. Stan slowed the boat down to head for the dock, and as he did so, Laura heard for the first time the soft pounding of sea waves in the distance and smelled the salt in the air. As they approached the dock, a young Mestizo man came out of the largest of the buildings and waited for them.

Stan cut off the motor, and they coasted towards the pier. When they got close, he threw a rope to the young man, who pulled them in and tied up the boat to one of the dock's four wooden posts. Tethered on the other side of the pier were two other motor boats. The young man smiled and greeted them in English and then began to help them out of the craft with their baggage.

Once they were all on the dock, Stan introduced the young man as Marcos Pinto, his right-hand man. Dressed in blue jeans, tennis shoes, and a green polo shirt, Marcos politely shook their hands.

"Marcos will take you to your rooms," Stan said. "The women will be in the Vanderbilt cabin and the men in the Mark Twain, which is right next to it. If it's OK with you, we'll have lunch in fifteen minutes. Afterwards, I'll give you a tour, first of the hotel and then of San Juan del Norte."

They all agreed to the plan, and as Stan went to check on the lunch, Marcos led them up the wooden stairs to the elevated canopied walkway along the bank of the river. Laura was impressed by the simple beauty of the construction and by the natural richness of the area. She loved the exotic green plants that almost smothered the sides of the elevated walkway and of the small cabins that looked out on the river.

The Vanderbilt cabin, where the three women were to stay, was the first one they came to. Marcos opened the door, and as they entered, they saw that it consisted of two bedrooms, a bathroom between the rooms, a sitting room with wicker chairs, and an outside porch overlooking the river. Two brightly colored hammocks hung from hooks on the outside balcony. Each of the bedrooms had two double beds, which were neatly made up with clean, white sheets and with mosquito nets hanging overhead.

The floor, walls, and roof of the cabin were a combination of rough wood, bamboo, and thatch. On the walls were framed, antique photographs displaying a street in old Greytown, riverboats, a ship with masts in the harbor of the town, and a glowering Cornelius Vanderbilt.

"This is a little paradise," Allison commented after she had walked out to the porch and looked out over the river.

In fractured but clear English, Marcos smiled and thanked her, "I'm glad you like it."

He then excused himself and went outside where Luis and Fernando were waiting to be shown their quarters in the Mark Twain cabin next door.

After freshening up, Laura, Allison, and Rosa walked back to the main lodge. When they entered, they saw an attractive black woman who looked to be in her mid-twenties dusting the small bamboo reception counter. She held a toddler of mixed race on her hip, and she smiled brightly when she saw them. "Welcome to the Rainbow's End Lodge," she said in English with a Creole lilt to it. "May I get you some fresh lemonade before you eat?"

"I would love some," Allison said as she went over to touch and admire the little boy. "He's so cute. How old is he?"

The woman was pleased at the compliment. "He's almost three."

Laura and Rosa also accepted the offer of lemonade, and as the young woman left to get it taking her son with her, the three women sat down in the brown wicker chairs of the reception area. Settling into the chair, Laura speculated to herself, *Could this little boy be my half-brother? Could Dad be so irresponsible as to father a child this late in life and in such sordid circumstances?*

Shaking these thoughts from her mind, Laura looked around her at the reception area. Like her cabin, it was built using sturdy, thick poles to hold up a thatched roof. It had wooden planks for flooring, and its walls were made mostly of bamboo. But unlike her cabin, the bamboo only rose in height to chest-level. This gave Laura the impression of being outside but also protected. As for furniture, besides the wicker chairs, the room also had a wicker loveseat with cushions, three low wooden tables, several small lamps, a bookstand, as well as a reception desk. Just as in the cabins, there were old photos of Greytown displayed in different parts of the room.

Before the young woman returned with the lemonade, Luis and Fernando had arrived from their cabin. Shortly thereafter, Stan also appeared and invited them into the dining room for lunch.

The dining room, like the reception area, had walls that were chest-high. In case of wind-blown rain or too many insects, curtains of mosquito net and transparent plastic could be pulled to enclose the open space between the walls and the ceiling. The tables and chairs in the room were of bamboo, and everything came together in beautiful simplicity. Several of the eight tables had been joined so that they could all eat together. On top of them were ample plates of chicken, fish, rice, and beans. Two large pitchers were filled with lemonade and water.

When they entered, Laura noticed three people who looked like foreign tourists sitting at two of the other tables. Stan introduced them as Peter Manning from Boston, and Madeline and Jean Paul Rostow from Montpellier, France. They all looked to be in their late twenties or early thirties.

"Peter," Stan explained, "is doing an article for a travel magazine in Boston about the Río San Juan and San Juan del Norte. I'll be taking him tomorrow to Bluefields so he can get a feel for that route and for him to catch a plane back to Managua."

Stan invited all three of the other guests to join them at the bigger table if they wished. The French couple politely declined. Peter, on the other hand, immediately accepted the offer and took the seat in front of Allison. Self-confident and talkative, he dominated most of the dinner conversation. He said that he had graduated from Boston University and had taken a job at a major Boston-based travel magazine to research new adventure opportunities for younger tourists. "They pay me to do what I love best," he said. "To travel!"

During the meal, Peter told them about other places he had visited both in Asia and in Latin America, but he said that San Juan del Norte was unique in its wildness, beauty, isolation, and low cost. "The infrastructure needs to be improved drastically before it can attract higher-end tourists," he said. "But even as it is now, it's a backpacker's paradise!"

While Laura kept one ear to Allison's conversation with Peter, she was also interested in Luis and Rosa's conversation about the leadership school they were hoping to start and Luis's efforts to identify students and select a location for the school.

The meal, served by the young Creole woman whom they had met in the reception area, was delicious and well-seasoned. When they were done, Laura complimented her father on the quality of the food.

"It's Amelia who does the cooking, so thank her," Stan said. He got up, went into the kitchen, and returned with the young black woman. "Marcos is my right-hand man, and Amelia is my left-hand woman. I don't know what I would do without the two of them."

"Is your son in the kitchen with you?" Laura asked.

"No, I'd never get anything done if he were," Amelia said smiling. "At meal times, my husband, Marcos, takes care of him."

Laura felt immensely relieved at this information. The little boy wasn't her father's but belonged to Marcos. "Well, I don't know how you do it," she said. "It was a remarkably good meal. Thank you so much."

"Wait until tonight," Stan said with obvious pride. "We will be serving her specialty—river shrimp with her secret sauce."

After the rest of them had added their appreciation for the meal and Amelia had returned to the kitchen, Allison asked her grandfather if they could see the rest of the hotel property and where he lived.

"Of course, we can go now if you'd like."

Stan began the tour with a visit to his private quarters which were located upstairs in the two-storied building next to the reception and dining room. Laura was impressed, as his apartment was neat, comfortable, tastefully decorated, and utilitarian. A queen-sized wooden bed, covered by a bright red bedspread was positioned against the back wall of a large room and faced towards the double doors that led to an outside balcony. On one side of the bed was a door leading to a bathroom that was partially open to the outside at shoulder level. On the other side was a closet for clothes and storage. In front of the bed, Stan had arranged a sitting area around a low table made of a single large piece of solid wood, which was heavily varnished. Two wicker chairs and a matching sofa with red and blue pillows gave Stan and any guest a comfortable place to sit.

In the left front corner of the room by a window, Stan had set up his small office, which consisted of a desk, chair, metal filing cabinet, and homemade bookcase. Laura quickly perused the bookcase and saw that it was filled mostly with volumes related to his work. There were dictionaries and grammar books in several different European languages, history books and guidebooks on Nicaragua, volumes on the flora and fauna of Costa Rica, and practical books on administration, repairs, and ecology. Mixed among these, however, were a Bible, a book on Liberation Theology, a collection of poems by Ernesto Cardenal, and several novels.

On top of Stan's desk, Laura noticed a lamp, a shortwave radio, and a laptop computer and printer. But it was the top of the filing cabinet that most interested her. Three framed photos faced towards Stan's desk: one of Elizabeth alone, one of all of their family together, and a third one of him with Allison as a toddler. It gave Laura comfort to know that her father cared enough about them to have their photos in a prominent place. The only other decoration in the room was a framed print above Stan's desk of a revolutionary Christ with a rifle in his hands. He looked remarkably like Che Guevara. In the picture's background, the poor of different races held up their agricultural and industrial tools in a revolutionary salute to him. Laura was relieved that nowhere in the room did she see pictures, clothes, or toiletries of other women.

"It's a lot neater than my room!" Allison exclaimed and smiled at her grandfather.

Stan laughed. "I knew that you were coming and didn't want you to have a worse impression of me than you already have!"

"Take a look at the view from the porch," Rosa called from outside the double doors where she was standing.

Laura and Allison went out to join her. It was a gorgeous view of the river in front of them, and to their right, of the breaking waves of the sea. "I can see why he loves this place," Rosa said.

When they came back inside, Stan led them back down the stairs to the lodge's main storeroom. At the back of it, he opened a door and turned on a faint light so that they could see inside. Laura could make out a generator, several large fuel containers, some propane tanks, and four shelves filled with batteries. Wires connected the batteries together and then headed outside through a large round hole that had been cut in the wall. "This is our power plant for lights, hot water, refrigerator, radio, and computer," Stan said with obvious pride. "The ice maker is run by propane gas. We furnish most of the ice for the town's bars and restaurants; also for the fishermen who need it to preserve their catch. Ice helps keep us afloat financially when we don't have many hotel guests."

"Does the energy all come from the solar panels on the roof?" Allison asked.

"Most of it, but some is also generated by a windmill we have on the beach. We tried a river turbine as well, but the current isn't strong enough to turn it sufficiently. We try to use our diesel generator as little as possible because of the high cost of fuel here."

"The light is a little weak for reading at night, but it is better than nothing," Peter said. "Now all you have to do is put in some type of internet access."

"It will come," Stan replied. "After we finish the landing strip, that's my next project!"

Closing the shed door, Stan continued the tour, leading the group over to a large fenced off area behind the hotel. "This is our food pantry. It's where we grow our vegetables and raise chickens and pigs for our hotel restaurant.

Within the fenced-off area was a greenhouse covered with a large plastic sheet and enclosed areas for different types of animals—a pig pen, a dog run, a chicken yard and house, a corral for four horses, as well as other enclosures for various wild animals. Two thin, sleepy dogs perked up when they saw Stan coming over to the fence, and they wagged their tails and ambled over to the gate when he approached it. "We have to always be on the lookout for panthers or river alligators. The dogs help keep them away with their barking, but sometimes they become meals themselves. I've lost a couple of dogs that way."

"Mom, look at the iguanas," Allison said, pointing to the largest of the pens inside the fenced in area. Dozens of iguanas scampered and sunbathed on stones and on tree limbs by a pool of water. "They look like little dinosaurs!"

"Those we sell in Bluefields, especially around Easter," Stan explained. "Some people consider them delicacies, and a few even like to keep them as pets."

Stan reached through the gate and patted each dog on the head and then turned toward a wooden sign cut in the shape of an arrow. "*Playa*—Beach 80 meters" was written on it. They all followed.

Curving back towards the river, they passed a rack of three faded canoes and kayaks that Stan said he rented to guests. The trail then followed the riverbank and finally ended at the beach. At different points on the path, Stan had placed rustic log benches for tourists to sit and enjoy the beauty of the place. He also had erected laminated signs explaining various plants or artifacts from the past.

At the point where the path arrived at the beach, there was a sign in Spanish and in English, "DANGEROUS OCEAN CURRENTS! SWIM AT YOUR OWN RISK!"

When they got to the beach, Laura saw no evidence of any houses or people. "It's so empty here. Who owns it?"

"That's always the basic question here in Nicaragua," Luis answered. "On this side of the river for about three kilometers towards Costa Rica, our family does. We also claim about half a kilometer on the other side of the outlet, but the mayor of San Juan del Norte disputes that. There is a small freshwater lake on it that the townspeople like to use for swimming. The truth is that boundaries here constantly shift over time, and that makes for confusion. After a big storm, the river sometimes changes course and seeks another outlet to the sea. Sometimes river sediment adds to your property, and at other times, floods take it away. What you see here today is far different from what my great-grandfather saw when he purchased his land."

"What would have it been like back then?" Allison asked.

"From what we can gather from old photos and maps, Greytown was located on a bay, its port protected by a spit of land on the other side where Vanderbilt had his operations," Luis replied. "That spit of land eventually expanded and closed making the lagoon we passed through coming here. A much wider and deeper Río San Juan would have passed by the town—not so silted up as it is now. Our property was across the bay from the town next to where Vanderbilt's Accessory Transit Company had its headquarters. You can still see remnants of the long wooden wharf that used to reach out into the water not far from here. Freight and tens of thousands of passengers from ocean-going schooners would have unloaded and loaded at it, including Mark Twain. There would have been a lot of activity."

Stan pointed out to the sea in front of them, "The *Cyane*, the ship commanded by our ancestor George Hollins, probably anchored right out there as it fired its big guns into Greytown destroying it. And down the beach a few years later," he said, pointing in the direction of Costa Rica, "William Walker landed with his men in an attempt to regain power in Nicaragua."

"So much history here, and yet now nothing remains—just miles of empty beach sand," Allison mused. "If you hadn't told us all these things, I'd never have guessed that this place had ever been populated."

Luis nodded. "What you just said, Allison, reminds me of 'Ozymandias,' a poem by Shelley I memorized as a youth. I'm sure you know it." He began to recite:

"I met a traveler from an antique land
Who said: 'Two vast and trunkless legs of stone
Stand in the desert. Near them, on the sand,
Half sunk, a shattered visage lies, whose frown
And wrinkled lip and sneer of cold command
Tell that its sculptor well those passions read
Which yet survive, stamped on these lifeless things,
The hand that mocked them and the heart that fed.
And on the pedestal these words appear:
'My name is Ozymandias, King of Kings:
Look on my works, ye mighty, and despair!'
Nothing beside remains. Round the decay
Of that colossal wreck, boundless and bare,
The lone and level sands stretch far away."

# CHAPTER 22

When they got back to the reception area from the beach, it was two-thirty. Stan said that he had to go to San Juan del Norte to make arrangements for his trip the next day to Bluefields. He invited anyone who wanted to see the town to accompany him.

"If we could go back to our rooms for a few minutes first, I'd love to go with you," Rosa said. "I've wanted to visit it for years."

The others agreed, and Stan asked them to be back at the dock in fifteen minutes.

When Rosa, Laura, and Allison got back to the boat, they found that the others were already waiting for them. As she approached the dock, Laura noticed for the first time the name of the blue-canopied craft that they had arrived on from Greytown. The words "Second Chance" were painted in blue letters on the back behind the motor. Curious about the choice of name, she asked her father about it.

"Moving to San Juan del Norte was a new start for me, so I named the boat that way," Stan answered. "I figured that we all need a second chance—myself, the Sandinistas, and Greytown—all of us."

"And some of us need a lot more than just two chances!" Luis joked, and Stan agreed.

Getting into the boat first, Stan then turned and extended his hand to help the three women, Luis, Fernando, and Peter enter. "Put on your lifejackets," Stan ordered. "They're under your seats. We've got a gung ho, local port director who checks on those sorts of things, and I don't want any trouble with him."

When they were all seated with lifejackets on, Marcos untied the rope that secured them to the dock and got into the stern.

Stan sat on the bow facing them, and as Marcos primed the engine, Stan explained what they would see. "Right now, we're at the junction of the Río San Juan and the Río Indio where they both enter the ocean. We'll go up the Río Indio about two kilometers to San Juan del Norte."

"Have you ever followed the Río Indio to its source?" Rosa asked.

"To its source, no," Stan answered. "But I have taken tourists and vaccination teams just about as far as one can go by small boat. The river parallels the coast for some twenty kilometers and then heads west into the Indio Maíz Biological Preserve. The area is now almost all protected virgin forest except for a tiny clearing here and there made by Indians or illegal farmers. You can go for about five hours before the river gets too shallow to continue. It's wild and beautiful."

The trip from the Rainbow's End Lodge to San Juan del Norte took only about ten minutes. The first signs of the town were some thatched huts that began to appear among the thick palm trees along the left bank of the river, but as they approached the town, the huts gave way to more substantial structures located closer together. Most of the buildings were of wood and galvanized metal, but several were constructed of cement blocks and had small docks.

"How many people live in the town now?" Laura asked.

"Maybe about fifteen hundred, I'd guess," Stan replied. "It's still new."

Marcos slowed down as they approached a concrete dock where a long, narrow passenger boat with a flat bottom was tied. Laura had seen several like it on the river from the helicopter and asked about it.

"They're made that way so that they can easily pass over the rapids on the way down," Luis explained. "The boats are the lifeline of the river, but they only make two trips here a week."

Once they came alongside the dock, they all took off their lifejackets. Stan got out first, and after tying the boat, helped everyone out of the bow onto the landing.

Once on land, Laura noticed that Stan was a popular figure in the town. The policeman at the dock and the three men drinking beer at the little outside bar all greeted him when they saw him. They also seemed to know Luis and saluted him as well.

Stan and Luis immediately returned their greetings, and then Stan called Allison and Laura over to introduce them to the men. Laura noticed the pride in his voice as he did so, and she was grateful for it. He then introduced the others. The men seemed to know exactly who Rosa was when he presented her as the wife of Felipe Gonzales. El Futuro was the biggest commercial enterprise on the Río San Juan, and all knew that Felipe was one of the most successful businessmen in Nicaragua. The three men were friendly, and Laura thought that one of them was perhaps a little drunk—not surprising, given the number of empty beer bottles on the table.

After the introductions were over, the drunk—the one Stan called Gancho, a tall, muscular man with Indian features and long black hair—reached out and touched Stan on the arm to get his attention. "How long do you think it will be before you'll be able to pay my wife for her work at Greytown?"

"I'm going tomorrow to Bluefields to try to get the money," Stan replied. "When I get back next week, everyone will get what I'm owing them." He patted Gancho on the back. "The airstrip is coming along fine. We had our first landing of a helicopter this morning."

Gancho nodded and then poured himself another glass of beer.

"Is the mayor around?" Stan asked the policeman. "I want my guests to meet him and see the town."

"He should still be at the *Alcaldía*," the policeman answered.

Stan thanked him and led Laura and the others towards the town hall. As they walked past a wooden police station on stilts, Laura surveyed the scene. The town was indeed small, and most of its structures were separated by wide-open spaces. One of these spaces was the town soccer field and a basketball court where a group of adolescents played. On the other side of the athletic field were a school and a church, both made of concrete blocks. Everything in the town was connected by footpaths and sometimes by elevated concrete sidewalks. Laura saw no streets and no vehicles—not even horses. People seemed to walk or ride a bike to wherever they had to go.

The Alcaldía itself was a small white building of concrete blocks, and two men sat outside the front door on blue plastic chairs talking animatedly to each other. One was a heavyset black man and the other a balding older man of mixed blood. When the balding man saw the group heading his way, he smiled broadly and stood up to greet them in Spanish. "So your family has arrived. We saw the helicopter as it circled earlier." He extended his hand to Laura. "Welcome to San Juan del Norte."

Stan introduced the friendly man as the town mayor, Mauricio Soto. The other man, Adric Williams, was much more reserved. He remained seated and only nodded his head in recognition when Stan introduced him. "Adric is the owner of the largest dry goods store in San Juan. He'll be going with me tomorrow to Bluefields." Stan then turned to Adric and added, "I was going to your store to tell you that we'll be leaving at eight o'clock, but now I don't have to. Try to be at the lodge a little before that if you can. That way we will make sure we arrive by early afternoon."

"Are all of these people going with us to Bluefields?" Adric asked with a tone of concern. He spoke in Creole English.

"No, just Peter here. We'll leave him off at the airport before our meeting. We'll also be leaving off Amelia and little Samuel. She wants to visit her parents for a few days in Bluefields."

"*Bueno, pues*—good, then. I'll be at your place before eight." Adric got up and turned to the mayor and said in Spanish, "We'll talk later." He then nodded to Stan and the others and left.

After Adric had gone, the mayor invited them all inside the Alcaldía which consisted of only two rooms and a bathroom. One of the rooms was just large enough for a big table with twelve wooden chairs around it. This, the mayor explained, served as the meeting room for the municipal council. Several large maps on the wall showed the town plan, the limits of the municipality, and ocean depths off the coast. The second room, a little bit larger than the first, had two desks, a few chairs, a file cabinet, and a table piled high with folders. A Nicaraguan flag and a picture of the Nicaraguan president were on the wall. Laura was surprised to see no employees or even basic office equipment like a computer, printer, or copying machine in the building. There was only an old manual typewriter.

The mayor and Luis seemed to be old friends, and as they entered the office, Luis asked him in Spanish what he thought about the airfield.

"Which one?" the mayor asked. "Are you talking about the one behind the town that has been promised for ten years by the government, or the one that our friend Mr. Stan is working on at Greytown?"

"The one at Greytown."

The mayor put his hand on Stan's shoulder and smiled broadly, "If Mr. Stan manages to succeed and planes actually land and take off from there, I'm going to suggest to the municipal council that we name it the Stan Hollins Airfield." The mayor turned to Laura and Allison, "Your father has been a tremendous asset to us here in San Juan del Norte. Not only is he building single-handedly our landing strip, he has also helped get money for our community center, our sidewalks, and a lot of other projects."

"A good bit of that money came from these two," Stan replied, pointing to Luis and Rosa. "The Romeros and Rosa and her husband have been particularly generous."

"I know that, and we are immensely grateful," the mayor said, thanking Luis and Rosa. "Any help you can give is greatly needed and well spent here."

"Now all we have to do is to convince them to help us to finish the landing strip and build the walkways to the dock there," Stan said, winking at them and at the mayor.

Rosa started to reply when suddenly, a young man dressed in a white medical coat appeared at the door looking agitated. "Excuse me, you're the people in the helicopter, aren't you?" he asked in Spanish.

Luis and Rosa nodded.

"We have an emergency, and I need your help."

"What's the matter, Eduardo?" the mayor asked.

"The little Sánchez girl was bitten on the hand by a coral snake about a half-hour ago as she was playing in the yard. The poison is extremely toxic, and she'll probably die if we don't get her antivenom serum quickly. The closest place that has it is the hospital in San Carlos." He turned to the visitors. "Is there any way that you could fly her there?"

"Of course, we can," Rosa said without hesitating. She turned to Fernando. "We can, can't we?"

"How quickly do we have to be there?" Fernando asked the doctor.

"Several hours, maybe. The girl and her parents are at the health center right now, and I've done all that I can."

Fernando quickly calculated in his head. "We can be in San Carlos within an hour or an hour and a half if we go right now," he said. "It depends on how fast we can get to the helicopter. First, we'll have to stop at the lodge to pick up our things."

Rosa took charge and said to the doctor, "Go get the little girl immediately, and we'll meet at Stan's boat at the dock. I'll go with the little girl to San Carlos to help." She turned to Laura. "You and Allison will stay here as planned, and tomorrow morning Fernando and I will return to pick you up."

"*Mil gracias,*" Eduardo said. "I'll call ahead to the hospital to make sure everything is ready when you get there." He then turned and rushed out of the door.

"We have a problem," Fernando said in Spanish to Rosa. "There's not enough aviation fuel at El Futuro for a return trip here and to get us to Managua. And probably not enough in San Carlos either. It might be at least the day after tomorrow before we can get back to pick them up."

"That complicates things," Rosa said, "but we have to take her to the hospital."

Laura heard the exchange between the two and remarked, "Can't we all just go now, sitting closer together?"

"No, it's dangerous. The helicopter is too small, and everyone has to be strapped in," Rosa replied.

"There's no need for you to come back at all," Stan interjected, turning to Rosa. "I can easily take Laura and Allison with me to Bluefields tomorrow morning in the boat. There's enough room, and from there we can fly on Costeña to Managua. Laura and Allison could probably even get to Managua tomorrow night if they had to."

"That sounds like a good idea, Mother," Allison said. "I'd love to do that and also see Bluefields. It would be an adventure."

"Are you sure it is safe?" Rosa asked Stan.

"It had better be," Peter said. "I'm going, too."

"Of course, it's safe," Stan reiterated. "I make the trip just about every month."

"And we can be in Managua tomorrow night or the day after tomorrow?" Laura asked.

"Don't worry, Laura," Stan said. "You'll be there."

"OK," Laura said, resigned to her lack of options. "It looks as if there's no other way."

"Let's get going then," Rosa said.

As they left, the mayor accompanied them to the dock, thanking Rosa profusely for helping. A few minutes later, Eduardo got there with the little girl and her parents who were carrying her. About a dozen of their friends accompanied them. The girl looked to be about ten years old, and her hand was purple and swollen. She was sobbing in pain, and Laura could see the fear in the eyes of her parents.

The father handed the child to Rosa in the boat and then got in and took her back immediately. Laura noticed that the doctor had wrapped the little girl's upper and lower arm with a tourniquet ending a little above the swollen bite.

"Land directly at the hospital," the doctor told Fernando, and then he turned to Rosa, "Keep the hand always below the heart to slow the advance of the poison, and keep the tourniquet on, but don't make it too tight."

"You aren't coming?" Rosa asked with concern in her voice.

"I'm sorry, I can't. I need to stay to call the hospital to warn them to get the antivenom ready. I also have two other seriously ill patients in the health center, and I'm the only doctor in the town." Turning to the parents he said, "Remember to tell them at San Carlos it was a coral snake. And don't worry, everything will be all right." And with that, he hurried away.

Once they were all in the boat, Marcos gunned the motor and headed to Stan's eco-lodge. When they arrived, Fernando and Rosa disembarked and hurried to their rooms to get their bags while the others waited. Within a few minutes, they were back.

As Rosa got back into the boat with Stan's help, she said to him, "You need to give me the name of the hotel where you'll be staying in Bluefields and the name and telephone of Amelia's parents."

He nodded. I have their number in my wallet.

Rosa then turned to Laura standing on the dock, "Promise to call me as soon as you arrive in Bluefields." She reached into her bag and took out a card and wrote several numbers on the back. "This is my house and my cell number," she said, handing it to Stan. "If I don't hear anything from you by four o'clock in the afternoon, I'll send out a rescue squad!"

Stan reassured her. "Don't worry. We'll be in Bluefields at the latest by three o'clock, and we'll call you. If we are delayed for any reason, you can get in touch here at the town number. I'll write all the information down that you need on our way to the helicopter. Everything will be fine."

Once they were all seated, Marcos opened up the throttle, and the boat headed towards the helicopter at Greytown.

Twenty minutes later, hearing the distant sound of the helicopter, Laura, Allison, and Luis came out of the lodge's reception area to the wharf to watch it rise into the sky and turn westward above the river towards San Carlos. "May God be with them," Allison said.

# CHAPTER 23

Laura and the others were sitting in the lodge's reception room when Stan and Marcos got back from taking the child to the helicopter in Greytown. They had brought with them Danilo and one of the women workers from the clearing. After reporting that all had gone well, Stan announced that he had to return to San Juan del Norte to take Danilo and the woman, pick up river shrimp from local fishermen to sell in Bluefields, and to get their documents in order for the trip. He would probably be there for a couple of hours, and he asked if anyone wanted to go with them.

Peter and Luis accepted the invitation. Peter wanted to take some more pictures for his article, and Luis needed to talk to the mayor about the leadership course he was planning. For their part, Laura and Allison decided to remain at the lodge in order to rest and enjoy it.

"In that case, I'll need your passport numbers to give to the police," Stan said to Laura. "They like to have a record of people coming and going."

Laura and Allison went to their room and got their passports. When they got back to the dock, Stan and Marcos were busy loading three large fiberglass containers into one of the boats tied at the other side of the wharf from the *Second Chance*. Stan told them that this would be the boat they would use to go to Bluefields. "It has a deeper hull and bigger engine than the *Second Chance*, and it was made for the open sea," Stan said. To Laura the boat looked to be about twenty-five feet in length.

Once the three containers were secure in the center of the boat, Stan and Marcos made several trips back and forth to the kitchen to get ice to put in two of them "to preserve the river shrimp for the trip," Stan explained.

When they were finished, and Luis and Peter had gotten into the boat, Stan started the powerful motor which had a much deeper sound than the smaller motor of the riverboat they had been in earlier. As it pulled away from the dock, Laura noticed for the first time the boat's name—the

*Samuel Pinto*—written on the back. She was surprised and felt hurt that her father had chosen to name his boat after the son of an employee rather than for his own daughter or granddaughter.

As the sea boat disappeared up the Río Indio heading to San Juan del Norte, Laura and Allison went back to the reception area where Amelia was standing at the door with Samuel on her hip, watching them. "Can I get you something?" she asked graciously when they came inside.

"I would love a glass of lemonade, if it's not too much trouble," Laura said. "They're so refreshing!"

"Me too," Allison said.

"It's no trouble at all. I'll be right back with them," Amelia said, turning towards the kitchen.

"Can I hold Samuel while you're gone?" Allison asked. "He's adorable!"

"Of course," Amelia said, handing him to her.

Instead of crying, as Laura expected, the little boy reached out trustingly to Allison with a smile on his face.

After Amelia had left the room, the little boy pointed to a colorful bird that had settled on the half-wall of the reception area and said, "Bird." He leaned out of Allison's arms as if to pet it. "Do you like birds?" Allison asked as it flew away.

"Like bird," he said.

When Amelia came back with the glasses of lemonade, Allison put Samuel on the floor so that she could take her glass from Amelia. When she did so, he got up on his feet and toddled over to the bookcase and pulled out a children's book with pictures. He then looked up to his mother, "Read me?"

"Tonight before bed," Amelia said, smiling at him. Her delight in her child was obvious to Laura, and for good reason.

He really is smart for his age," Laura said. "I see that you're teaching him English."

Amelia nodded. "I grew up in Bluefields, and it's my first language." She paused and then asked, "Have you ever been there before?"

"Never," Laura said. "We always planned to visit it and the Corn Islands when we lived in Managua, but we never got around to it."

"You'll see it tomorrow. It's totally different from the rest of Nicaragua," Amelia explained. "More like the Caribbean islands. A lot of people there like me still speak English."

"Why 'Bluefields?'" Allison asked. "Is it named for some type of agriculture?"

Amelia laughed. "Actually it's an English corruption of the name of a Dutch pirate, Abraham Blauvelt. He used to hide in the bay there when he wasn't attacking Spanish ships."

"Dad says that you are going to visit your parents for a few days," Laura said.

Amelia nodded. "They're anxious to see Samuel. The last time they saw him was six months ago."

"It is amazing how well he takes to strangers," Allison commented.

"I guess it's because there are so many different people who stay at the hotel. He's a trusting little boy."

"Unfortunately, I'm just the opposite!" Laura admitted with a nervous laugh. "I'm actually a little scared about this trip tomorrow in such a small boat. Isn't it dangerous to take a small child out on the ocean like that?"

Amelia smiled. "To tell you the truth, I never think about it much. I've done it so many times. If we went the river and land route by way of San Carlos, it would take us three days. By sea, we can be there in five hours. The Lord will protect us."

"Amen!" Allison said. "Are you a Christian, Amelia?"

Amelia nodded. "I grew up Moravian in Bluefields, but there're only a few of us here in San Juan del Norte. Marcos is Catholic, but he doesn't go to church much."

"How did the two of you get to working for my father here?" Laura wondered.

Amelia seemed surprised at the question. "Mr. Stan has never told you about that?"

"No, I don't think so," Laura answered.

"Mr. Stan kind of adopted Marcos a few years ago," she said. "He wanted to help him, since he accidentally killed Marcos's father during the war."

"Marcos is the son of the soldier my father shot?!" Laura asked. Her face and voice showed her surprise.

Amelia nodded. "Señor Luis helped track down Marcos's mother in San Carlos, and Mr. Stan offered to do what he could for them and then invited Marcos to come to San Juan del Norte to work for him in the lodge. Mr. Stan's been like a father to him, teaching him English and about the hotel and tourist business."

173

Laura digested this new information. "I never knew that. I knew that my father had killed a soldier that night but never that he had helped the soldier's child."

"That's a wonderful story," Allison said to Amelia.

"And how did you meet Marcos?" Laura asked.

"Mr. Stan and Marcos came to my father's store in Bluefields to sell their river shrimp and iguanas. Marcos started to come back every couple of months to bring tourists or to make more sales, and we started to go out together. Four years ago we married, and I moved to San Juan del Norte. Samuel was born, and we named him after Marcos's father."

"And the boat, the *Samuel Pinto*, was that named after Marcos's father or your son? Laura asked.

"After Marcos's father, three years before Samuel was born."

"I never knew any of this," Laura reiterated, feeling a lot better now about the boat's name.

"I'm surprised that Mr. Stan never told you."

"It's just that we haven't communicated much in many years. For a long time, he hid from us the whole story of what happened that night on the river when my husband and Marcos's father were killed."

"Has it been a good life for you and Marcos here, Amelia?" Allison asked, quickly changing the subject.

"It has for the most part, but I miss my family and my church in Bluefields. That's why I look forward so much to these trips. I will introduce you to my parents tomorrow when we get there, if you'd like. They are very good people." Amelia went over to the bookcase and picked up Samuel, who had pulled out several books and was flipping their pages.

"We'll look forward to that," Allison said.

With Samuel on her hip, Amelia excused herself, "I would love to talk with you more, but right now I've got to go fix the meal for tonight. Mr. Stan wanted it to be something special, like river shrimp, as it would probably be your only chance to eat it."

"I'd be glad to watch Samuel while you fix dinner," Allison offered.

"Are you sure?" Amelia asked.

"Of course! I'll take him to our cabin and read to him from the book he took out." Allison turned to Samuel. "Would you like for me to read to you?"

Samuel nodded affirmatively.

"Then it's settled," Allison said.

Amelia was pleased. "Thank you so much. It's such a big help. When Marcos gets back, I'll send him over to get him." She turned to Samuel, "Now you be good, OK?"

"OK," he said.

Taking Samuel and his book with them, Allison and Laura returned to their room. While Allison read to Samuel and played with him on her bed, Laura stretched out in one of the two hammocks on the little porch of their cabin and nodded off to sleep listening to the lapping of the river water against the banks and to the muted roar of the ocean in the distance.

It was six o'clock when Allison woke her up and told her that the *Samuel Pinto* had returned from San Juan del Norte and Marcos had picked up Samuel.

# CHAPTER 24

At six-thirty, Laura and Allison joined the others for the special dinner of river shrimp. Marcos had pushed together all of the tables in the dining room so that everyone, including the French couple, could eat together.

"Have you heard anything about the little Sánchez girl?" Allison asked her grandfather as she took her seat beside him.

"We have, and it's good news," Stan answered. "We called Rosa on her cell phone from the town. It looks like everything will be all right. She said that they were still at the hospital but would be leaving soon for Managua so they could get back before nightfall."

He then looked at Laura who was seated in front of him beside Luis. "Rosa was concerned that you were still fearful about the trip tomorrow, and she wondered if it might not be better for you to wait another day and take the public boat up the river to San Carlos and then the plane from there to Managua."

"No, it will be all right. Amelia made me feel better about it all." Laura smiled at Amelia who had just served her a plate of rice and a river shrimp the size of a small lobster. Marcos, behind her, brought in more platters of salad, beans, and fried potatoes to the table.

"I'm really looking forward to the adventure," Allison said, "but I wish that we didn't have to leave so soon. It's so beautiful and full of history here."

"It's true," Peter said. He was seated on the other side of Allison. "The town just needs a museum to tell it all."

"After the airfield and the internet," Stan said, smiling, "that's our next project. Our idea is to put a kind of welcoming center for eco-tourists next to the Alcaldía. It'll have it all—the geological makeup of the area, its fauna and flora, and its history to the present. We'll start with the Indians and cover everything from then on—the coming of the Spanish, their wars with the pirates and British and Miskitos, Vanderbilt's Transit Route, the invasion of William Walker, the inter-ocean canal, the Contra war, the building of the new town, and hopefully, the completion of the landing strip!"

"Just who is this William Walker you keep talking about?" Peter wanted to know. "You've mentioned him several times."

"The short answer is that he was the epitome of American arrogance and Manifest Destiny," Stan replied. "In the 1850s, he tried to take over Nicaragua and then make it a part of the United States. He was a little man with a huge ego."

"An American Napoleon?" the Frenchman joked from the end of the table where he was sitting.

"Kind of," Stan replied. "He was an American mercenary born in Nashville who was hired by a general in León representing the Liberales to attack his Conservative enemies in the city of Granada. Walker and his hundred and fifty or so men were successful in taking Granada, but Walker had his own ambitions and they were different from his employers in León. He wanted to create a Central American empire with him as president and maybe annex it to the South before the U.S. Civil War. Among his first decrees when he became president of Nicaragua was to make English the official language and to reintroduce slavery."

"A real progressive," Laura joked, serving herself the potatoes.

"Afterwards, he and his men were defeated by a coalition of Central American forces, but he kept trying to return until finally he was captured by the British who handed him over to the Hondurans to be tried and executed because he had invaded there, too."

"One of the things I've always found so interesting about him," Luis interjected, "is that he did so much, so young. He was a seminary-trained minister, a medical doctor trained in Germany, a lawyer in Nashville, and a journalist in New Orleans and San Francisco—all of that before he became a soldier of fortune and then president of Nicaragua. He also wrote books. When he was executed, he was only thirty-six years old!"

"Amazing!" Peter replied.

"To me," Stan said, "Walker and my ancestor Captain Hollins, along with Cornelius Vanderbilt, were the forerunners of American imperialism here. Later, U.S. Marines occupied the country for twenty-three years, and then we supported the Contras. It seems that we're always trying to impose our will and our ways on other people."

"True," Luis said, "but to be fair to your country and its citizens, often the interference is welcomed and actually helps."

"Like when?" Stan wanted to know.

"Like much of the time," Luis answered. "Walker was bad, but it was Vanderbilt who helped organize and finance the Central American armies that eventually got rid of him. Vanderbilt hated Walker because he had commandeered one of Vanderbilt's boats to attack Granada. Also, because he had sided later with Vanderbilt's business rivals to take over the Accessory Transit Route in order to bring in more mercenaries from the U.S. Contrary to popular opinion, the U.S. Government never supported Walker either. Actually, the U.S. Navy captured him when he tried to return to Nicaragua to reclaim his presidency. That happened right here in San Juan del Norte. They sent him back to the U.S."

"But their actions were in their own self-interest!" Stan argued. "What about the evils of the invasion of our Marines and our propping up Somoza and financing the Contras?"

"Interference for sure," Luis admitted, "but interference supported by many in our country. Remember, too, that while the U.S. propped up Somoza, it was also the U.S. that finally helped convince him to go. A lot of your government's foreign policies I don't like, but I and many other Nicaraguans are grateful for many of its ideals—for example, your support for democracy, human rights, transparency in government, and a free press. We are also grateful for the many years of financial assistance to our country from your government and from American organizations and citizens—including you, Stan." Luis looked straight at Stan and smiled. "Stan, *you, too,* have often interfered in the affairs of our country—first, by starting Acción, and now with all of your projects here in San Juan del Norte—but we praise you for it."

"What's your point?" Stan asked.

"My point is that we all try to impose our ideas and projects on others because we believe in them. Like Walker, we're all little men with big egos."

"But Walker's plans were against the interests of the Nicaraguan people. Acción and the airfield are in their interests."

"It's really all in the eyes of the beholder, isn't it?" Luis said. "Walker, Vanderbilt, Somoza, the Contras, the Sandinistas, the U.S., you, me—we all claim that what we do is in the interests of others, but we all have our own selfish agendas, too. We all say that we want to do good, but much of the time, we wind up hurting others in the process. Look at my brothers, for instance. They had opposing visions of the good, and in their desire to impose their views, they killed others. Stan, you yourself killed someone in self-defense."

"And I've spent my life feeling terribly guilty and trying to make amends for it, just like I have for the actions of my country," Stan replied.

Laura bit her tongue as she felt a sudden surge of anger within her—a deep anger that she had repressed the whole trip. It was a resentment that had started when her father yanked her out of school her senior year of high school, one of the most critical times of her life. It grew at Clay's death, which Laura blamed on Stan's insistence that Clay accompany him on that fateful river trip. Finally, when Laura discovered the lies of her father and his betrayal of her mother, it had burst forth into the open. Now, it burst forth again at his hypocrisy. She looked at her father icily and blurted out, "You're always talking about all this guilt of yours about being American—about Captain Hollins, Vanderbilt, Walker, the Marines, and the Contras! I wish that you felt the same guilt and desire to make amends for Clay's death and for the way that you've treated Mother!"

A heavy silence fell around the table as everyone was astonished by Laura's sudden and unexpected anger—so uncharacteristic of the professional, thoughtful, and private woman that she normally was.

Stan's face got red as he looked at Laura across the table and shook his head. "Unlike Marcos, you will never forgive me, will you, Laura? Clay's death was not my fault."

"And your lies about what happened? Were they not your fault either?" Laura had become oblivious to the others at the table, as had Stan.

"There were justifiable reasons at the time."

"What could possibly justify that?"

"I thought it was necessary to protect the Revolution, to protect Luis and myself. And what I said was the truth, even though it wasn't all of the truth. The Contras *did* cause the death of Clay. If they hadn't attacked that night, he wouldn't have been killed."

"And what's your excuse for your betrayal of Mother?"

"It was difficult for me when she chose not to return to Nicaragua."

"I can't believe that you are putting any blame on her," Laura retorted. "She's been a saint the way she has stuck with you all these years after the way you've treated her."

"I know that, Laura," Stan said, trying to regain his calm. "I want to see her and ask her forgiveness, but she didn't come with you."

"The truth is that she didn't come because she feared you might be living here with another woman. She didn't want to put pressure on you, but wanted to leave you free to choose." Laura paused and then added, "From all that I've heard so far today, you have already made the choice to reject us again and not go back with us."

"I'm not rejecting you. I'm deeply thankful for your coming," Stan said. "But first, I have to finish this airstrip. I have to get money to pay the workers and complete it. I want to leave something of worth before I die. Acción was to be that, but it was taken from me."

"Stan," Luis corrected, "it wasn't taken from you. You resigned."

"Because I didn't have your support," Stan said.

"Because you misused the money of other people," Laura retorted.

"I disagree, but that isn't the point," Stan said, struggling again to remain calm. "The point is that my life up until now has been a failure. I want at least one success before I die!"

"Stop it, both of you!" Allison interjected, close to tears. "You love each other. Why do you keep hurting each other like this!" She turned to her grandfather. "Please, come home with us for treatment. The mayor and others can finish the landing strip."

"They can't, Allison," Stan replied, his voice now soft. "The town has no money and no one else wants to help. I have to pay the workers what I owe them and finish the job. My meeting tomorrow in Bluefields with a possible investor is my last chance. I have to resolve this before I do anything else."

"Who's this investor in Bluefields?" Luis asked.

"Someone Adric knows."

Stan then got up abruptly from the table, looking uncomfortable. "I really don't want to talk about these things anymore. This was meant to be a fun feast, and I'm sorry it's ending this way. Hopefully, tomorrow we'll all have cooler heads. Anyway, we all need to go to bed so Amelia can clean up the kitchen and get ready for the trip."

Stan moved behind Allison and hugged her shoulders. "I know you love me, Allison, and I love you, too. But I have to finish what I started."

The French couple got up next. They were wide-eyed during the emotional exchange between father and daughter and seemed relieved to get away.

"We'll meet here at seven for breakfast," Stan said. He then went into the kitchen to talk to Amelia and Marcos.

As Allison got up, Peter said to her, "It's too early for me to go to bed, no matter what time we're getting up. Why don't you stay a little longer so that we can talk."

Allison looked across the table at her mother for guidance.

"No, it's time for bed," Laura said, still furious at her father and mistrusting Peter's motives.

Before leaving, they thanked Amelia and Marcos for the excellent dinner. Wanting to be alone, Laura went directly to her room, but Allison and Luis stayed to help Amelia clear the tables. When they were done, they also headed to their cabins for the night.

# CHAPTER 25

The next morning, Laura woke up early. Maybe it was the loud yells of howler monkeys or the grating calls of roosters. Perhaps it was her apprehensions about the upcoming trip or her regrets about the night before. She looked at her watch and then nudged Allison in the other bed. Like most young adults, Allison was a late sleeper. They quickly dressed, finished packing their knapsacks, and went to meet the others for breakfast.

The breakfast consisted of hearty servings of eggs and *gallo pinto*—rice and beans mixed together. After they had finished, Stan gave them each a bag and said, "We'll stop at a little island near Monkey Point for lunch. Amelia has packed us some sandwiches and bottles of water." He was friendly and acted as if nothing had happened the previous evening.

When Laura and the others who were going to Bluefields got to the *Samuel Pinto,* Adric Williams was on the wharf waiting for them along with Marcos. As they all gathered by the softly rocking boat, Marcos got into the craft and took off the lid of one of the three fiberglass containers he had already secured to the boat. From inside, he pulled out a half-dozen orange ponchos and lifejackets and handed them to everyone who was making the trip. Amelia put the smallest lifejacket on Samuel, but it still engulfed him.

Laura looked up at the sky. "Why the ponchos," she asked. "It doesn't look at all like rain."

"One never knows around here," Stan said. "Anyway, it will help keep you dry from the ocean spray."

Marcos asked each person to hand down their bags and lunches one by one. As they did so, he placed them in yellow plastic sacks and put them into the same container in the stern of the boat from which he had taken the lifejackets. "We don't want them to get wet," he explained. Getting out of the craft, he kissed Amelia and Samuel and then helped them into the boat along with Laura and Allison.

Stan assigned each of them their seats. Adric was to be at the bow and was to be the lookout for floating debris in the water. Peter and Allison and Laura were to sit on the seat behind him, and Amelia and Samuel were to be behind them with their backs against the first of the three containers. Stan took his own position at the controls, standing in the back of the boat near two large transparent plastic tanks of gasoline.

"What's in the other two containers?" Peter asked Stan.

"River shrimp to sell in Bluefields."

"No iguanas?" Allison asked.

"Not this time."

Luis, who had taken breakfast with them, now came to the dock to see them off. He was leaving the next day for El Futuro on the public boat. "Don't forget to call Rosa as soon as you get to Bluefields," he said to Stan. "She's expecting you to be there by three o'clock by the latest."

"Stan looked at his watch. "Don't worry, we'll be there way before then. It's a five to six-hour trip, maximum, and it's only seven-thirty now."

After examining the ropes that secured the containers to the boat to make sure they were tight, Stan started the engine. It rumbled, and the water boiled up behind the boat. Marcos then untied the rope that held the craft to the dock and tossed it to Adric. Stan, standing at the controls, put the boat in reverse, and they slowly eased away from the pier. At that moment, the French couple came out on to their cabin's balcony and waved and took some pictures of them. Laura and Allison waved back.

"*Vayan con Dios*—go with God," Luis called out to them above the rumble of the motor.

Once in the main flow of the river, Stan guided the boat eastward where the river drained into the ocean. In front of them, Laura could see the waves breaking over the shallow sand bars and wondered where they would pass.

When they got to the end of the river channel and were even with the beaches, Stan yelled for them to hold on tightly. "I'm going to gun the engine, and we may scrape a sandbar or two getting out to sea."

He then scanned the channel to find the route with the deepest water. When he had chosen his path, he pushed the throttle to its maximum, and the boat lurched forward. Laura and Allison held tightly to their seats and to the side of the boat as it roared and sped in the direction of the sun, which was now only a little above the horizon. As they raced through the breaking waves to the deeper ocean, their faces were whipped by the spray. Allison grinned in delight.

Once in the deeper, smoother water, Stan pulled back on the throttle handle and turned the boat parallel to the empty beaches that stretched for kilometers and kilometers in a curve as far as the eye could see. To their right, Laura and Allison looked up at the bright orange and yellows of the young morning, so beautiful against the blue sky. Above them, white seagulls hovered gracefully in the air streams. Laura, for the first time that morning, relaxed.

As the outboard cut through the waters heading north towards Monkey Point, Adric sat at the bow as a lookout. From time to time, he yelled something to Stan and motioned to him with his hand to go to the right or to the left in order to avoid some of the flotsam in the water. At times, it was a patch of seaweed, and at others, a broken palm tree trunk that had come down one of the rivers and was carried to sea.

To pass the time, Laura and Allison played peek-a-boo with little Samuel behind them, and Peter took pictures of the coast, which gradually became smaller as they headed across the half moon bay towards Monkey Point and then Bluefields. After about an hour in the boat, Laura noticed that she could no longer see land and that the waves were getting larger. Looking eastward in the sky, she no longer saw the soft hues of the morning, but a gathering of large dark clouds advancing towards them.

Stan also took notice of the clouds but seemed unconcerned and continued at the same speed in the same direction that the boat's compass pointed—straight north. The roar of the motor and the banging of the bottom of the boat made hearing each other difficult.

Within fifteen minutes, the winds started to pick up, the clouds in the distance lit up with lightning bolts, and the waves grew larger. In one of the cresting waves, not more than thirty meters away, Laura was aghast to see the form of a large shark swimming parallel to the boat. She pointed it out to Allison, and her fears began to resurface. "I knew that we should never have come on this trip," she said, grasping Allison's knee for reassurance.

"It will be OK, Mother," Allison said, patting her leg. "You heard Amelia. They've made this trip countless times."

Laura looked back at Amelia, who smiled at her, but Laura noticed that she had put the hood of the poncho over her head and had wrapped the bottom of the poncho around Samuel, holding him tightly to her.

Within another half-hour, almost all of the blue sky over their heads had been covered with the dark incoming clouds, and it began to drizzle. Soon the sky darkened even further, and the drizzle turned into heavy drops of stinging rain. Breaking waves began to splash into the boat, and water sloshed at their feet.

Laura looked back at Stan for reassurance. He ignored her look and held tightly to the controls, staring fixedly ahead at Adric, who with one hand grabbed on to the boat for security and with the other, made signals from time to time for Stan to move to the right or to the left.

Stan yelled something to Amelia, and Amelia nodded. She then said to Laura, "Please hold onto Samuel. Mr. Stan wants me to bail."

She stood up and turned towards Stan, holding on to one of the ropes securing the containers with one hand to balance herself. With her other hand, she reached out to grasp the improvised plastic bailer that he handed to her. She then sat down and began to scoop out the water and throw it overboard. As she did so, Samuel reached out for her and cried. Laura held tightly to him and tried to comfort him.

As the waves got bigger and more water came into the side of the boat, Laura began to fear that the boat might capsize if one of them broke too closely to its side. Stan must have sensed the same danger as well, as he slowed down and turned the boat into the waves rather than continuing parallel to the coast.

From then on, they began to climb to the crest of one gigantic wave after another and then slam down on the other side into the valley between them. The boat shuddered each time, and Laura held on tightly to the seat and to Samuel as Amelia continued to bail. It was like riding a bull in a rodeo. This went on for some fifteen minutes, and then they all heard a terrifying sound—the powerful motor of the boat began to sputter.

"Hang on, I've got to change the gas tanks," Stan yelled. He killed the motor, and fighting to hold himself upright in the midst of the recurring waves, he worked frantically to transfer the gas hose from the now empty gas tank to the full one. As Stan unscrewed the cap of the full tank and stuck the hose into it, Adric let out a loud curse and pointed frantically at a monster wave that was approaching. Before Stan could re-screw the cap, the wave hit them with a wallop that knocked him off his feet and overturned both gas containers. Fuel poured out of the topless tank into the seawater in the bottom of the boat.

The same gigantic wave jerked loose the rope that tied down the front fiberglass container and it flew out of the boat striking the three women and Peter, knocking them off their seats. Recovering from the shock of the hit, Laura realized to her horror that she was no longer holding on to Samuel. She looked frantically for him and screamed as she saw his orange vest bobbing in the sea some ten meters away from the boat near the white fiberglass container that had hit them. "Samuel is in the ocean! Do something! Save him!" she shrieked to Stan.

Stan got to his feet, and seeing what had happened, immediately tore off his rain poncho and dove into the sea. Although hindered by his shoes and the lifejacket, with four powerful strokes, he reached the frightened Samuel, grabbed him and took hold of the dangling rope that had once held down the fiberglass container. Above the roar of the waves and of the rain, he yelled to Adric, "The gas is spilling out. Upright the gas can!"

As Adric scrambled to the stern past the terrified women and over the two remaining containers, Peter grabbed the boat's ringed life-buoy and heaved it to Stan in the water. Stan reached out and grabbed it, still managing to hold on to Samuel and the rope attached to the container. "Pull us in!" Stan yelled.

Peter started to pull, but when Stan and Samuel were halfway to the boat, another massive wave broke and knocked Peter almost into the water. He instinctively grasped the side of the boat to save himself, and as he did so, he dropped his end of the rope. That same wave pushed Stan and Samuel much farther away from the craft.

Meanwhile, Adric was on his knees in the water and gasoline mixture in the stern of the boat, trying to upright the plastic tank that still held some gasoline. When he was finally successful, another powerful wave smashed the boat and again almost capsized them.

"Quickly, quickly," Amelia shouted to Adric. "They're almost out of sight!"

Adric screamed back, "Grab the oars, and paddle hard to turn the boat to face the waves. Otherwise, we'll turn over!"

Allison grabbed the two paddles attached to the inside of the boat and handed one of them to Peter. He scrambled behind her and they both paddled furiously on the left side trying to get the bow to face the never ceasing, enormous waves rolling one after another towards them.

After what seemed like an eternity to Laura, Adric finally managed to re-attach the gas line. He then pressed the starter button, but there were only whirrs. Adric then checked the connections, pumped the gas, and then tried again and again. After five more sputtering attempts, the gas began to flow, and the motor finally caught. It was the sweetest sound that Laura had ever heard in her life, and all of them let out shouts of relief.

"Thank you, Lord," Allison said, exhausted from paddling.

But by the time the motor restarted, Stan and Samuel had disappeared from view.

# CHAPTER 26

Stan cursed as he saw the giant wave break on the boat and then tear the rope from Peter's hand. He cursed again as the same wave hit him with ferocious force and almost tore Samuel from his arms. As they swirled in its foam, Stan fought to hold on to Samuel and at the same time not to be scratched and choked by the desperate boy clinging to his head and neck.

When the wave had passed, Stan bobbed to the surface, gasping for breath. He freed himself from Samuel's frantic grip and disentangled them both from the ropes attached to the life-buoy and to the container. Samuel's eyes were wide with terror.

"Hold on to this, Samuel, not to my neck!" Stan said as he repositioned the screaming child's hands and arms around the life preserver.

Stan then kicked off his shoes and maneuvered himself behind Samuel so that the boy couldn't grab him anymore. Placing his arms around him and his legs underneath him, Stan made a kind of chair with his lap for Samuel to sit in.

"Everything will be all right. I'll hold you up from behind," he said to him reassuringly.

When Samuel sensed the security of Stan's arms and legs holding him, he quieted down. Fear, however, still showed on his face.

The wave had pushed them some fifty meters from the boat, but Stan could still see Adric trying desperately to get the fuel lines connected to the motor. He could also hear the now faint but frantic cries of Amelia above the roar of the sea. "Don't let go of him. Please hold on to him, Mr. Stan."

"I want Mommy," the little boy whimpered as he heard his mother.

"I will get you to her soon," Stan reassured him. "Just hold on tightly to the ring until they come and get us."

It was then for the first time that Stan noticed a four centimeter cut on the side of Samuel's head that was bleeding. It didn't look deep, but the blood concerned him. Stan surmised that the edge of the container must have hit the little boy in the head as it knocked him off the boat.

Stan and Samuel waited, and minutes seemed like hours as the motor didn't start, and the boat didn't come. Instead, each of the incoming waves pushed them farther and farther away from their rescuers, and the boat became more difficult to see because of the sheets of rain and the many wave crests separating them.

As the distance between them and the boat lengthened, Stan's own sense of anxiety and helplessness began to increase. He thought about trying to swim towards the boat, but quickly rejected that idea. He knew that doing so would be exhausting and useless. He would never be able to drag Samuel the distance under his arm or overcome the force of the oncoming waves.

He also didn't want to let go of the ropes to the container or to the life-buoy. Both were too valuable to him as flotation devices. Thinking of them, Stan tied the rope attached to the container to the round life-buoy and then attached the buoy rope to Samuel's waist and to his own waist. That way they wouldn't escape from him, and Stan would keep his hands free to hold on to Samuel.

As he held the little boy wedged firmly between his arms and his legs, Stan checked Samuel's lifejacket, which was too bulky for him. He adjusted the top so that Samuel's head could not slide down inside, and he tightened the lower straps to make sure that he would not slip out of it. When he had done the best he was able, Stan talked to the little boy, trying to comfort him. "You're doing great, Samuel. Your lifejacket won't let you sink in the water and neither will I. We'll just stay here for awhile, and pretty soon, they'll get the motor started and come get us and pull us out."

The little boy said nothing but shivered in fear. Blood still oozed from the side of his head down his neck onto the lifejacket.

When the next large wave broke, Stan held on tightly to Samuel as they both swirled under water and were jerked by the pull of the attached container and ringed-buoy. Coming to the surface again, Stan cleared the stinging saltwater from his eyes, as Samuel coughed and cried. When Stan looked back to where the boat had been, he was horrified to discover that he could no longer see it! He looked in other directions, in case he had become disoriented, but the boat was nowhere to be seen. Nor could he hear any motor.

Instinctively, Stan yelled into the wind. "We're here! We're over here!" But he could hear nothing in response except the sounds of breaking waves, claps of thunder, the whimpers and coughs of Samuel, and the pounding of the heavy rain like a machine gun on the fiberglass container floating near them.

# CHAPTER 27

Amelia, who had kept her eyes on the location where she had last seen Stan and Samuel, motioned frantically for Adric to go in that direction. The others also stood up in the boat, holding tightly to the side, looking for signs of the white container or orange lifejackets in the dark seascape of high waves and deep troughs. Several times one of the women yelled out that she thought that she saw something, but it always turned out that it was only another whitecap of a breaking wave.

They searched desperately and systematically, going five minutes in one direction, five minutes in another—north, south, east, and west. For close to an hour they searched, but they saw no sign of Stan and Samuel. Complicating matters, they could see no more than thirty meters because of the driving rain and giant waves. In every direction they looked, they saw only rolling walls of water, dark clouds, heavy rain, some ocean debris, and the fearful expressions on their own faces.

Adric finally called to Amelia and Laura. "We're about out of gasoline," he said pointing to the transparent tank that was now only about twenty percent full. "We can't search any more. We have to head for the shore."

"But we can't give up!" Laura protested. "We have to find them."

"Maybe they're heading with the currents towards the shore," Adric suggested.

"And maybe they are heading out to sea," Laura retorted. "We have to keep searching! They're bound to be close-by!"

"I'm heading towards the shore," Adric said with firmness. "If we don't, and we run out of gas, there's no way we can keep from capsizing." He looked at the compass and turned the boat due west.

"But we can't stop looking," Amelia implored. "It's my son out there!"

When Adric ignored her and kept going in the same direction, Amelia crawled over the containers to the back and tried to wrest the controls from him.

"Stop it!" Adric yelled, as he pushed her to the bottom of the boat. "You're going to kill us all."

Laura turned to climb over the containers and help Amelia, but as she did so, Peter grabbed her at the waist and pulled her back. "He's right," he yelled. "We have to use the little gasoline we have to get us to shore."

"Take your hands off of me!" Laura screamed, trying unsuccessfully to get out of his grip. "We have to keep looking!"

"We've looked for the last hour and haven't found anything," Peter yelled back, protecting himself from her fists. "Be reasonable! They have lifejackets on. Maybe they'll drift to the shore. Anyway, maybe we can get some help there."

Allison joined the fray, pulling at Peter's arm. "Leave my mother alone," she yelled at him.

"We're all going to die if you don't get some sense in your heads!" Peter screamed at them, pushing them both down onto the seat. "We don't have enough gas to search without risking our own lives. We have to get back to shore as soon as we can."

As Adric kept the craft heading toward land, the hard lurching of the boat began to diminish as they now rode the waves instead of fighting them. Amelia, crying uncontrollably, crawled forward over the containers. "Keep looking for them and pray," she said to Allison and Laura through her sobs.

Laura both looked and prayed, but as the minutes passed, a terrible dread, much darker even than the black clouds overhead, began to seep into her spirit. She began to think the unthinkable. *What if Dad and Samuel are lost at sea and never found? It would be my fault for having let go of Samuel.*

"Go to the front of the boat and watch out for debris," Adric yelled to Peter above the sounds of the wind and motor.

Peter immediately obeyed and moved clumsily to the bow, hanging on tightly to the metal handle there. For some twenty minutes, he surveyed in front of them, looking for land and for dangers to avoid. He also scanned the ocean on the left and right, searching for Stan and Samuel. For twenty minutes, he saw nothing and was silent. Then suddenly, as the rain began to slacken, he shouted, "I think I see land!"

Adric let out a whoop of joy, and soon all of them could see the gray coastline in the distance. Laura searched for evidence of houses and boats where they could get help, but she could find no sign of human habitation. Her heart sank again.

In another twenty minutes, the boat had come within a hundred meters of the shore. Adric slowed the motor and yelled for everyone to hold tight. "I'm going to go full speed so we can land on the sand. It's going to be a hard impact, so be prepared!"

Peter returned from the bow to his seat, and they all held on to the side of the boat and to the planks under them as tightly as they were able, preparing for the shudder of the landing.

Adric opened up the throttle, and they roared through the breaking waves. In the final seconds, about fifteen meters out, Adric cut off the outboard motor and raised the propeller out of the water. They landed with a hard thud and scraped the beach, coming to a stop on the sand some five meters from the water. Then, there was stillness.

"We made it!" Adric yelled victoriously.

Peter also let out a whoop of relief.

The women, however, were quiet as they got out of the boat—shaken, aching, sopping wet, and despairing.

"We've got to find someone with a boat to help us look for Dad and Samuel," Laura said as her feet touched the sand.

"I don't think you will find anyone. The area is deserted," Adric replied. "We're still a long way from Monkey Point."

When she heard that, Laura fell down on her knees in the sand and sobbed, "I'm so sorry, Amelia. I just couldn't hang on to him when the container hit us. I'm so sorry."

Allison knelt beside her mother and put her arm around her. "It's not your fault, Mother. It's not anyone's fault."

As for Amelia, she said nothing but only looked out at the sea. "He's in the hands of Mr. Stan and of the Lord."

"Yes!" Allison stood up, and then she said with conviction. "And they can make it!" She looked at her watch. "It's still daylight and the wind and rain are dying down. The water is warm, and the waves will bring them to shore. They have lifejackets on, and Grandfather is a survivor. He will protect Samuel, and God will protect them both!"

# CHAPTER 28

As time passed, Stan's certainty of a quick rescue began to fade, and he began to ask himself fearful questions. *What if Adric is unable to start the motor, or what if they don't have enough fuel to come to get us or for them to get back to shore? What if they can't find us? What if they have capsized? What if another huge, crashing wave pulls us into its churn, and we can't get back to the surface in time to breathe? What if the wave rips Samuel from my grasp or hurls an uprooted tree from some riverbank or coast into the backs of our heads like a battering ram? And what about the danger from sharks? Is the blood coming from Samuel's head wound enough to attract them?*

Stan knew and feared the bull sharks that lurked beneath them. Not only did they patrol the coastal waters off Nicaragua and the rest of Central America, they were extremely adaptable and even swam up in the fresh water of the Río San Juan as far as Lake Nicaragua. Aggressive, solitary hunters, they sometimes attacked humans. He remembered what had happened to an Argentine from Tandil who had chartered one of Jimmy Langston's fishing boats and had fallen overboard, drunk. Before they could pull him out, he had lost his right arm at the elbow to the bite of a bull shark. The man bled to death before Jimmy could get him back to Barra del Colorado.

Stan was not ready to die, and he certainly didn't want to die in that way. Stan feared death. He always had as long as he could remember. It was not so much pain that terrified him but the unknown that awaited him beyond death's doorway. In Stan's more rational moments, he thought that this life on earth was all there was and that there was no after-life. But at other times, in the loneliness of the night, he felt deep in his bones that religion was right, and there was a Creator-Sustainer God and an afterlife. While that thought comforted many, it made Stan feel uneasy and vulnerable. He was afraid of how that God would judge him.

Despite all of his brave posturing, Stan was deeply ashamed of his life—not only for his treatment of Elizabeth, but for the pretense and selfishness that permeated his thoughts and actions. For all of his talk about justice, liberation, and concern for the poor, how much did he *really* care about them? Like Elizabeth said that day on the beach in Miami, not much. It was mostly playacting so that he could feel superior to others—especially his parents. He really only cared for himself and for what others thought of him. While Stan wanted to be different, he realized he had no power to bring about the change. All he could do was pray to a God he wasn't even sure existed—to a God he feared.

Stan prayed now as he had never prayed before in his life. He prayed for courage. He prayed for forgiveness and mercy. He prayed for protection. He prayed for the wisdom that would enable him to get them out of their dilemma. Most of all, he prayed that he would see his family again and be able to bring Samuel back safely to his mother and father.

*But meanwhile what should I do?* Stan imagined that they were some ten to fifteen kilometers from the shore and that the ever tricky currents could either take them farther out to sea, or eventually carry them to the beach. If the current carried them out to sea, Stan knew all would be lost, unless Adric or some other search party found them.

Stan imagined that he could perhaps make it to the shore on his own by swimming and resting, but abandoning Samuel was not an option. He could never face Marcos and Amelia without him. He had been responsible for the death of Marcos's father. He would not be responsible for the death of Marcos's son. Samuel and he would both survive or die together.

As he thought of Samuel, Stan turned his attention to the little boy's needs. He knew that the orange lifejacket would keep Samuel afloat, but there was the double danger of sharks and of hypothermia for him to consider if Samuel stayed long in the water. Even though the ocean was relatively warm, being in it for a long time, and especially at night, would be dangerous for a small boy. Stan somehow needed to keep Samuel warm, perhaps by rubbing his legs and arms, or by finding a way to get him out of the water. The only way he could do the latter was to put Samuel in the container. Emptied, it was big enough to hold him, and inside, Stan thought, Samuel would be protected from hypothermia and perhaps even sharks.

Stan's spirits rose as he considered making the container into a boat for Samuel. The main problem was to find a way to keep the container upright in the waves. With Samuel inside, it would quickly tip over, and the little boy would fall out, as Stan would be unable to stabilize it by himself. He needed something else to brace and balance it. Perhaps he could find a floating coconut tree to act as an outrigger. Earlier in the day he had seen several in the ocean, and he knew from experience that the beaches of the region were littered with hundreds of them, swept in by the currents. That was what he had to do. He had to find a tree.

With this objective in his mind, Stan turned Samuel around so that they could face and brace themselves for the waves that came towards them, billowing and falling, billowing and falling. He scanned as far as he could see for signs of the boat or signs of flotsam that could be used to brace the container. He also kept his eyes peeled for sharks, but he had no idea what he would do if he saw one.

For a good hour, Stan's eyes swept the seas and the sky, but all that he could see were whitecaps and an occasional patch of green seaweed. He kept up his chatter to Samuel, who from time to time complained about his head or said that he wanted his mother or that he wanted to go home. But for the most part, Samuel was quiet and had stopped trembling and trusted himself to Stan's lap and Stan's reassuring voice.

# CHAPTER 29

The rain stopped, and Adric took charge of the situation on the beach. "The first thing we have to do is to make a fire to dry out and to warm up. It will also serve as a signal. All the wood will be wet, but we can use some of the leftover gasoline to start it."

"You do that," Laura said, still angry at him, "but I'm going down the beach to search for help for my father and Samuel." She headed towards the boat and started to open one of the containers.

"What are you doing?" Adric asked when he saw her struggling to take off the lid of the front container. He went over to stop her.

"I'm getting out our packs," Laura replied. "I want to get some dry clothes and my binoculars."

"You're opening the one with the river shrimp," he said. "The packs are in the other container." He put the lid back on the front container and then opened the one behind it. Reaching in, he pulled out the different bags and backpacks and put them on the wet sand.

"If you have any paper or notebooks in these, we can use them to start the fire," Adric said.

Peter came over and unzipped his bag, which was considerably bigger than the others. He fumbled around inside and then pulled out a loose-leaf notebook that he had used to make notes on his trip. "This should help some," he said as he tore out a wad of clean pages and handed them to Adric.

Laura, meanwhile, had taken out the binoculars from her pack and scanned the long beach north and south searching for signs of people and houses. She didn't see anything definite, but she decided to go south towards San Juan del Norte. If Stan and Samuel made it to shore, it would most likely be in that direction. Anyway, she just wanted to do something and to get away from Adric and Peter. Allison and Amelia agreed to go with her.

"While the women go south, why don't you go north towards Monkey Point and look for help," Adric said to Peter. "I'll stay here and gather some wood for the fire and cook some shrimp for our supper tonight."

Peter agreed.

"But all of you should be back within a couple of hours. You don't want to be wandering in the dark!" Adric admonished.

Laura emptied her pack except for one change of dry clothes and then put her lunch and binoculars into it. She advised Allison and Amelia to do the same so they could get out of their wet clothes farther down the beach. Once they had done so, all three women took off towards the south with Laura in the lead. As they walked, Amelia kept repeating her soft pleas to God, "Please Lord, please Lord, please Lord." Allison put her arm around her.

When they were about a half-kilometer away from the boat near a grove of palm trees, Laura suggested that they change into their dry clothes before continuing forward. Amelia and Allison concurred, and each went modestly behind one of the trees and stripped, putting on the dry garments.

When she had changed, Laura went back to the middle of the beach, took out her binoculars again, and surveyed once more the beach and the ocean looking for signs of Stan and Samuel or of other people who might help them. She saw nothing. She then turned the binoculars back north to where the boat was. There was yet no fire, and at first she could not see Adric either. Then, scanning the tree line, she was able to see him as he dug in the sand near two palm trees.

"What are the chances we will find someone to help us?" Allison asked Amelia as they joined Laura again on the beach. "You know this region."

"Not good," Amelia answered, her voice cracking. "There's no village that I know of between San Juan del Norte and Monkey Point. We may find an isolated fisherman's shack, but that's all. We have to depend on God for a miracle!"

Laura wanted to follow up with a question about the chances of Stan and Samuel surviving, but she knew that she couldn't. The answer would be too painful for all of them.

"I know Mr. Stan will never let go of Samuel," Amelia said, as if anticipating the question. "If God wills that they survive, then they will survive together. The weather is so much better now."

"And Rosa will be worried, since it is way past the time that we were supposed to call her from Bluefields," Laura said, adding to the encouragement. "And she'll start looking for us soon, as she said."

"We could write a big SOS in the sand with our feet," Allison suggested. "They might see it from a plane or a helicopter."

"That's a great idea, Allison," Laura replied, wanting something concrete to do. "Why don't you do it by yourself so we don't all mess up the beach? Maybe, you could also make an arrow pointing to the boat."

Allison went to a part of the beach that looked like it was safe from the tide and began to shuffle her feet in the sand, making the large, curving shapes of the letters S . . . O . . . S, being careful to walk lightly between the letters. She then went back over the same path two more times to make the letters deeper and more visible. Next, she dragged her foot to make a giant arrow pointing north towards the boat.

When she was finished, the three women continued their trek down the beach for another two kilometers. Every now and then, Laura stopped to look out into the ocean with her binoculars for a flash of orange or of the white container. Then she looked down the beach for a sign of a house or boat. Once she thought that someone must be near because the beach sand had been considerably disturbed, as if a boat had been dragged through it. Amelia, however, burst her hope when she explained that the tracks were of a giant sea turtle that had come to the beach to lay her eggs.

When they came to a shallow river traversing the beach and still had not found any sign of Stan and Samuel or someone to help them, Laura suggested that they turn back. "It's going to get dark soon, and we've been walking for over an hour. We need to get back." Allison and Amelia agreed.

The way back was twice as tiring and discouraging to them. Their hopes of finding someone to help were dashed. Also, each of the women was weighed down from carrying their packs and walking in the wet, heavy sand and by their fears for Stan and Samuel's survival. When they got back to the SOS sign, Amelia stopped near the water and knelt down facing the ocean, her hands up in the air pleading again and again for God's mercy. Allison knelt beside her and held her, praying out loud with her.

Laura sat down in the sand behind them and pulled her knees up to her forehead. "I'm so sorry, I'm so sorry," she said through her tears.

When they finally got back to the boat, it was almost dark, and both Adric and Peter were standing by a roaring fire. Sparks flew up into the air in spirals of smoke as the coconuts, bark, and broken branches crackled fiercely. A large heap of driftwood was drying out beside the fire. Adric had cooked a half-dozen river shrimp and had laid them on one of the wooden seats of the boat. Next to them were several plastic bottles of water.

"We saw you coming, and we wanted to have a meal ready for you," Peter said. "I take it that you found no one."

"No one," Allison said.

"I didn't either. The beach is empty."

Laura made no comment.

Peter sensed her continued anger towards him. "I'm sorry that I had to hold you back in the boat, but none of us would have made it if we hadn't turned to shore when we did. There just wasn't enough gas."

"You don't know that," Laura replied. "What we do know is that leaving them behind in the water has drastically cut their chances of survival."

Overhearing, Adric responded angrily, "I'm tired of all of this. We did our best to find them. If we hadn't turned to come ashore when we did, we would still be adrift or maybe even dead. The stark truth is that your father has incurable cancer and not long to live anyway."

"That is the coldest thing I think I have ever heard anyone say," Laura said with disgust. "Yes, my father may be dying, but Samuel has a long life before him."

"That's enough, Mother," Allison said putting her arm around her. "It's no one's fault. It's not yours, it's not theirs. We did all that we were able to do. We are safe, and Stan and Samuel's lives are in God's hands."

# CHAPTER 30

As much as Stan talked to Samuel, he talked an equal amount to the God he wasn't sure existed. He prayed for protection from sharks, and he prayed for the *Samuel Pinto*—or at least a sturdy tree trunk—to appear. Each time a rolling wave raised them high, Stan scanned the waters. Each time he was disappointed, for wherever he looked, there was only water.

Then suddenly, when he had almost lost hope, one of his prayers was answered. While the *Samuel Pinto* never appeared, the tree did. It was the splintered trunk of a coconut tree floating on the crest of a wave not more than twenty meters from them. At first Stan thought it might be a large fish or even a shark, but then as the wave rose again, he was able to make out its roots. He let out a shout of thanks that frightened Samuel by its suddenness and made him start crying once more.

Stan decided that he had to get to the trunk as quickly as he could before it passed them by or crashed into them. He explained to the little boy his plan so that he wouldn't be afraid. "Samuel, I want you to hold onto this ring tightly, and together we're going to swim to that tree over there in the water. I'm going to put my arm around your chest so you'll be safe. Is that OK?"

Samuel nodded.

Stan turned on his side and wrapped his right arm around Samuel's chest and the ring. With his left arm, he did an awkward side stroke and kicked hard, maneuvering as best he could towards the log. The effort was exhausting, as he had to pull both Samuel and the container. He took five strokes and then rested; five more strokes and then rested.

Finally, after some ten minutes of struggle and mouthfuls of salt water, Stan was able to come parallel to the tree trunk. He grabbed it with his left arm, and he celebrated his victory, panting in exhaustion.

When he had partially recovered from his efforts, Stan thought through what he had to do next. The first thing, he decided, was to pull the container and the tree close to one another. Then he would use the rope still tied to the container to bind them together. That way, he figured, he could make the container and tree trunk into a kind of awkward outrigger canoe.

"Samuel, we're going to make us a boat, and you're going to be the captain," Stan said to the young boy. "I'm going to need your help, though. I have to have both my hands free, so what I'm going to do is let you float on your own for a short while. Don't worry, though, I've tied you to my waist so that we won't be separated. I want you to be brave and not cry. I won't be holding you like I am now, but I'll be near you, and I won't let you get hurt. Everything will be fine, and then we will be able to get you to your mommy sooner. Is that OK?"

Samuel's face was crunched as if he were about to cry, but he didn't. He didn't say anything but just continued to hold tightly to the ring that helped keep him afloat.

After untying the rope that connected the container to the lifesaving ring, Stan let go of Samuel and of the ring so that they floated on their own, but they were still connected to his waist by five meters of rope. Samuel didn't cry.

With both hands now free, Stan pulled the fiberglass container towards him with the rope that was attached at the other end to one of the container's handles. When the container bumped against the log, he looped the loose end of the rope twice around the middle of the trunk and then under the container to the handle on the other side and back again over the top of the container to the log. He then pulled the two together as tightly as he was able and tied several knots to secure them.

Once he was finished, Stan reached up and grabbed the handle of the container. After several unsuccessful attempts, he was finally able to place his knees onto the splintered tree trunk, pushing it under water while tipping the container towards him. Stan pulled off the snap-on lid of the container, sliding it into the ocean from under the rope. Holding on to the side of the container with his left hand, he used his right to sweep out the ice and water and dozens of river shrimp from inside it into the ocean.

"That was the easy part, Samuel, now comes the really hard part."

Steadying himself on the log, Stan reached deep into the container and pulled out a false bottom, letting it float away like the lid. From beneath that bottom, he pulled out the seven packets of cocaine wrapped in plastic that he had hidden there two days before. He threw them one by one into the sea.

As the packets slowly floated away past Samuel, Stan felt a mixture of remorse and of relief. "You're a valuable little boy!" Stan exclaimed.

Once the container was empty, Stan pulled Samuel back to him using the rope around his waist. "Now it's time for you to get into your boat. You'll be the captain, but I want you to sit down and stay still inside. Otherwise, you might tip your boat over. Once you're in there, you'll only be able to see the rope and sky over your head, but I'm going to be outside right here hooked to you with this other rope. You won't see me, but I promise you that I'll be here. If you wonder if I'm still here, you can pull on the rope and I will pull back. I'll be your boat's motor and rudder guiding you to the shore and to your mommy."

Stan used all of his strength to raise the little boy out of the water until he was standing on the log against the container, supported by Stan's right hand.

"I want you to get in the box. OK?"

"OK."

The little boy put his left leg over the top as Stan steadied the container with his left hand and pushed Samuel's bottom with the right. Samuel then lowered himself inside and disappeared.

"Can you sit down and be still?" Stan asked.

There was a pause and some movement inside.

"OK," Samuel said.

There was another pause and then the voice of Samuel came through the container, "Cold."

Stan saw that the rain was still coming down with force into the container. "If there's still ice in there, you can throw it out. There will be a lot of rainwater to drink if you need it."

There was movement again, and a chunk of ice went out into the ocean. Then Samuel sat down again and was still.

Stan then turned the log and the container so that they pointed in the direction the waves were heading, and he began to kick slowly.

"I'm right here, Samuel, and we're going to ride the waves together until we get to the shore."

All of Stan's thoughts and efforts now were concentrated on Samuel—on reassuring and protecting him. Stan's main tasks were to keep the container level and the log pointed to land.

Often, the container tipped in the waves, and Stan would steady it. Several times, Samuel pulled at the rope in order to see if Stan was still there. Whenever he did so, Stan pulled back and talked reassuringly to him. "I'm here, Samuel. Don't be afraid. Don't be afraid." Soon Samuel's fears must have subsided as the rope pulling and calls for reassurance from inside the container ceased.

At the same time, Stan found his own fears disappearing. It was something he could not explain. In place of his terror of failing, of dying, and of God, Stan felt a growing sense of peace welling up within him. The waves that before were so threatening now became allies, lifting and carrying them towards the shore. The dark, silent underwater world that before had caused Stan such fear when his head was submerged was now a refuge from the cacophony of the storm. The God whom he doubted, now surely existed. The God whom he feared, now became to him the God who loved and cared for him.

Stan had an assurance and peace that he had never experienced before in his life. It was as if he and Samuel were being held in the arms of a loving Father. Stan no longer needed to prove himself or to be right or to be praised; he no longer needed to fear death or to fear God—just to let go and trust. It was strange, but somehow the former Stan was no more, and it felt as if a new Stan had taken his place. Stan laughed out loud at the irony of it all. Here he was lost at sea and dying of cancer, but he now felt free, unafraid, loving, and profoundly loved for the first time in his life! Adding to his comfort, the heavy rain stopped.

As night came on, Stan talked constantly to Samuel, letting him know that he was still there and that they were safe and all would be well. He told stories to him and expressed his hopes for him. He sang the songs that Elizabeth had sung to Laura as a child. Most of all, Stan expressed gratitude. He thanked God for the container, the life-buoy, the ropes, the log, the lifejackets, the slackening of the storm, and for the waves carrying them towards land. He thanked God for life, for the constant and undeserved love of Elizabeth, for Laura and Allison, for Amelia and Samuel, for the friendship of Luis, for the forgiveness of Marcos, for the gift of the inheritance from his father, and most of all for God's love for him, despite all that he had done to ignore, deny, and dishonor it.

As he continued to kick and then rest, and then kick and rest, Stan didn't even search anymore for a boat to save them. He knew deep in his spirit that he was already safe and that all would be well. He knew also that what was actually carrying them to the shore was not his own efforts, but the waves of God's grace.

As the waves became gentler and the night quieter, Stan relaxed even more, and turned on his back and looked up at the sky. The clouds had parted, and pinpoints of starlight sparkled in the sky and on the water. A white seagull hovered overhead in the light of the moon, and as Stan watched her, she spiraled down and came to rest on the ocean near him. And then, while Stan and the seagull observed each other, Stan heard the sounds of land—of monkeys and of gently breaking waves on the sand.

As he turned over again and looked in front of him, Stan saw the most beautiful scene he had ever seen in his life—the beach shimmering in the moonlight. Stan put his feet down, and his toes touched sand.

"We're home, Samuel," he said, as he steadied his feet. Chest deep in water, Stan pushed the log and container the final few meters to the shore. This time, however, no harsh undertow pulled him back into the deep. This time, the waves pushed him gently forward. When the front of the log scraped the sand, Stan reached into the container and pulled out a wet and half-asleep little boy whose hair was caked with dried blood, but who no longer bled. Stan carried him out of the water and on to the beach. Hugging him tightly to his chest, Stan fell to his knees onto the sand and wept tears of joy and gratitude. He then placed the little boy gently on the ground and lay down beside him and fell asleep.

# CHAPTER 31

Stan awoke suddenly with a tug from the rope that still connected him to Samuel. The little boy had moved some five meters away and was playing with a glistening seashell that he had found on the beach. When Samuel saw Stan sitting up, he asked, "Go see Mommy?" as if nothing had happened.

"Yes," Stan replied, "but we have to find her first. She's looking for you as well."

Stan got up and held his watch close to his eyes so that he could see what time it was. It was 4:30 a.m. He shook his head in disbelief as he recalled what they had just come through, and thanked God again that he had been able to get Samuel safely to land.

Stan looked back out at the sea; it was now calm. The only waves breaking did so with a comforting soft, steady sound as they touched the sand. The night sky was clear and the stars shone brightly. The sea breezes now caressed rather than menaced. It was as if the last twenty-four hours were a nightmare that had never happened.

But it had happened! The container and the log that had saved them were still there on the sand as proof. A rope still tied him to Samuel. Stan slowly untied it and took off Samuel's lifejacket and his own and placed them in the container with the life-buoy ring. He then pulled the container farther onto the beach beyond the reach of the tide.

"We won't need these anymore," he said to Samuel. "Now we have got to figure out what is the quickest way to get you to your mommy. She wants to see you very badly."

Stan thought of the last desperate look that he had seen on Amelia's face. He knew that the agony she felt as she saw them disappear was overwhelming. He wondered what had happened to her and his family. *Have they made it to Bluefields or Monkey Point? Have they come ashore because they had so little fuel left? Or, have they been carried out to sea or capsized? Please God, don't let it be that!*

Stan's fears were calmed by the thought that if the currents brought Samuel and him to shore, surely they would also bring the others to safety. Also, Rosa would know that they hadn't made it to Bluefields and would start a search for them.

"Please God," he prayed out loud, "just one more request—that they be safe."

Stan tried to figure out what his next steps should be. Looking for any signs of human life, he searched the ocean, the land, and the sky for the lights of boats, airplanes, or houses. To the south was nothing but darkness. To the north he saw what he thought might be a flickering of a fire on the beach with a thin column of orange against the horizon. He decided that north was the direction that he should go.

Stan lifted Samuel on to his shoulders. "You get to ride piggyback for awhile. We have a long walk ahead of us, but we'll find someone to help us get you to your mother."

The wet sand was heavy, and Stan's bare feet were sensitive to the shells, rocks, and sticks that lay hidden in it. That coupled with his weariness made Stan's progress slow.

Within twenty-five minutes, they came to a wide but shallow stream of water that cut the deserted beach and entered the ocean. Stan dipped his hand into it and after tasting it first, gave both himself and Samuel a drink. He then picked up Samuel again and carefully crossed the stream to the other side.

Out over the sea the faint pinks and blues of pre-dawn turned into the strong oranges and yellows of dawn itself. Looking down the beach in front of him, Stan could now see wisps of smoke rising where in the night he had seen only a thin column of orange.

"It's a fire, Samuel. There must be people there who can help us." A new quickness came to his stride as he walked in the direction of the column of smoke. Soon, in the morning light he noticed other footprints in the sand, and then he came upon the large SOS sign. He let out a cry of glee. "I know it's them, Samuel. I know they made it to safety."

# CHAPTER 32

It was as light was dawning that Laura first saw what she thought was a lone figure coming towards them in the distance. She had gotten up to collect more branches to put on the fire, and then she had sat down in the sand by Amelia, who was still praying and scanning the ocean for signs of Samuel and Stan as she had done all night. The others were still sleeping—Peter and Adric on the north side of the boat, and Allison on the south side near where Laura and Amelia were sitting.

Laura, like Amelia, had been unable to sleep and had occupied herself by keeping the fire blazing and going over and over in her mind that split second in which she had let go of Samuel. Because of her, both Samuel and her father were now lost at sea. Amelia and Allison continued to reassure her that it wasn't her fault, but it did no good. She knew that it was her fault. She cried often during the night, and for the first time in many years, she prayed. She also constantly swept the ocean and the beaches with her eyes looking for any hopeful sign of Samuel and of her father.

"Amelia, look down the beach," she said, grabbing her shoulder. "There's someone coming towards us."

Amelia stood up and strained her eyes to make out the figure. "Is it one person or two?" Before Laura could answer, Amelia let out a shriek of joy. "It's them! It's them!" She ran towards her son, and Laura ran after her.

"It's your mommy, Samuel," Stan exclaimed in delight when he saw them. "We made it home!" He swung Samuel from his shoulders and held him to his chest as he too ran as quickly as he was able towards them.

The meeting of the women with Stan and Samuel was full of tears of joy. Amelia grabbed her son and hugged him to her breast, smothering him with kisses. Stan embraced Laura and didn't want to let her go. All four of them fell to the sand on their knees, crying and laughing and hugging like crazy people.

Allison, Peter, and Adric heard the noise and jumped up, at first confused as to what was happening. When it became clear to Allison, she ran towards her grandfather and embraced him and her mother, overflowing with happiness.

When they were able to regain their composure, they began walking back towards the fire, hand in hand and still laughing. Peter took out his camera and snapped some pictures of them coming towards them. He then came over to shake Stan's hand. "I knew you would make it," he said. "What a story this will be!"

Adric also came over and congratulated him.

Peter asked Stan to tell them how he and Samuel had survived, but Laura insisted first on cleaning Samuel's cut and giving them something to eat and to drink. She pulled out the bottle of water that she still had in her pack and gave it to Amelia to use to clean the cut. She then got out a sandwich and another bottle of water and gave it to her father and to Samuel. As they ate, Laura kept touching them to make sure they were real. Her face was alight with happiness.

After munching hungrily on the sandwich, Stan answered Peter. "It was God's grace that saved us—by way of the ropes, the life-buoy ring, the container, a log that appeared, protection from the sharks, and the waves carrying us to shore."

"We looked and looked for you, but we couldn't find you," Peter said. "We were almost out of gas, so we decided that we had to come to shore. Otherwise, we might have overturned or been swept out to sea."

"You and Adric decided that," Laura interjected. "Amelia, Allison, and I wanted to keep looking."

"It's all right," Stan said. "It was the right decision. I'm just so glad that you're all safe. Can you imagine what it would have been to survive and then to find out that you hadn't?" He hugged Laura and Allison again.

"And little Samuel here is the bravest, most trusting person I know. He obeyed everything I said to do and even slept through most of the ordeal inside the container." Stan laughed. "He just wanted to be with his mommy."

Amelia hugged Samuel to her. "Thank you, thank you, Mr. Stan."

"And where's the container?" Adric asked.

Stan looked at him and smiled knowingly. "I emptied everything out into the sea to give Samuel room to sit."

"Everything?" Adric asked.

"Everything," Stan replied. "All of the shrimp and all of the white lobster."

Adric shook his head in astonishment at what Stan had done and just now had said.

"White lobster?" Peter asked. "Isn't that the name they use here for cocaine?"

"It is," Stan said. "That's what it was."

"I don't understand," Laura said.

"About a month ago, I found a bale of it washed up on the beach when I was coming back from Costa Rica," Stan explained. "I thought it was going to be my financial salvation. Selling it, I would have money for the airstrip and maybe even for my cancer treatment. I hid it under false bottoms in the three containers and was going to deliver it yesterday to a buyer that Adric knows in Bluefields."

Laura couldn't believe what she was hearing. "Are you saying that you were dealing in drugs?!"

"I guess you could say that," Stan answered matter-of-factly. "It was the only way that I saw to finance the airstrip project."

Adric spoke angrily in Spanish to Stan. "I can't believe that you are telling them this."

Stan smiled. "And I can't believe that I was actually going to do it!" With that, he got up and walked over to the boat. "I've got to destroy all of it."

Stan took off the lids of the remaining two containers. He peered into them and was surprised to see that their false bottoms had been removed and that they were now empty—except for some lifejackets, ponchos, and a dozen or so shrimp. He turned to the others and asked, "Where are the packets?"

No one said anything.

Stan looked straight at Adric. "You're the only one who knew they were there. What did you do with them?"

Adric stared daggers at him but said nothing.

"I think I know," Laura said. "After Amelia, Allison, and I left to find help, I looked back here with binoculars and saw Adric burying something in the ground."

"Where?" Stan asked.

Laura looked behind them to the low sand dunes where the forest met the edge of the beach. She pointed to a spot about thirty meters away. "I think it was over there by those two palm trees."

As Adric watched helplessly, Stan walked over to the forest with Laura, and she pointed out the approximate spot. Coconut branches were strewn over the area, but it was clear to Stan that the sand under them had been recently disturbed. Stan got down on his hands and knees and started to dig. Within less than ten seconds, he came upon the first of the plastic packets of the drug.

Peter, who had followed them with Allison, raised his camera to take a picture.

"No pictures of this," Laura ordered.

He put down the camera.

When Stan had dug out all of the remaining thirteen packets of cocaine, he asked Laura and Allison to help him carry them over to the bonfire that was still burning with considerable force. They did so, and when they got close to the fire, they arranged them on the sand beside those that Stan had already put down.

"Now I want you all to get back and not inhale any of the smoke that is going to spread."

Adric was besides himself with anger, "You're going to burn them just like that? They're worth tens of thousands of dollars!"

"I *am* going to burn them 'just like that,'" Stan replied. "If I don't, the drugs will ruin hundreds of lives."

"Then how are you going to pay what you owe to the workers on the airstrip?" Adric asked.

"I don't know," Stan said. "But I do know that I have to burn them." Stan threw two of the packets on the flames, and they ignited almost immediately.

"You fool!" Adric yelled. "The dealers will kill you when they find out that you did this."

Stan smiled and threw two more packs on the fire. "I'm already a walking dead man."

"They'll come after me, too. I told them that you could be trusted," Adric pleaded. He picked up a paddle from the boat and came towards Stan.

"What are you going to do, Adric?" Stan asked. "Kill me in front of my daughter and granddaughter and steal the cocaine? How do you think that you'll get away with that?"

"You owe me, too," Adric answered. "You promised me a thousand dollars for making contact with the buyers."

Laura, Allison, and Peter came towards the fire and stood between Adric and Stan. Peter picked up a heavy branch from the fuel pile. "Put the paddle down," Laura ordered Adric. "I'll pay you whatever he owes you. Just forget that this ever happened, and we won't get the police after you for your threats and involvement in drug trafficking."

Adric looked at her and then at Peter with the raised tree limb in his hand. He lowered the paddle as he spoke to Stan, "If God didn't want you to have the cocaine, it wouldn't have washed up from the sea in front of you. I expect to be paid for my troubles and the danger you have put me in."

"I said that I will pay you the thousand," Laura reiterated. She turned to her father. "Who else knows about this?"

"Just Adric and myself," Stan said. "Everyone thinks that I am getting the money for the airstrip from a foreign investor in Bluefields."

"And that's the way it will be," Laura replied. "Except I'm the foreign investor now." She picked up two cocaine packets at the feet of her father, looked at them carefully, and then threw them into the fire. Allison also threw in several.

When all of the packets were burning, Stan backed up mesmerized and watched all of the money, hopes, and pain associated with the packets go up in smoke. He laughed. "It's like a thank offering of incense to God."

Adric turned his back on them, unable to watch.

When the packets were finally consumed by the fire, Peter asked, "Now what?"

"First, let's see what our situation is with the boat and fuel." Stan went to the boat in order to investigate if it had been damaged. Satisfied that it hadn't, he examined the two fuel containers. One was empty, and the other held about five centimeters of fuel. "One possibility is to use the gasoline that we still have and go as far as we can towards Monkey Point, hugging the shore. We won't make it, but we'll get closer, and then we can walk the rest of the way. At Monkey Point, we probably can buy more gas to get us to Bluefields."

"I'm never getting in that boat again, nor is Allison," Laura said, shaking her head with determination.

Stan smiled and nodded. "Or we could wait here, hoping that someone comes to look for us and will see the fire and the boat."

"I vote for that," Laura said. "Rosa and Felipe will be worried that we didn't call yesterday, and they'll get in touch with Luis and with Amelia's parents. Then they'll start looking for us. I know Rosa!"

"Amelia?" Stan asked. "What is your vote?"

"It's a long way to walk with Samuel," Amelia said, "and I don't want to get into the boat again with Samuel without gas."

"Allison and Peter?" Stan asked.

"Stay here at least for today," Peter replied. "If no one comes by tomorrow, we can always start walking. I presume we still have some shrimp left so we won't go hungry."

Stan nodded. "When I looked in the container, we had about a dozen."

"I agree with staying today," Allison said. "I also think that we should build the fire as large as we can and make a big SOS nearby. We can use clothes and brush to make it more visible against the sand."

"So it's decided," Stan said without asking Adric's opinion. "We'll stay here today and make some signs to draw attention. If no one comes, then tomorrow we'll head towards Monkey Point." He looked at his watch. "It's now almost eight o'clock. Let's get busy. Peter and Adric, you help me get branches for the fire, while you girls make the SOS."

Peter followed Stan back to the forest bordering the beach. Adric stayed where he was, still glowering at them. He was not going to accept orders from Stan.

Within half an hour, they had stacked a large pile of broken limbs and trunks by the fire, and Stan and Peter began to throw them in to build it up.

As for the women, they traced out a large SOS in the sand and made it more visible by putting extra clothes, lifejackets, packs, and sticks inside the letters. Then they sat down and played with Samuel and watched the sea and air for signs of a rescue party.

# CHAPTER 33

It was ten-thirty when they saw the chopper. Allison, who heard it first, shouted from the ocean's edge where she was standing and pointed into the sun. When they observed the speck northeast of them over the ocean, it was some ten kilometers away, heading south. Excited, they all stood up and began to wave anything they could find—oars, lifejackets, clothes, and branches to attract attention. For several minutes, Laura feared it was too far away to see them and that whoever was inside was concentrating on looking for a boat on the sea. But then the helicopter suddenly changed its course and came towards them. When it did so, they all let out a cheer.

Laura ran to get her binoculars from her pack, and when the helicopter got close enough to hover near them, she focused the lenses on it. It was Felipe's helicopter, and Laura could even make out Fernando who was piloting it. In the co-pilot's seat was a man with binoculars looking at her and waving. She imagined that it must be Felipe, but she couldn't tell for sure.

The helicopter landed some thirty-five meters from them on the brown sand, slinging stinging grains of it in their direction. Laura and the others lowered their heads and covered their faces to protect themselves, and Amelia turned her back to it in order to shield Samuel.

After the engine was turned off and the blades slowed down, Laura saw a man and a woman come running towards them, ducking below the blades. Fernando followed them. It was only when they got closer that Laura recognized who they were. It was her mother, Elizabeth, and Antonio Lopez.

When Elizabeth reached Laura and Allison, she encircled them both with her arms and held them to her, weeping in joy. "You're safe! Thank God, you're safe!"

Stan came up behind them and put his arms around all three of them.

Elizabeth looked up at him through her tears and smiled. She released the girls and hugged him tightly and kissed him.

"Is anyone hurt?" Antonio asked as he watched.

"Just Samuel who has a cut on his head," Laura said. "It could have been so much worse. We're just happy to be alive and that you've found us!"

"What happened?" Antonio asked as he came over to examine Samuel.

"Unbelievable things!" Laura replied. "We ran into a terrible storm, and somehow Samuel was knocked overboard along with a container. Dad saved Samuel's life and swam with him over ten miles to shore. Our boat almost capsized."

"We didn't have enough gas to make it to Monkey Point or to go back to San Juan del Norte, so we decided just to wait here," Stan added. "We thought Rosa and Felipe would send Fernando to look for us when we didn't call from Bluefields. But we certainly didn't expect the president's advisor and Elizabeth to come looking for us, too!"

"Mrs. Hollins and I insisted on coming," Antonio said. "When Rosa called and asked for help, I thought that I could organize a government rescue effort in Bluefields if needed."

"And do you think I would possibly not come if you were in danger?" Elizabeth asked.

"They were my lookouts," Fernando said. "It was Mrs. Hollins who saw you first on the beach."

He, too, came over to examine the cut on Samuel's head. "I have a first aid kit in the helicopter. It looks like he's going to need some stitches, but right now we can put some ointment on the cut and bandage it."

He started to walk back towards the helicopter and then paused and turned around again. "We brought a thirty-gallon container of gasoline and some food and water in case we found you drifting at sea," he said to Stan. "We attached it to a long rope so that we could lower it to you. I can bring that too."

"Wonderful," Stan said. "That's enough fuel to get the boat back to San Juan del Norte. I wasn't feeling good about leaving it here."

"After what you've just been through, you're not thinking about going out to sea again in that boat, are you?" Laura asked her father, alarmed. "We're not letting you out of our sight again."

"It'll be fine. The day is beautiful, and I can't leave the boat and motor to be stolen. I have too much invested in them for that.

215

"Why don't you let Adric take the boat back to San Juan del Norte for you," Laura suggested. "That way we can all stick together as a family, and he can keep it as security for the money that I promised." She looked at Adric to see if he agreed.

"Is that OK with you?" Stan asked Adric.

Adric had a scowl on his face, but he agreed. "There's certainly no reason for me to go to Bluefields now."

"Then that would leave eight of us for Fernando to carry back in the helicopter," Antonio said. "He could take four of you now and then come back within a couple of hours and take the other four of us." He unselfishly put himself in the group that would wait.

"Why don't the rest of you go first, and Stan, Laura, Allison, and I will wait," Elizabeth countered. "It's been so many years since we've been together as a family, and we have so much to catch up on." She laughed. "It's also my chance to see the Atlantic Coast of Nicaragua for the first time!"

"I agree with Elizabeth," Stan said. "Samuel needs to see a doctor, and Amelia's family probably is frantic with worry. She can then get in touch with Marcos and Adric's family and tell them the plans."

"OK," Antonio said. "First, let's get Samuel taken care of and get the gasoline. Then the rest of us will load up and be on our way so you won't have to wait too long for Fernando's return."

Antonio, Stan, and Fernando walked to the helicopter in order to get the first aid kit and the gasoline. As they did so, Amelia and Peter went to the boat to get their packs and to gather up their loose clothing from the SOS sign.

A few minutes later, Stan and Antonio returned to the boat with the first aid kit and the gasoline container. As for Fernando, he stayed at the helicopter to radio to Bluefields the news that they had found the missing persons and to prepare for the return trip.

After Stan had set down the gasoline by the boat, he went back to where Antonio was washing Samuel's wound with bottled water from the helicopter. Once the wound was clean, Antonio put some ointment on it using gauze. He decided not to bandage it because it was no longer bleeding.

When Antonio was finished, Stan picked up Samuel and hugged him. "We've been through a lot together, little man. I'm so proud of you!" He then handed Samuel back to Amelia and said, "When you call Marcos, don't forget to leave a message for Adric's family about his returning today by boat."

Amelia nodded and embraced Stan, thanking him again. "I will never forget what you did for Samuel," she added.

As Stan, Laura, and Allison accompanied the travelers to the helicopter, Stan joked with Peter. "This might have been a little more adventure than you bargained for when you came to San Juan del Norte."

Peter laughed. "What an article I'm going to write!"

When they got to the door, Laura hugged Amelia and Samuel. She then came over to Antonio and embraced him. In a low voice she said, "It means so much to me that you came searching for us. I can't begin to tell you how much it means."

"Of course I came," Antonio replied for her ears only. "You're very important to me, Laura." He then added for all to hear, "Rosa and Felipe and I will be waiting for you at the Bluefields airport."

The doors of the helicopter closed, and the Hollins family returned to where Adric was waiting behind the boat by the gasoline.

When Fernando saw that they were at a safe distance, he started the rotors. A few minutes later, the helicopter lifted off.

After the wind turbulence on the beach had subsided, Stan picked up the gasoline container Fernando had brought from Bluefields, and with Adric's help, he filled one of the boat's fuel tanks.

"If you stay close to the shore it should be more than enough to get you to San Juan del Norte," Stan said to him, "Now all we all have to do is shove the boat back into the water."

With the help of the women, he and Adric pushed the boat the five meters to the water and then out beyond the softly breaking waves. Adric pulled himself into the boat, and after putting on his lifejacket and hooking up the gasoline lines, he started the motor.

"How far down the beach did you make shore?" he yelled above the rumble to Stan.

"About four or five kilometers—maybe a kilometer on the other side of the first big stream you see cutting through the beach. You'll see a log attached to the container and inside it are life preservers."

Adric nodded and yelled, "When will you be back in San Juan del Norte?"

"I don't know. Not before I have the money to pay you and the workers. I'll get in touch with the mayor and Marcos. You can keep the boat as security until I pay you all."

Stan waved as Adric revved up the motor and then slowly headed south. Stan grinned ironically at Allison and Laura. "You can be sure that it's going to take him awhile to get back. He'll be looking for those seven white lobster packets that I dumped into the sea."

# CHAPTER 34

After Adric and the boat had left for San Juan del Norte, Stan suggested that they all go over to the dunes and sit under the palm trees. "We've got a couple of hours to wait for the helicopter to return, and that way we can get out of the sun."

"It *is* hot," Elizabeth said. The sun was now almost overhead, and its light and heat were reflecting off the sand and the water.

As they walked to the forest edge near the dunes, Stan spontaneously put his arm around Elizabeth's waist. Laura and Allison, who followed behind, noticed and smiled at each other.

Stan found a small dune with blades of green grass popping out, not far from the spot where Adric had hidden the cocaine. It was a comfortable place in the shade of the palms, blessed by the soft music and caresses of a light breeze. Stan sat down between Elizabeth and Laura, while Allison leaned against the trunk of a palm tree, as they faced the wide brown beach and the vast but now calm sea. The view reminded Stan of that last tumultuous time he and Elizabeth had sat together on the park bench by the ocean in Miami.

"You know, I always wanted to come to visit the Atlantic when we lived in Managua, but we never did," Elizabeth said. "It's so beautiful and peaceful here."

"Today it is," Laura said, "but yesterday the storm almost killed us."

"Actually," Stan said, "yesterday the storm saved me."

"What in the world do you mean by that?" Laura looked at her father quizzically.

Stan smiled. "What I mean is that yesterday that storm helped me wake up. You might even say that it baptized me. It changed me from one person into another." He was silent for a few seconds, and then he reached out and found Elizabeth's and Laura's hands in the sand and squeezed them. "I really don't know where to start. I guess I'll just go to the heart of the matter and say I'm so sorry for the way that I've hurt you both over the years. I've been a pompous, self-righteous, driven, selfish ass."

Allison shook her head, giving her grandfather a supportive smile.

Stan smiled back at her. "And I'll probably continue to be an ass! But even so, something changed inside me yesterday in the storm." He paused for a moment as he searched for what he wanted to say. "It's really hard to describe. I guess the closest is to say that I learned what love is. I got out of myself for a little while and cared—really cared—about someone else. All I could think about was getting Samuel back to his mother and reuniting with you and asking you for your forgiveness."

Both Elizabeth and Laura squeezed his hands.

"I know now what Jesus meant when he said that only after you lose yourself can you find yourself," Stan said, looking out at the wide sky and sea. "Losing yourself gives you such freedom and joy!" None of the others said anything.

"Yesterday, I also learned not only what it is to love, but what is to be loved," Stan added. "Again, I don't know how the transformation occurred, but it did. At first I was so desperate and fearful, scared of sharks, of drowning, of losing Samuel, of death and judgment, and then suddenly I was at peace. I felt God's love. I felt his grace in the miracles of the container, the ropes, the lifejackets, the log showing up, and in the waves carrying us to shore. I began to trust God, much like Samuel trusted me. Somehow, in the midst of the terror, I felt a deep tranquility. I still do."

"That's wonderful, Stan," Elizabeth said. "I think that the happiest moment of my life was seeing all of you from the helicopter, safely on the beach."

"It amazes me that all of you came to Nicaragua when you found out that I was sick," Stan said. "I don't deserve that. I know how I've hurt you with my unfaithfulness, my lying, and my responsibility for Clay's death."

"You weren't responsible for Daddy's death, Grandfather," Allison said.

"Allison is right," Laura added. "You weren't responsible, even though I've done my best to blame you all of these years. Yesterday I learned my own lesson about responsibility and guilt when the wave knocked Samuel out of my grip." She looked at her father. "I'm sorry, too."

"The past is the past," Elizabeth said. "I'm just so grateful that we're all safe and together."

They sat together for a while enjoying the moment. Several seagulls alighted on the beach near the water and walked back and forth looking for morsels to eat.

"But we still have to figure out what we're going to do next," Laura said. She looked at her father. "Are you going to come back to Nashville with us for treatment for your cancer?"

"Yes, if it will make you happy. I just don't want to be a financial burden on you." Stan smiled. "I may have been transformed, but I still have a lot of pride!" He paused and added, "You know, it's the strangest thing, but after this experience, I'm not worried anymore about the cancer."

"But we are," Elizabeth said.

"And you won't be a financial burden either because you turn sixty-five in a month and will be eligible for Medicare," Laura added.

Stan laughed out loud. "You know, that's true! I had forgotten about that. Come to think of it, it's the one advantage of getting older!"

"So it's all taken care of," Allison said gleefully.

"But what about my responsibilities for the hotel, for paying Adric and the workers at the airstrip?" Stan asked. He looked at Laura. "Were you serious when you told Adric that you would take care of that?"

"Very," Laura said. "I haven't even touched your father's legacy to me, and I'll also talk to the Danforths and to Felipe and Rosa about the airstrip. In the big scheme of things, it's not a lot of money. Now that I've been there, I agree with you that an airstrip is important for the town, especially for medical emergencies."

"Maybe Antonio could help, too," Elizabeth suggested. "He seems to really care for you," she continued, looking at Laura. "He was so worried about you and insisted on dropping everything at his office to come this morning."

Stan was fascinated. "Now wouldn't that be something?!"

"What do you mean?" Laura asked.

"I mean if you and Antonio ever got together. He's a powerful person in the government. Add to that your friendship with Rosa and Felipe." He paused as if thinking. "That would be fantastic—the philanthropist, the government planner, and the successful businessperson together. Then things could happen—not only in San Juan del Norte, but elsewhere."

"Antonio's a good man," Elizabeth added.

Laura blushed. "What's everyone trying to do? Be matchmakers! Antonio's a great person, but his life is here in his country, and my life is in Nashville with my family and friends and Clay's Foundation."

"That's something to think about," Stan said. He turned to Elizabeth. "Unfortunately, I didn't think about those things when we married. I was always so selfish, insisting only on fulfilling my own dreams. I really never seriously considered yours."

"We're all that way!" Allison interjected. "Maybe if we adjusted our lives to God's perspective on things, then we wouldn't be so unhappy all of the time."

"Yesterday, I would have said, 'Yeah, right!'" Stan said. "But you know, today I'm not quite so cynical. My ways haven't always turned out so well." He squeezed Elizabeth's hand again.

"What about the hotel and the landing strip and your other projects in San Juan del Norte?" Elizabeth asked. "Is that just what you want, or do you feel that it is also what God wants of you?"

Stan pondered. "That's a good question, Elizabeth, and I'm not sure I know the answer yet. Saving Samuel and asking your forgiveness were clear priorities for me. Now what I need to do in San Juan del Norte no longer is. I guess I feel that my projects there are good things, but they are also thoroughly contaminated by my sense of guilt and by my desire for praise and recognition and to prove myself right."

"Getting treatment for your cancer has to be in there somewhere as a top priority," Laura said.

Elizabeth nodded. "And afterwards, if you feel God's leading to you is to come back to San Juan del Norte and complete your work, then you should come back!" She paused a moment and then added. "And if you want me to come with you, I will. Laura and Allison don't need me so much anymore."

Stan looked at Elizabeth in astonishment. "You'd do that for me?"

"No, not just for you. But I would do it for God and you."

Stan put his arm around Elizabeth and squeezed her. "I'll never understand how you've put up with me all of these years."

Elizabeth grinned. "It hasn't been easy! Let's just say that both you and I are God's work in progress!"

"You'd love his hotel, Nana," Allison said. "It's eco-friendly and simple, but elegant in its own way."

"I just hope it stays in business long enough for you to see it one day," Stan said to Elizabeth.

"Why wouldn't it?" Elizabeth asked.

"Our room occupancy is so low, especially in the dry months when it's hard to get down the river. Without the airport, there just aren't enough tourists."

They were all quiet in their own thoughts when suddenly Laura exclaimed, "I've got an idea, Dad. Luis is looking for a place for his school, and Rosa and Felipe are willing to finance it, so why don't you rent out the hotel to him in the dry season? That will give you a steady income in the off-season months, and it will help him and help San Juan del Norte and the rest of the river as well."

"That's a great idea, Mom," Allison said. "Luis would love it. The hotel's on his family's property, he's an investor in it, and it's just the right size for the number of students he wants."

Stan thought a minute and then said, "It *is* a good idea, Laura. It's just strange that neither he nor I ever thought of it! Having the school in San Juan del Norte would bring attention to the area, and students could take part in local projects. The lodge could be a school half of the year and a hotel half of the year. It would be a huge catalyst for the region! Marcos and Amelia could run it all."

Laura nodded. "I think that the Danforths may want to become involved, too, as Luis's project sounds fascinating."

Stan got up and danced a little jig. Laughing, he pulled Laura to him, "I don't think I've ever been so grateful and happy in my life." He then reached down and pulled up Elizabeth and Allison. He embraced each of them. As they hugged each other, they looked like a football team huddling together to plan their next play.

For the next hour, they talked about many things while they waited for the return of the helicopter. Stan used the time to ask about Elizabeth's family and about old friends that he hadn't been in touch with for years. He also asked about Allison's studies at Davidson and about Laura's projects with the Clay Danforth Foundation. They kidded each other, laughed, held hands, and walked down the beach together, living in the joy of the moment.

# CHAPTER 35

When they heard the helicopter in the distance, all four of them ran towards the smoking coals of the fire and waved shirts to make sure Fernando could see them, now that there was no boat on the beach. He must have had no trouble because he came straight towards them, hovered and landed, again throwing up the stinging sand.

After the motor quieted, yet while the blades still circled overhead, Fernando got out of the helicopter, bending to avoid the blades as he came towards them. "You're going to have quite a welcoming party in Bluefields," was the first thing that he said to Stan in Spanish. "Rosa tried to keep the press away, but she wasn't able to. *El Diario* and *La Prensa* have asked for interviews and so have a couple of TV stations."

"But why?" Stan exclaimed. He was truly puzzled.

"The news got out late yesterday when Antonio started a government search. It's such a great story! You saving Samuel and making it to shore in such a storm," Fernando said.

Stan was not happy. "I really don't want to do an interview," he said. "I didn't save Samuel. It was God who saved us both!"

"You're just modest!" Fernando replied. "But don't worry. Antonio insisted that they could only take pictures now. You can decide later what you want to do about an interview after you've rested in Managua. Señor Felipe has arranged with the director of Costeña to have one of their Cessna Grand Caravans take you all back together from Bluefields, as not everyone can fit in the helicopter."

Fernando picked up Allison's and Laura's bags to carry them to the helicopter. Laura, however, stayed behind as the others followed him towards the machine. She took some pictures of them with the helicopter in the background, and when she caught up with them again, she asked Fernando to do her the favor of taking a photo of all of the family together with the still smoldering bonfire and the ocean in the background. "This is the happiest day of my life," she said, "and I want to record it with a photo."

Fernando gladly did so. Afterwards, he packed the bags underneath, and then they all climbed in. Stan got into the co-pilot seat and strapped himself in while the three women did the same in the back. As the helicopter lifted off and rose up into the sky, Laura took several more pictures of the beach, while Stan looked far out to sea. He thanked God for rescuing them all and for the healing and good that had come out of this disaster.

A few hundred feet above the ground, Fernando turned the helicopter north towards Bluefields. Instead of following the curved coast, Fernando headed in a straight line, passing over the enormous Indio Maíz Biological Preserve of dense virgin forest. As they flew above it, Stan pointed out the tiny, isolated settlement of Monkey Point way to the east on a high coastal bluff. This was where they were to have stopped for lunch in their boat trip to Bluefields the previous day.

Soon the carpet of green forest ended, and they were over the placid waters of Bluefields Bay. The bay near the forest was a lovely blue color, but turned to a muddy brown as they approached Nicaragua's main Caribbean port and home to forty-five thousand inhabitants. "We'll set down at the Bluefields's airport at the south of the town," Fernando explained.

As they got closer, Laura saw that the airport consisted of a single runway and a small terminal on a high point at the edge of the city. Fernando hovered over the concrete ramp for a moment and then slowly descended between a large Russian military helicopter from the Sandinista days and a Costeña Cessna Caravan. As he did so, a small crowd of some two dozen people emerged excitedly from the terminal and shaded their eyes as they looked up at them. Several of them had cameras and at least one person a television camera.

"Wait until the rotors stop before you get out," Fernando reminded them. "As for your bags, I'll take care of them and put them in the Costeña plane you'll take to Managua."

Once they were on the ground, Stan got out and opened the door and then helped the rest of his family descend. They all thanked Fernando as Antonio, Felipe, Rosa, Peter, and Amelia carrying Samuel came rapidly towards them with big grins on their faces. Accompanying them was a man in military uniform and two people whom Stan recognized as Amelia's parents.

It was joyful chaos when they met—tears and hugging, congratulations and expressions of thanks. Samuel reached out to Stan, who took him and hugged him. Amelia's parents cried and thanked Stan effusively.

"After what Amelia told the press about how you saved Samuel," Antonio joked, "you're no longer just '*el yanqui bueno*,' you're '*el yanqui superhéroe*!'"

Stan felt a hot flash of embarrassment come to his face. "They've got it all wrong," he said. "It was really Samuel who saved me!"

Antonio seemed confused by the remark, but added, "They're insisting on interviewing you, but I told them not now."

"Thank you!" Stan said. Two days ago, he would have relished such positive adulation, but today it seemed so false, ridiculous, and embarrassing.

"Maybe after you rest a day or two in Managua," Antonio suggested. Stan nodded.

"Speaking of Managua, we'll leave in about fifteen minutes, if that is OK with you," Felipe said to Stan. "We have a plane ready." He pointed to the Grand Caravan.

"But first," Rosa suggested pragmatically, "you might want to freshen up in the restrooms in the terminal."

"How can we ever repay you for all you and Felipe have done for us?" Elizabeth asked Rosa and Felipe as they walked arm in arm to the terminal.

"You don't have to. You're family to us, and anyway, we're the ones in debt to you, and we always will be."

When Stan and the others returned outside, Stan was immediately surrounded by the pushing reporters and photographers. Even though Antonio had made it clear that Stan was not going to do an interview, they still peppered him with questions and insisted that he pick up Samuel so that they could take pictures of them both.

Stan took Samuel from Amelia and answered politely and modestly as the TV camera filmed. "I did nothing heroic. All I did was to hold onto Samuel and trust God to deliver us, and he did. Samuel, here, was the one who was particularly brave."

With Antonio's and Felipe's intervention, Stan was finally able to get away from the reporters and join the others at the Cessna. When he got to the plane's steps, Felipe motioned for him and Elizabeth to get in first and the rest to follow. Stan hugged Amelia and Samuel one last time and told them that he would see them soon. Then he followed Elizabeth up the three steps into the plane. Bent over because of the low ceiling, they went to the front and took their seats right behind the two pilots, who greeted them with bright smiles and thumbs-up. The Hollins were followed by Peter, who took the single seat across from them. The rest sat in the seats behind them.

As the pilots went through their checklist, Stan and the others buckled up their seat belts. The pilots then revved up the motor and taxied out to the runway. The takeoff was noisy but smooth, and as the plane circled the airport and headed towards Managua, Stan could see people still outside the terminal waving at them. He and Elizabeth waved back.

Stan then turned and looked at his daughter and granddaughter seated behind him and he beamed. They smiled back, and Laura patted him on his arm. "It's the happiest day of my life, too," Stan said to Laura, remembering her earlier remark.

During the forty-five minute journey to Managua, Laura conversed animatedly with Antonio, who sat across the narrow aisle from her. Allison looked out the window at the mountains, fields, and forests of Nicaragua; she also secretly eavesdropped on her mother and smiled to herself.

As for Stan and Elizabeth, they talked little during the trip but said much. Stan reached out and held Elizabeth's hand, taking comfort in the feel of the gold wedding band that was still on her finger. He rubbed it with his fingers and then squeezed her hand three times—their private signal from years back for "I . . . love . . . you." Elizabeth returned the three squeezes and then looked at Stan and smiled through her tears. Her face incarnated the mixed happiness and sorrow of true Joy.

# EPILOGUE

# CHAPTER 36

When they got to Managua, Rosa and Felipe made sure that the Hollins family felt entirely at home, reiterating that they could stay at their house as long as they needed. They also made sure that no reporters bothered them so that they could adjust to each other and have a taste of normal family life once more. At Antonio's suggestion, Stan issued a press statement thanking everyone for their help and interest, but he gave no interview.

A few days later, as scheduled, Allison left on her flight back to Nashville, as she had to get back to her classes. Elizabeth and Laura, however, changed their return tickets for a week later, and they purchased another one for Stan. They needed the extra week in Nicaragua to give Stan time to put his affairs in order so that he could leave for an extended medical stay in Nashville.

Laura insisted on turning over to Stan all of the hundred and fifty thousand dollars her grandfather had left her in his will and that made it possible for Stan to resolve all of his financial obligations to Adelante, the laborers, and Adric. "I don't need the money as the Danforths have always been generous to me," she told her astonished father. "What is left over of the money from your obligations," she said, "you can use for your medical treatment or in any way you please."

Since Stan had to return to San Juan del Norte for a few days to settle his affairs, Felipe suggested that both he and Elizabeth accompany him by helicopter. "It will be faster for you, and it will give Elizabeth a chance to see a little of your life. As for me, I have to go to El Futuro anyway, and I've always wanted to see San Juan del Norte for myself."

Felipe also suggested that they pick up Luis again at El Futuro, and while they were in San Juan del Norte, they could all discuss together Laura's idea of using the installations of the Rainbow End's Lodge for Luis's leadership training school. He added, "Rosa also wants me to see if the Greytown landing strip is a project that our foundation can support.

She insists that the town needs some way to deal with medical emergencies like that of the little girl who was bitten by the snake."

Elizabeth and Stan immediately accepted Felipe's offer with gratitude, and two days after Allison returned to the U.S., the three of them left for San Juan del Norte. During the two and a half days they were there, Stan paid off his debts to Adric, the workers, and Adelante, and he left sufficient money with the mayor and the town council to finish the clearing and hardening of the landing strip. He also promoted Marcos to the position of manager of the Rainbow's End Lodge and left him money for operating expenses.

In their discussions with Stan and Marcos, both Luis and Felipe agreed that the lodge would be a perfect place for the training center, and they offered a generous sum for its half-year rental. They even allowed that some of the rooms in the hotel still be offered to guests during the rental period, as they could use bunk beds instead of single beds for the students. Luis also invited both Marcos and Amelia to be part-time students in the first class.

After visiting San Juan del Norte, Felipe was pleased with the difference that the elevated sidewalks he had financed there had made and agreed that his foundation would finance a similar elevated path from the dock to the landing strip in Greytown. He also promised the mayor that he would work with him and the town council to pressure the government to follow through on its earlier commitment to build a more permanent airport behind the town and improve its communication and health facilities.

As for Elizabeth, she loved the short visit to San Juan del Norte. Spending time with Amelia, Samuel, and Marcos, she was impressed with their love for and gratitude to Stan. She also greatly enjoyed the simple beauty of the lodge that Stan had created and appreciated his efforts to help the town.

The day they left Greytown to return to Managua was also highly emotional for her, as well as for Stan. Amelia, Marcos, Samuel, the mayor, and some three dozen of the townspeople came by boat to Greytown to say goodbye. The mayor made a short speech praising all of the help that Stan had given the town and wished him a quick recovery from his illness and a rapid return to San Juan del Norte. Both Stan and Elizabeth had tears in their eyes as they embraced each person there.

Meanwhile, back in Managua, while her parents were in San Juan del Norte, Laura spent her days with Rosa and Marta and the evenings with

Antonio. Antonio invited her out for dinner both of the evenings that her parents were gone, and the two of them talked long into the night about their love for their former spouses and the hurt they had felt at their losses. They also talked about their appreciation of each other and of their desires to get to know each other better. Laura even invited Antonio to come to Nashville on his vacation to see her and to meet her in-laws, the Danforths.

Antonio did come to Nashville on his next vacation, and both the Danforths and the Hollins gave their enthusiastic approval to his courtship of Laura. So did his own family and that of Flavia. Two years later, when the Sandinistas returned for their second chance at governing Nicaragua, Antonio left his government position and moved to Nashville where he accepted a position as an economics professor at Vanderbilt University. In a small ceremony, he and Laura were married.

Stan was able to attend the wedding in a wheel chair, but three weeks afterwards, surrounded by his much loved wife, Elizabeth, his daughter, Laura, his granddaughter, Allison, and his new son-in-law, Antonio, Stan died of complications from his cancer.

At the suggestion of Luis Romero, the Clay Danforth Foundation together with Felipe and Rosa's Foundation financed the building and furnishing of a memorial to him in San Juan del Norte, now also called San Juan de Nicaragua. The new Stan Hollins Historical Museum was much as Stan had envisaged it, celebrating the town's history as well as the flora and fauna of the region. It also had a separate room with five computers for public internet access by satellite.

The museum and the internet were inaugurated on Stan's birthday, eighteen months after he passed away. Among those present for the ceremony were Rosa, Felipe, Marta, Luis, twenty students in Luis's second leadership program, and most of the people of the town. Elizabeth and Allison were also there, as were Laura and Antonio. The honor of cutting the ribbon was given to the Pinto family—Marcos, Amelia, Samuel, and Samuel's new baby brother, Stan Pinto.

The End

CPSIA information can be obtained at www.ICGtesting.com
Printed in the USA
BVOW071850061112

304844BV00002B/102/P